SLICE GIRLS

ANTHOLOGY

Edited by
CARMILLA VOIEZ

MOCHA MEMOIRS PRESS

OTHER MOCHA MEMOIRS HORROR ANTHOLOGIES

Slay: Stories of the Vampire Noire

Black Magic Women

The Grotesquerie

In The Bloodstream

Ghosts, Gears, and Grimoires

Dedicated to the millions of women still fighting for an equal world.

LILIES OF THE FIELD

BY MEI KERR

AH, I SEE HIM. HE'S RIGHT THERE.

He can't see me yet. The bar is poorly-lit, and there's the usual noise and whooping around Lulu-Lily when she dances.

"Hallo shuai-ge," she croons as they wave fifty-dollar bills at her. Lulu-Lily, real name Lu Mei, has two children struggling in school. She comes from some backwater in China and made it all the way here in the hope that her children would do better.

Of course, her husband is 'at home working.' Sure.

Lulu-Lily winks, waves, teases, bends over, wiggles... and nods, imperceptibly, at him.

I wave at him. I am pleased with what I see. He's a big, fat, bald white man, exactly the kind we need. The online profile listed him as British, and he's almost a stereotype of that particular kind of British sex tourist – pasty white, ugly, carrying an enormous belly on top of skinny hairy legs. The top of his head is already sunburnt, though he can't have been here that long.

I grin at him over my braces. I have my best denim miniskirt on, the one so tight it's hard to sit down, and a pink crop-top with lace trim. Lulu-Lily and Diamond-Lily did my hair in two French braids and put glittery *My Little Pony* barrettes in it. We decided on the high heels together, the kind I could pretend to wobble and trip on.

I giggle as I stand up. "Sorry," I say, wobbling. "New shoes. Hi, John."

"Hi, Lilibet. You're very pretty." He smiles faintly.

Ah, this one will be one of those pretend-nice ones. That's good. It's more satisfying. The ones who just outright grab you are no fun. They just don't last long enough.

I giggle – hee hee hee – and bring up a blush. "You handsome." You have to use weird pidgin English with these guys. Somehow speaking good English intimidates them. They want their Suzie Wong Me Virgin Girl type.

"You buy me drink?"

"Oh, I don't know... how old are you?"

"I eighteen. I good girl."

"You're eighteen, yes; that's good."

Sure it is. I'm fourteen and I look it. I've been fourteen for the past four thousand years.

"What'll you have?"

"Bourbon Coke."

He laughs and orders. I sip my Coke gingerly. There's no bourbon in it. But there's an extra something in the bottom of his beer-glass. Tequila-Lily knows what she's doing.

I've been doing this so long, it no longer disgusts me when his hands start to move – on my back, my thigh, my knee. I only avoid him when he tries to touch my face. I hate their filthy hands on my face.

He starts to tell me stories – the drug does that – complaining about his wife, his children, his job, his life. Men are an endless metronome of the same complaints, particularly those who have it all. If they have a job, a home, a family, a car, be sure they'll have more to fucking drone on about than a homeless guy washing dishes for food.

Blah, blah, blah, and I giggle and nod and smile until he wants to leave the Lilies-of-the-Field and go 'somewhere private.' We stand up, and he pitches face forward to the ground.

Brit Reported Missing.

David J. Travers, 47, senior accountant, father of three, has been reported missing for three weeks. He was last seen in Changi Airport, Singapore, on two-day stopover on his way to a business conference in Bangkok, Thailand. He did not check in for his connecting flight.

Travers' wife, Mrs. Dorothy Travers, will be arriving in Singapore to assist in investigations.

Local police urge for witnesses to come forward.

"Wake up, John Smith. C'mon. It's no fun if you're asleep. Wake up, Mr...Travers. David? Dave? Davy-boy. Wake up!"

I sometimes wonder what they see. The set-up has been the same for centuries, since the days we bound our feet and played the zither for them. They are stripped naked, bound and suspended from the ceiling by ropes and chains, legs and arms splayed out. And when they open their eyes, they see us.

Today it's me and Diamond-Lily. I'm still in my pink sparkly outfit. Diamond-Lily always wears black when she wears anything at all. She has Smash out today, her favorite toy; it's an aluminum baseball bat and nine-inch nails duct-taped together. I just have my fish knives. My work needs to be clean.

I've just finished shaving his legs. Electric razors make the job so much faster these days.

I think he's screaming, but it's hard to tell with the gag on. Diamond-Lily smiles, baring her pointed canines. "So," she says. "Let's get to it. Who do we have, Lilibet?"

I pick up my iPad. There are dancing rainbow unicorns on the cover, which seems to terrify him somehow. He wriggles furiously as Diamond-Lily takes her stance and brings Smash up over her shoulder.

"Vietnam, 2002. Bao Linh, thirteen. Let's give her the right thigh."

"You got it."

The satisfying crack of Smash snapping John Smith's femur, the wet squelch of the nails driving into flabby muscle, and his muffled shriek. It always makes me happy. I set to work with my knives, carving into the meaty flanks Diamond-Lily has just tenderized. Fried in garlic and butter, perhaps. Diamond-Lily likes hers raw, but the rest of us find cooking fun.

"Thailand, 2004, Pornthip Saethang, sixteen. That lasted two years, every couple of weeks."

Smash strikes John Smith in the left tibia, smashing it. He screams and tries to form words around the ball gag. Diamond-Lily, because she gets off on it, removes the gag.

"...please I swear, I promise I won't..."

"Philippines, Marizel Mendoza, twelve, 2007. Singapore, Eliza Tham, fifteen, 2010. Back to Marizel in 2013, when she was eighteen. Got tired of her, huh, John Smith? Thailand again, 2016..."

Diamond-Lily leaves the gag off so he can scream his head off. The iron nails give him a good mincing, and the bat leaves bone splinters. His right tibia has broken straight through the skin, but I can cut around it. I've done this a long time. As long as the carcass is plump enough, I can get good steak out of it no matter what the condition. At a pinch, we can create hamburger mince and sausage.

"Okay, Diamond. It's time to carve. He'll bleed out otherwise."

"Damn. Already?" But she obliges. A good strike to the spine breaks his back and leaves him paralyzed and without sensation from the waist down.

"Adrenaline," she says. "He's passing out."

Adrenaline – the greatest invention since birth control. I jab him directly in the heart, and he starts back awake, sweating, moaning, blubbering all over his fat doughy face.

He subsides a little when he realizes he can't feel the pain anymore. Usually at this point they're grateful to have their spines broken.

Until, that is, they realize what I'm doing.

There's not much left to his legs. Nicely filleted rounds of steak from his thighs and strips from his calves are now laid out on the gleaming steel table beside me. I've already started marinating some in teriyaki. The calf muscles get very tense, you see. Too tough.

The grill is already hot. The aroma of minced garlic battles with the stink of fear, urine and shit. It's the reason we tie them up with legs splayed open. You don't want to contaminate your meat.

He's trying to say something. Perhaps he thinks it's a dream.

"Hey," Lulu-Lily calls down the stairs to us. "She's here."

Diamond-Lily looks at me, and I nod. "Okay," she calls up. "Let her come in."

Missing Brit's Wife Appeals for Witnesses.

Mrs Dorothy Travers, 28, wife of missing Brit David J. Travers, today held a press conference appealing for witnesses to come forward. Mr. Travers was last seen at an airport in Singapore four days ago, did not make his connecting flight, and has not checked into his hotel.

"My husband is a hard working, honest man, and we want to know what has happened to him," Dorothy Travers stated in an emotional speech. "We are prepared for the worst. We just need to know."

Witness statements so far say Mr. Travers may have been sighted in Desker Street, Singapore, a well-known red-light area. No leads have been reported.

We always save the best part for the one who deserves it most.

Mrs. Dorothy Travers is exactly what you'd imagine: a short, plump, pretty woman in a floral dress too old for her young face. When she speaks, her accent hints she is – was – Eastern European. Her hips tell you she has borne too many children in too short a time. Her eyes tell you she knows it.

I take her hands. She's trembling. When she first found us, she was also shaking, but with rage, clutching a crying baby.

"They are all bastards," she wept. "Men. All of them. My father, he beat us. My priest, he touched me. And now... and now..."

The story has been repeated through all the ages of man. The Liliths, we die and are reborn, over and over again, and our task has never ended.

She looks at me, her eyes wide and frightened, but her mouth set and determined. I gently put a clean fish knife in her hands.

"Grip it tight," I say. "Are you ready?"

"I think so." She pauses, smiles faintly. "When I was little, my grandmother killed pigs with knives like this."

"That's right. That's exactly right."

Removing a penis is very easy. It's soft, mostly skin. A sharp pair of gardening shears could do it. I give them the fish knife because it's slow. Sometimes, they request we don't break their spines first, but this usually backfires. The pig just blacks out from the pain anyway, and we don't want that.

David J. Travers hangs there, watching helpless as his wife carefully slices off his genitals.

He's still screaming, but I severed his vocal cords. The wives tend to prefer silence while they work so they can concentrate. I teach her where to cut, how to slice neatly.

Diamond-Lily gives Dorothy a seat at the table as she removes her rubber gloves.

"It'll just be a minute," she says cheerfully like the barmaid she is, while Dorothy tucks her legs neatly beneath her skirt and stares up at the bleeding, mutilated creature she married, slowly dying.

The grill sizzles as I toss on seasoning and spices. It's ready in seconds. Not much to it, after all.

I serve it to her on a china platter. Dorothy nods and picks up her knife and fork.

David J. Travers dies, screaming silently to the end while his wife quietly consumes his severed penis.

A body was discovered washed up on Changi Beach early Saturday morning. The identity of the corpse has not been established as it is said to be in poor condition. The Coast Guard confirms the body has been in the water for eight weeks or more and has been partially consumed, likely by fish and parasites.

Residents of the area took to social media, speculating that this is the body of the missing Brit, David J. Travers.

His wife could not be reached for comment.

MEI HAS BEEN PUBLISHED in two short story compilations by Monsoon Books and was made writer and editor of the local Comics Association in 2005.

2

JENNY

BY DAN ALLEN

EARS BUZZING, HEAD THROBBING, AND MY MOUTH tastes like ass. Hangover, that's what this is. Another goddamn hangover. Where am I? Hard, cold, musty – the basement floor. How did I get here? I can't quite open my eyes. This one's a doozy, all right. And my nose, what the fuck happened to my nose? Did I get punched? Probably fell again. I really need to stop drinkin'. Hope it's not busted... What the hell? I can't move my arms. Don't fuck with me now, God. Don't tell me I'm paralyzed. I got work in the morning and I can't afford to miss another day.

What about my legs? They good? Yep, they look fine, but I can't wiggle my toes. Wait a minute. What the hell is on my foot? It looks like... blood. Shit, something chewed off the bottom of my toe or... maybe it's melted. I don't know. I can't turn it to see. It's going to hurt later, that's for sure. There's a puddle under my foot. I wish I could see it better. If only I could move a little. I need to get away from that puddle. It smells bad, toxic, like chemicals. Damn, I'm dizzy. I might need to sleep this off a little while longer.

"Jenny? Is that you, baby? I need some help here." I must still be drunk. It looks like she's wearing a gas mask. "What happened to me last night? No? You're not going to tell? Do you know where my clothes are? Can you at least throw a sheet over my balls? I'm feeling a little exposed here, if you know what I mean." That was funny. She's not even laughing. Why is she not laughing? "Come on, bitch; help me off the goddamn floor."

"Hush. One question for you, asshole. Do you see?"

I don't understand her. Never really have. "Are you pissed at me or something? Hey, what's in the jug? Muriatic acid? What the hell, Jen. Be careful with that stuff. No! Don't pour it on my feet! Quick, get some water and wash it off." Whoa... wait a minute. What's with the syringe? "Jenny, honey, you know I don't like needles. No, don't do it. Please, Jen, not in the neck..."

Spinning, turning, Jennifer's face revolving around me. Faster, faster. I'm drifting, falling, slipping into the dark. "Why are you doing this? Why?" I'm mumbling, and I don't even know what I'm saying. Maybe it's gibberish. Are my lips even moving?

BASTARD. Only two windows in the entire basement and I'm stuck under one of them. It's morning. Sunlight burns through my eyelids, but the heat on my forehead and inside my brain is not from the sun. I'm fevered. Sweat trickles into my eyes. It stings, but I can't move my arms to wipe it away. I can't feel anything below the neck. Not my arms or legs or my mutilated toe. I guess I should be thankful, but I'm not.

"Do you see?"

She's yelling, telling me to wake up. Fuck her. I'm pretending to sleep. She slaps my face, once, twice, then grabs a handful of hair and lifts my head.

"Look."

She points at my legs. My foot is covered with a million tiny white bubbles. They jump and pop and sizzle and... my fucking foot is dissolving! The toes are still there, white and cleaned of flesh; the rest is a gory mess of ligaments and cartilage and pink... Pink what? Jello? No, it's not fucking jello. I can't feel my stomach, but I know I'm going to puke. Maybe I'm hallucinating. This should hurt. Why don't I feel any pain? The injections, of course. Duh. Jenny grabs my neck and squeezes.

"Look, asshole, if you barf, you'll choke to death and die. I won't save you. No goddamn way."

She leans close. Maybe I should spit on her, show her I'm still the boss. It might be my only chance. I listen instead. Her voice is seductive, her breath warm, and for a moment I think she might save me.

"It would be a shame if you died now. I have so much more work to do."

She reaches for the gas mask, slips it over her face and morphs into an alien. I'm high, so goddamn high, hallucinating, wasted. What's in the syringe? Something that paralyzes for sure, else I would be dead from the shock and the pain, but also some kind of narcotic to mess me up. Again, I should be thankful but I'm not. The jug of muriatic acid appears. She dribbles some over my shins, calves, and one big drop on my thigh.

"Just a little, right, asshole? One for the road? We wouldn't want the fun to end too soon, would we?"

I see the needle. Where did she have that hiding? Wow, I'm spinning. She must've upped the dose. I'm going to kill her. Yes, that's what I'm going to do, soon as I get out of here. Strangle the bitch. Laughing? Do I hear her laughing? Why is she laughing? What's so funny?

THERE'S THAT WHORE AGAIN, light. I don't know what's worse, the pounding inside my skull or the sun burning through it like a laser beam. Good news is I don't feel fevered anymore, just cold. Really, really, cold.

"Open your eyes. I know you're awake."

Oh, yes, Jenny. The love of my life. How could I forget? She's behind me. Her hands slide through my hair, under my ears, against my cheekbones.

"Sit up, asshole." She jerks my head and forces my shoulders off the ground. She tugs again. Any harder and the bitch is going to decapitate me.

"Do you see?"

My legs are foaming and alive with activity. My drugged-out mind finds it fascinating but no, this is my flesh dissolving, and I scream. She punches me hard in my temple, just above my left ear.

"Shut up and look."

I open my eyes. A coin-sized hole in my thigh spews pink foam, like a tiny volcano erupting melted flesh. I risk a glance at my lower legs. A patchwork of smoldering acid splotches burns through the remaining soft tissue, working on muscle below the bubbles. Further down, my ankles and feet are clean and white, like the plastic skeleton we hang at Halloween. A black curtain falls and I'm falling too...

I'M GASPING, choking, sucking in breath. A needle sticks out of my chest, much larger than the ones before.

"Adrenaline. I need you awake for this one."

The gas mask comes out again. This time I see a swamp monster. The beast twists the cap off a new jug. Careless splashing over my already decimated lower legs, my thighs, even some on my balls. The beast fills my bellybutton hole, closes the jug, and pulls off the mask.

"Please, Jenny. Please. Not my testicles. I don't know what I did, but I'm sorry. God knows, I'm sorry."

I think the bitch is smiling, I'm not sure. My vision is blurry, and my eyes are full of tears, or maybe it's toxic fumes.

"Do you see now, Asshole? Do you see?"

"No, I don't fucking see."

She leans over me, closer now. Maybe she's going to bite my nose. I wouldn't put it past her. I close my eyes. I'm not going to give her the pleasure of seeing my fear. Something brushes my cheek, my lips. Did she just kiss me?

"There's not going to be a needle this time. I want you lucid. I want you to experience it all, baby."

"Go to Hell." Go to Hell? Is that the best I can do? Clicking on the wooden stairs, high heels? Is she going out? She can't leave me like this.

"Wait, Jenny, come back!"

* * *

Dan Allen writes dark speculative fiction. Visit him at www. danallenhorror.com for more.

3

JAGGED JAWS

BY CARMILLA VOIEZ

"Do you remember Daryl Smith?" Clare asked, handing me a cup of fruit tea.

Despite the distance of decades and many conversations with counselors, all of which ended in tears, I couldn't prevent my own fear and disgust from slapping me across the face. I was thrown straight back to that time and place, powerless.

"Are you okay?" she asked. "You look as though you're about to throw up."

I forced myself to nod. This wasn't a conversation I felt ready to have, not twenty years after the event and probably not after another fifty. The shame of it had burrowed its roots deep into my psyche. The packed soil of all my experiences since, that I'd used to insulate me from the pain, shook and cracked when I heard his name again. All that work rebuilding myself had never gained any solidity because the foundations were as shaky as ever.

"What about him?" My voice felt thin, insubstantial.

Clare studied my face. The weight of her stare pinned me, squirming on the kitchen stool. Did she know?

"He got married. They're expecting a baby."

Daryl was in Clare's year at school whereas I'd been in the year above. We'd all left that concrete-blocked structure long ago, but I guessed she'd kept in touch.

Daryl had been a friend of my school sweetheart, Stuart. He was a troubled kid from a trouble-making family with a pleasant face and saccharine charm. Although it was hard to recall his facial features clearly, I could remember dark hair, tanned skin, and roguish good looks. When I tried to picture him it wasn't his face that sprang to mind; it was a part of him that hung midway between head and ludicrously expensive trainers.

I wanted to be alone so I could stamp down the memories and trample them deeper, but I was cradling a freshly made cup of rhubarb tea, and Clare had been bugging me for weeks to meet up for a chat. I couldn't simply leave, not without explaining why.

"They've got a croft in Thorne village. It's a lovely place. She's a landscape gardener. Although, I guess she'll need to take it easy for a while, and play a more managerial role."

I stared at the pink liquid in my cup, pretending to care, while any possible response that I might have offered refused to form in my throat. Clare's chatter tightened its grip on me, squeezing.

"Anyway, they're having a party the weekend after next, and I can bring a guest. Do you wanna come? There might be lots of the old crowd there, maybe Stuart. They're still friends. Daryl was talking about Stuart the other day. He's single. He works for the MOD. Apparently, he's still gorgeous..."

I couldn't hate her. She was trying to be sweet. She'd watched me sprint through relationships since school with long fallow periods between, and assumed I was still in love with the boy I'd lost at fifteen.

It wasn't her fault that I'd never trusted her enough to tell her why sustaining adult relationships was an impossible task. She was supposed to be my best friend, but she knew nothing. That's why she couldn't understand my rage.

"Aww come on. It'll be fun, like old times."

"Excuse me," I said, grasping my stomach and fleeing to the bathroom.

I CAN'T REMEMBER EXACTLY how Clare convinced me to go, but there I was feeling shabbily dressed outside a rather grand stone cottage. My only consolation was that Clare was doing a superb impression of the Cheshire cat beside me. I'd rarely seen her so excited.

Could you call someone a best friend if you only had one friend? My life had become so tiny over the years that I had all my fun by proxy, listening to her stories. I knew all her disappointments. Her volatile relationships with work colleagues; the lovers who failed to call and the ones who wouldn't stop calling. It was refreshing to see her face without any shadow of sadness and it almost made me forget my own for a moment.

The door was ajar. I guessed this was the sort of area where you didn't have to lock up your bargain-basement possessions for fear of theft. The music wafting into the garden was as bouncy as my friend. I gripped a chilly bottle of Lambrusco tighter in my fist and stepped inside.

It was busy. Half-remembered faces mingled with strangers as Clare and I wove between them towards the kitchen to drop off our bottles and greet our hosts. My saliva tasted metallic. Would Daryl recognize me or I him? Who else would I know at this party, and could I depend on Clare to stick beside me this time? One thing I knew for certain, I'd be mixing my own drinks.

A beautiful couple rested against a polished oak workstation at the center of the kitchen. Between making drinks and smiling graciously at guests, they pawed at each other's arms and gazed into each other's eyes. The wide-smiled, floppy-haired, pretty boy was unmistakably Daryl. The woman, presumably his wife, had flame-colored tight curls and golden freckles on her heart shaped face. Her clothing and posture were effortlessly elegant and strong. The only hint of softness, other than her kind eyes, was the curve of her belly shielding the undoubtedly healthy baby growing within.

The woman glanced across at us and smiled. "Clare."

"Hi, Amanda... Daryl. Great party. Congratulations. We brought some wine. This is Pam. Do you remember Pam?"

The name and my face did not invoke any sign of recognition. The smiles were professional, like photographs of catalog models in a family setting. I couldn't believe he didn't recognize me at all. I wanted to growl something at him, but I kept silent.

"Can I get you drinks?" Daryl asked.

I shuddered and saw the mug of cola in my hand again.

"Red please?" Clare answered.

"... Pam?" Daryl asked. Staring at my face as if trying to recall who I was.

I shook my head. "I'm fine, thanks."

Clare reached out and squeezed my hand. Neither Amanda nor Daryl lost their smiles.

"You must show... Pam the garden, Clare. We'll catch up later," Amanda assured us.

"It's Amanda's showcase garden. Her pride and joy. She uses it to display her talents to prospective clients. It looks even better in daylight," Clare gushed as we stepped outside.

Fairy lights twinkled in the trees and yellow stone pathways guided feet between closely cropped, lush lawns. The heavy fragrance of flowers gave a magical feeling to the place as though we'd accidentally stepped over the rainbow into Oz, or fallen down a rabbit hole into Wonderland. I was enchanted. For a moment, I let my guard slip and felt happy.

"Clare... *Pam?*"

I turned and saw sparkling green eyes and recognized him immediately.

"Stuart."

I felt unsteady. The ground moved beneath my feet. His hair was darker than the ash blond I remembered, a light brown with soft highlights that might or might not have been natural. I hadn't seen him in twenty years, but I'd never forgotten his smile. I still felt as though I might drown in it.

"Long time, no see," I said, trying not to shake.

"Oh my God. It is you? How have you been?"

I nodded. "Busy. You?"

"Oh, you know."

I didn't.

Amanda grinned at me. "I'll just be a minute. You guys can keep each other company, right?"

"I'll look after her," Stuart said, but his eyes looked predatory.

I reached into my bag and touched the bottle of anti-anxiety pills; it was enough to know I had them with me. I withdrew my empty hand and attempted a smile. Being close to Stuart made my skin tingle. His eyes only left my face for a second to appraise the rest of me; his trademarked mischievous sparkle had not faded.

"You look good," I told him.

"You too. How long has it been?"

"Nineteen years and two months." My reply was instant. "Not that I've been counting."

"You haven't changed a bit," he said.

"Oh, I have," I replied.

He glanced over his shoulder. "Daryl and Amanda have a lovely place. Have you been here before?"

"No. Clare brought me."

His nod was so slight I might have missed it if I hadn't been staring.

"Want a guided tour?"

He showed me the garden first, Amanda's Magnum Opus. There was a well-stocked shed, unlocked. The walls were covered with gardening tools that reminded me of instruments of torture. I wondered for a moment what that said about me. A summer house and barbecue stood beside a pond full of Koi carp surrounded by ornamental reeds and grasses. It was heavenly. I could imagine sitting here on summer days, kids racing around and behind me on trikes. Sadness stabbed my chest. I could never have this. It was my mirage in a desert.

He held my hand when we entered the busy house. My palm sweated in his soft grip. Everything inside had been as carefully planned as the garden, and I could only imagine how a toddler's crayon scribbles across those pale walls would be received.

There were three bedrooms, including one in the process of having wallpaper stripped. I remembered the first (and last time) we'd been together in Stuart's bedroom, and a fat tear rolled down my cheek.

"I'm so sorry, Pam. I was a kid."

"So was I."

He squeezed my hand. "I know. Look, can I take you to dinner?"

"So, what did you say?" Clare asked.

I shrugged. "What could I say?"

"A thousand different things, but I hope you said yes."

"I did."

She made a high-pitched sound and wrapped her arms around me. "That's wonderful. I'm so excited for you. We need to buy you a new dress... and shoes... maybe you should get your hair done."

"Slow down."

"I'm just excited for you."

She took the kettle to the sink and filled it. It was our ritual, drinking tea together, fruit tea normally. She thought it was good for us, cleansing. God knows I needed a good cleanse.

"Really? Coz I'm fucking terrified."

She cocked her head and stared at me for a moment before switching the kettle on.

"Why?"

"Because I think I still love him, and that scares the shit out of me."

"It'll be fun. It's exactly what you need."

I couldn't grasp how this feeling could ever be described as fun. It was like waking up from a nightmare and not knowing whether I was still dreaming. I felt hot, sweaty and sick. It wasn't fun at all. It was torture.

Stuart had broken my heart when he was fourteen and I was fifteen. Whether it was Stuart's betrayal or what followed that royally fucked me up, I wasn't quite sure, but I couldn't help wondering how different my life would have been if I had never met Stuart or Daryl. Now I was about to enter the lion's den once more.

Clare poured boiling water into two mugs. The water was dark. It looked like thinned blood.

"When are you having dinner?"

I sighed. "Saturday."

"You don't have to sound so miserable about it."

I didn't have the right words to explain how much he'd hurt

me, or how the memories of him had frozen my heart. That's why it had endured, stayed fresh. My love for him had been cryogenically preserved.

"What happened between you?"

"Don't you know?" My heart raced. I grabbed the bottle of Xanax and popped a pill into my mouth.

"I just thought you broke up. Is there something else?"

"He called me a slut."

"Oh, Pam... He was fourteen. It won't be like that now."

Once the words came, I couldn't stop them tumbling from my jagged jaws.

"He was my first. I loved him. Fuck, we'd been going out for two years before. After, he wouldn't talk to me. He talked to everyone else, though. Told them what we'd done. Said I was easy. Said I was a slut. I was fifteen."

"He didn't mean it. People say stupid things. He was probably as confused as you were. I know he hurt you. Put it behind you. Maybe this is the closure you need to move on, with or without Stuart."

She stood up and walked around the table, wrapped me inside her arms and hugged me. My cheek squashed the cushions of her breasts.

"Poor baby. It's ancient history; don't cling to it. Give him a second chance."

Stuart hadn't been the only boy to call me a slut. Stuart said it because I said yes and Daryl because I'd said no. It was a word that communicated hatred and was used to make women (and girls) feel worthless. The trouble was I did feel worthless. I still felt worthless. Sometimes words had an awful lot of power.

I held my face over the steam that rose from my blackberry tea. The word was one symbol, the mug another. I could tell Clare about the word but not about the mug or what Daryl did to me. Those were secrets I planned to carry to my grave.

. . .

SATURDAY CAME TOO QUICKLY. I wore trousers, a blouse, and flat shoes. Stuart was at the table when I arrived. He stood up; that smile appeared again, and I was lost. I looked down at my plain clothes and wished I'd been brave enough to don the figure-hugging dress Clare had made me buy.

We sat simultaneously, his knee brushing against mine. I buried my face in the menu as my cheeks ripened. I'd had my fair share of awkward first dates. I just hadn't had many second dates and, for the life of me, I couldn't figure out what this was. Could old lovers have first dates?

A shadow hovered beside me. I shivered, but it was only the waiter.

"Would you like wine?" Stuart asked.

"White please," I replied.

Stuart read a French name from the menu. The waiter nodded and withdrew.

"I don't know what to choose."

"Are you still vegetarian?" Stuart asked.

I looked up from the menu. He remembered. I nodded slowly.

"The roasted vegetable lasagna is supposed to be excellent. I'm afraid I'm still a carnivore. Do you mind?"

"I'll have the lasagna, thank you. Do you come here often? Wow that line was cheesy." I giggled self-consciously.

"Before I became a bit of a hermit, it was a fairly regular haunt. It's near work." He reached across the table and brushed my thumb with his. "Guess what?"

The question transported me to a happier time.

Stuart and I sat together in a youth club, Nineties pop blared. We were sharing our first kiss. His cheek brushed mine as he whispered the words in my ear. "Guess what?"

"What?"

"I love you."

I COULDN'T SPEAK.

"I've been really nervous about tonight. I managed to convince myself you wouldn't come, not that I'd blame you."

His words washed over me. He was right. I shouldn't have come. Yet, when I tried to leave, my muscles couldn't comply. I sat there, nodding like one of those toys on the back shelves of cars.

"I thought about contacting you lots of times."

My eyes misted.

"I was just a stupid kid, but... I really did love you."

A tear pushed under my lashes and rolled down my cheek. He grasped my hand.

"Shhh, don't cry."

I brushed the tear away, denying my grief.

The shadow returned. A twist of expert hands and a cork was pulled from the bottle. Glug, glug, said the wine as it was poured into my glass. I picked it up and downed the liquid. The waiter smiled and refilled my glass.

"Are you ready to order?"

"Umm..." I tried to clear my thoughts. Reality felt far away. "Vegetable lasagna, please."

"Steak, rare with a pepper sauce."

"Fillet or Sirloin, sir?"

"Sirloin."

"Very good. Is the wine to your satisfaction?"

"Yes, thank you," I answered before Stuart could reply. I wanted the waiter to leave so Stuart and I could be alone, but I wanted him to stay so I wouldn't start weeping again.

I didn't know what to say to Stuart, the one person I had truly loved, but who had betrayed me and in doing so caused all the evil of my life to unfold. I wished I'd never met him, but if I hadn't, I wouldn't remember his soft lips against mine every time I heard the right song.

Stuart squeezed my hand again. His face framed a smile that could melt the Arctic tundra.

"This is a mistake."

"Stay for dinner at least. Call it my apology, and if you don't want to forgive me... Well, at least I tried."

"I want to forgive you." The words came out with my breath. I inhaled to reclaim them, but it was too late. I wanted to tell him that everything was his fault, but it wasn't. It was about time I stopped blaming Stuart for every failed relationship in my adult life and looked elsewhere.

"What do you want?" My voice was harder than I intended.

He emptied his wine glass. His eyes looked softer than before as if shrouded by mist.

"I want a second chance."

"DID YOU SAY YES?" Clare asked.

"I didn't say no," I answered, staring vacantly at the cat on my lap who was shedding pale fur all over my clothes.

"When will you see him again?"

"I said I'd call him."

"And have you?"

"Not yet."

Clare sighed, impatiently. "What are you waiting for?"

"There's something I need to take care of first." I brushed the cat from my lap and stood up. I left the kitchen, knowing Clare was sitting open-mouthed behind me.

"Pam?"

I didn't turn around. I left her flat without my jacket. The air was warm anyway, and I didn't feel I would need it. I had my handbag, clutched in my fist, with enough money to get where I needed to go. It was going to be okay. I would say goodbye then I would be free. After that it was up to me.

WHEN I ARRIVED at Daryl's, I still wasn't sure what I had planned. One car was parked in the generous driveway, and the house seemed deathly quiet. Perhaps they were both out. I stood in front of their rustic-looking front door and let my mind drift. It traveled back in time and for once I let it.

I WAS HOLDING that mug again. *Cola bubbles spluttered upwards, bursting in the air. I took a sip and then another. The friendly conversations around me became homogeneous noise. I didn't suspect a thing.* I hadn't heard of date rape drugs back then. In fact, it took me over a decade to accept that what happened that day wasn't my fault.

My head swam, and my limbs felt impossibly heavy. I asked if I could lie down for a while and a friend helped me stumble up the stairs and onto a single bed.

I thought I'd sleep it off. Wake up fresh and apologize. It wasn't my first migraine, although this felt different. I was too muddled to try and work out what was wrong. Sleep... that's what I needed. I sank into the mattress.

I FELT SICK. What was I doing here? What did I plan to say if Daryl or his wife came to the door? I couldn't tell them about that day. Twenty years and many hours of therapy later and I still didn't have all the pieces. More was conjecture than not, but a nightmare couldn't have haunted me for all those years or provoked the overwhelming shame, fear and anger that I harbored. I was a victim, and the only way I could get past this was to make Daryl pay. I pressed the doorbell.

THE DOOR OPENED *and a sharp chill entered the room. I shivered, trying to burrow further into the sheets. My eyelids changed from red to black as a shadow passed behind them. I tried to open my eyes, but they were too heavy. The mattress dipped as someone sat beside me, leaned over me. Sweat and musk filled my nostrils when a hand touched my hair. I was trapped. Pinned to a strange bed, unable to see or move, unable even to open my mouth and ask who was there. I was living a nightmare and I couldn't wake up.*

"You got away last time," the male voice whispered.

Got away? I knew at once it was Daryl and remembered what I had tried to drive from my mind. It had happened within a week of Stuart's betrayal. A sharp kick and a swift sprint and it had been left behind. A frightening moment, a warning but nothing more. At least not until now.

"This time, you're stuck here. Just you and me."

I shook my head or hoped I was moving it. I would deny him to my final breath. Never surrender.

"You're a filthy slut. Don't pretend you're a virgin. I know what you did."

Bile rose in my throat. I tried to swallow it down, but a lump of it lingered there, burning.

"I'll give you a choice. Suck me or fuck me."

NO ANSWER. I pressed the doorbell again, longer this time, letting the sound of it break through the words in my head, the scream I'd been unable to articulate. The scream that might have saved me and brought footsteps hammering up those stairs.

I skirted the house and stood in the garden. Flowers jostled for my attention. Their bright colors calmed my mind. I wandered towards the shed. It smelled peaty inside, rich, earthy, musky.

THE STINK *of Daryl made me want to vomit. Old cheese and sweat. Did he ever wash? His skin pressed against my mouth, prying open my lips. I wanted to bite down hard. I wanted to hear him scream, but my jaw was unwilling or unable to do my bidding. It yielded to his will not mine and opened around him.*

TOOLS HUNG from hooks against the rough wood. Spades, hoes, forks, shears and secateurs, all clean, sharp, oiled, and ready to be used. I could destroy their dream garden; dig up plants, cut blooms from their stems. Maybe Daryl and his wife would look at the wreckage, terrified, not knowing what could have sparked such wrath, but they might assume it was an act of jealousy, report the damage and move on. Amanda would mourn her wasted hours, tears spilling on parched earth, but that would give me no satisfaction. Amanda wasn't the person I needed to punish. There were other ways I could use these tools to make sure I targeted the right victim.

I took my time, handling the tools and weighing in my mind what they might be used for. The rope would be perfect. He should be powerless, unable to move, just like I had been, but what next? How much did I want to hurt him? Did I want him dead?

I wondered how I would tie him up. I couldn't access drugs like the Rohypnol he'd slipped into my mug all those years ago. I lifted a heavy shovel off the wall. Perhaps an old-fashioned whack to the back of the head would suffice.

Daryl didn't deserve a moment longer in paradise. I would make him powerless then kill him, and if Amanda returned too soon, I would have to slaughter her as well. If not, I would let her and the baby live. No one would suspect me. Only Daryl and I knew my motive, and he would carry the knowledge to his cold grave.

I'd need a plan. I couldn't just wait in the shed for someone to arrive. It would more likely be Amanda who came here first. It was her shed and tools I'd co-opted as weapons. The super-fit, gardening-crazy wife, even with child, would be stronger than me. They both would. Against the two of them, I wouldn't stand a chance.

I returned the shovel to its hook and left. The sun was still high in the sky when I checked my watch, four o'clock. I needed to do some reconnaissance, study them and learn their habits. I'd need warmer clothes and a lot of patience. I decided to return the following day.

THIS TIME, when I rang on Daryl's door he opened it. He looked at me without the slightest recognition in his eyes. I chose to play on his poor memory.

"Is Amanda there?" I asked.

"No. She won't be back until six."

"She asked me to look at the azaleas. Is it all right if I go ahead?"

He looked puzzled for a moment then nodded. "Sure... Do I know you?"

"I'll leave you to figure that one out while I check on the flowers. Come and find me when you have." It was a risk. He might phone his wife to confirm my identity, but the sparkle in his eyes suggested he approved of my game.

He nodded. "Tea or coffee?"

"Tea, please."

"I'll leave the door open."

To the shed! I lifted the shovel off the hook, some rope, an evil-looking pair of shears and a ridiculously sharp pair of secateurs. I looked at each in turn. The spade for the initial blow or two, or however many it took to knock him out; the rope for tying him up so he would be helpless, and the evil looking gardener's scissors, both pairs, for snipping, cutting, biting. I wished I'd been able to bite him before, hurt him, crushed him, pierced his skin rather than letting him use my mouth for his pleasure. This time, it would be very different. This time, my jaws would not be pliant, they would be jagged.

I took the shovel into the house but left the other tools on the doorstep. I figured I could explain away one tool. He was in the kitchen, sat on the counter again, sipping from a steaming mug.

"So, what's your diagnosis?" he asked, nodding towards a mug beside him that looked like hot, milky tea but would never be tasted.

"Sick."

"Amanda will be disappointed. Are you uprooting them? You know the tools should be left outside right?"

I stared at him. "Remember yet?"

He slipped off the counter and stood before me, puffing himself up to look as large as possible. His charming smile chilled me. He shook his head and held the second mug towards me.

"You got me. You'll have to tell me."

With my left hand, I took hold of the mug and threw the hot liquid at his face. The spade I thrust down hard on the exposed skin of his left foot. He bent forward and I swung the shovel in a wide arc, behind me then over my shoulder, hitting the back of his head before he could straighten his body. The blow wasn't well-aimed, and I sliced his left ear with the edge of the blade. He dropped to the floor. Blood pooled in his earlobe. He was shaking, but he was still conscious and trying to get back up. I couldn't let him do that. So, I hit him again.

"YOU'RE AWAKE," I said.

He shook his head. His mouth hung open, and drool dripped from his chin. He struggled to focus on my face. He was on his knees. I'd used the rope to tie his wrists to his legs and around his waist. The knots were tight, restricting his movements to twitches.

"You hit me," he said in a slow, measured tone as if trying to solve a math problem. "Why am I tied up? What did I ever do to you?"

"You stole my power to say no," I told him.

He stared at me until the soft light of recognition danced in his eyes.

"Remember now?" I asked.

"You were Stuart's girl."

I nodded.

"Shit!" He struggled against his bondage, tugging at the ropes and testing the knots. I let him. After a few minutes, he stopped and sat still.

"What can I say?" he asked.

I shrugged. "Silence would be golden, but you can sob and plead if you want."

The smile returned. He looked more confident than ever. It made me want to crush his skull.

"Amanda will be home soon," he said, calmly.

"Not for another three hours," I replied.

"You're pissed at me. I get it. But what are you going to do? Do you want me to apologize? Of course, I'm sorry. I was a dumb kid. I was experimenting. I didn't expect you to be so..."

"Easy?" I swallowed my scream.

"I was going to say docile, subdued, but maybe you're right. Maybe you didn't want to resist. Stuart told me..."

"I don't want to hear what that wanker told you!" I screamed. "Shut your fucking mouth or I'll fill it."

Daryl was tied up tight, and his head must have hurt like hell; his cheek was swollen and his ear still bleeding, but I couldn't see a trace of fear in his eyes or smile.

I picked up the secateurs and brandished them in front of his face, hoping for some acknowledgment that I had the power. He was at my mercy, and I really wasn't feeling merciful.

"You need to put this all back before Amanda arrives," was all he said.

I screeched in frustration. I wanted him to beg, plead, tell me while choking back tears that he was sorry, but he gave me nothing.

I paced the room. Looking down from time to time to catch him wriggling his arms, trying to get free. The moment my eyes settled on him, he'd freeze and smile up at me like a trusting child, wondering what the next part of the game might be.

I strode across the room towards him and stabbed the metal points into his cheek.

His neck muscles strained as he tried to move back; his eyes grew wider and, for a moment, I felt gratified until I heard his unshakable voice, still the epitome of calm and reason. "Be careful with those," he said. "They aren't toys."

"Why aren't you afraid?" I asked him.

"You're owed your little tantrum. I figure I should let you get it out of your system so we can talk."

"What? I'm going to kill you."

He pursed his lips before shaking his head slowly. "No, you're not."

"I fucking am," I said. "You raped me."

"I did not!"

"You drugged me and stuck your penis in my mouth. Oh, and by the way, you stank. You should fucking bathe once in a while."

"You wanted me. I just made it easier for you. You still want me. Come on. I'm helpless. Why don't you come and sit on my lap?" He actually smiled, the filthy bastard.

I screamed again, shaking with anger. "How can you say that? When you tried to rape, yes rape me, that first time on the building site, I kicked you in the balls. You had to fucking ruffie me to get anywhere. That's rape, you asshole."

"I gave you a choice."

"I was virtually unconscious."

"Not so unconscious that your eyes didn't beg me to come to you or that your lips didn't moisten at the thought of my flesh between them."

"You sick wanker. I'll show you what I think of your cock."

I rushed at him again. This time, I sliced through the denim that covered his lap. He wouldn't stop grinning, so I elbowed him in the mouth. That shit-eating smile returned immediately even though blood coated his teeth. I dropped the secateurs and put my hands over my ears. I knelt before him, terrified of the power he still wielded.

"It's okay," he said. "I understand."

"You really don't." I started to sob.

"Let's end it now. Untie me. Leave before Amanda gets home. You can come back earlier tomorrow, give us more time to play."

I shook my head. "Shut up!"

"I can see if Stuart wants to join in too."

"Shut up! Shut up!"

"A reunion."

"Shut the fuck up!"

I didn't know what to do. I wanted to run away. No, I wanted to use the shovel to smash in his skull. No, I wanted to cut his dick off and stuff it in his mouth. All I could do was kneel there, staring through hate-filled eyes at his idiot smile and unfailing self-love. I almost wished Amanda would return so at least this moment would be over, and I would be dragged from this hell into caged safety. How could he be so unafraid, so cocksure?

I leaned forwards, so my forehead rested against his chest. I reached for the secateurs and uncovered his crotch. I moved back a little so he could see what I could see, how small and non-threatening his penis looked, asleep on his testicles. It wasn't a weapon. It wasn't a god. It was a pathetic worm.

"If you cut a worm into two, both halves survive," I mumbled more to myself than him.

He wriggled, trying again to pull his hands free of the ropes.

"I'm not afraid of you," I told his flaccid penis.

The wriggling grew more urgent. Perhaps Daryl sensed the change in me. I squeezed the handle of the secateurs, and its jaws closed around empty air. His body jerked as he struggled more desperately. I lifted the head of his cock and held it between the thumb and forefinger of my left hand. The fucking pervert started to harden. Even now he was excited. I saw before me every evil deed that men had committed against women – every rape, every child bride, every acid burn, every stoning. I held all this wickedness between my finger and my thumb. I could uproot it. I let my right hand relax, and the jaws of the gardener's tool opened.

"No," he whispered. "Please."

It was a tight squeeze, but I managed to push his member between the hungry metal jaws. I looked into his eyes, wide with fear and disbelief, then squeezed. My ears rang with the echoes of his scream.

So much blood. A laugh bubbled in my stomach, rose through my chest and escaped my lips. Daryl was silent. His head drooped as if staring at his crimson thighs. His body shook, but it was impossible to tell whether he was still conscious.

So much blood. I left footprints of it across the kitchen floor. I checked my watch. If Amanda returned at her usual time, I had a little under an hour. I couldn't clean this mess in that time. The jerking movements of Daryl's chest and stomach had slowed, but blood still flowed from his raw wound. He would bleed out soon.

I realized I was holding something soft in my left hand. I glanced at the purple flesh and dropped it onto the vinyl, repulsed. Disembodied, it looked uglier than ever. The secateurs were still clutched in my right fist. They would be covered in prints. I dropped them into the sink and filled it with hot water, rubbing the taps after. I had to go. The house was remote enough that Daryl's scream, however piercing, should not have been heard. Any witnesses who saw me leave would be unlikely to recall my features, Daryl hadn't.

I was mesmerized by the gentle twitches of Daryl's shoulders. Blood pooled on the floor, reflecting the afternoon sun in its dark depths. I shook myself into action. My clothes were covered in his blood, hands too, dark and red. I wondered whether any had splashed on my face. I visited the downstairs bathroom and cleaned myself as well as I could, leaving stains on the previously pristine cream hand towel. I grabbed a coat from the cupboard and wrapped it around myself.

I WAITED in my flat for the police to call. I saw a news report. Amanda looked devastated. Reading between the lines, it seemed she was the prime, if not only, suspect. Poor woman. The ringing of my phone startled me. This was it. I couldn't escape the consequences of my actions. It had taken the police longer than I expected. Red soaked my vision, and I felt like Lady Macbeth, marked by blood as a murderer. I couldn't open my front door afraid people would see me and know what I'd done. My fridge was empty, and I was making short work of the frozen food and tins. Soon I would starve if I couldn't find a suitable disguise and take the short walk to the local shop.

The phone. It was still ringing. Whoever it was, didn't seem to be giving up easily. Shaking, I lifted it from the table.

"Hello?"

"Pam. How are you?"

It was Stuart. He sounded close to tears. For a moment, I wondered why.

Stuart told me, the words of a rapist, a self-satisfied prick, a dead man. *What did Stuart tell you?*

"I saw the news. I'm sorry," I said.

"I can't believe Amanda would do such a thing. They seemed so... Can I see you?"

I swallowed hard. I couldn't think of anything we had to say to each other. The idea of touching him made me want to throw up.

"I don't think so, Stuart. Look, I have to go."

I hung up. I'd thought punishing Daryl would free me, but I was more trapped than ever, unable to leave my flat, unable to drink a mug of tea without seeing Daryl's expiring corpse and the blood. So much blood. I had been powerful. For a moment, I had been a god. Daryl would never hurt a woman again, but his blood would never be washed from my soul.

I picked up the phone again and dialed Stuart's number.

"Actually, how does one hour sound?"

"Great. Let me know your address."

"No, I'll come to yours."

This time, I chose darker clothes. The kitchen knife fitted neatly into my bag.

. . .

STUART LIVED in a flat not much bigger than my own, but in a much better part of town. This was commuter-ville, and the only people wandering around at this time of day were mothers pushing baby carriages.

He assured me his family home was more impressive but, with child support, it would take him a while to get back on top. I found his apologies confusing and shook my head.

"I made some biscuits," he said. "Want tea or coffee with them?"

"Let me make the drinks," I said. "What do you want?"

He looked confused but nodded. "Black coffee please."

As I brought the drinks across to the circular table, he was tipping hot biscuits onto a plate.

"They smell good."

He beamed with pride. "I like cooking."

"The perfect boyfriend, huh?" I teased.

He shrugged. "My ex-wife didn't think so."

"What happened?"

He passed me a plate, ignoring the question. "So, you heard about Daryl?"

"Yes. Was he a good friend of yours?"

"I don't know why Amanda did it," he said, softly, as if to himself.

"Maybe she didn't."

"The police aren't looking for anyone else."

"She still might be innocent."

"I guess, but Hell hath no fury, right?" He pulled a face.

I sighed, loudly. "Indeed."

"I wish I knew how to apologize to you. I feel like such a shit."

"Explain it. I never did understand what I did wrong. Why did you break up with me?"

"You didn't do anything wrong," Stuart said.

"Then why? Why did you spread those rumors about me? Do you know what horrors you unleashed?"

He cocked his head. "Huh?"

"What people do to sluts?"

His face crumpled. His brow creased. The corners of his mouth turned downwards. He looked comical for a moment. I laughed. His eyebrows lifted and his eyes opened wider, reversing the lines. He looked ridiculous. I lifted my hand to my lips to catch the giggle that escaped.

"Are you feeling okay?" he asked.

I turned away from him and stared at the wall. A few photos of two pretty children were pinned to the faded wallpaper.

"It's your fault," I said.

"What's my fault, Pam?"

"When you use that word... it means... public property. Do you understand?"

"I'm sorry, Pam. I'm not sure I understand a word you're telling me."

"Daryl..."

Stuart grabbed my arm and spun me round to face him. "What about Daryl?"

Tears swelled in my eyes. The grief I had been clinging to for twenty years poured out of me. "He said I deserved it. He called me a filthy slut. He said you told him..." I never did find out what he had said. "What did you tell him?"

Stuart backed away. His face turned towards his mobile phone on the kitchen counter beside the oven. I shook my head, warning him not to move. He inched away from me, although his eyes never left my face. He looked terrified. What sort of monster had I become that this gentle boy was trying to hide from my anger?

I reached inside my handbag and drew out the knife. His eyes dropped from my face to the weapon. His pulse fluttered in his throat, and I could hear his thoughts; he knew what I had done, and he wasn't accepting any responsibility for my actions. He'd spread lies about me, made me a pariah, made me public property. He'd had his fun then discarded me like a soiled tissue. I wouldn't let him tell any more lies about me. I wouldn't let him pick up that phone and tell the police I was a murderer. It wasn't murder. It was justice.

What was the right way to deal with such a spreader of lies?

I lunged at him, but he pushed me away. I fell to the floor, and my knife skidded across the vinyl. I crawled towards it, but he grabbed my ankles. My chin hit the floor and I bit my tongue. I spat out blood then glanced over my shoulder. Stuart looked pale, and his torso shook violently. He sat on the floor with his phone in his fist. I kicked out and knocked it from his fingers then kicked again, busting his nose.

The gentleness left his eyes. He snarled as he loomed above me. Blood from his nose dripped onto my clothes and skin as he grabbed the knife. He looked at me as if he was convinced this was all a dream and any moment he would wake up. My tongue throbbed and the reassuring words I tried to offer flapped around my mouth unintelligible.

"Fuck it," I cursed.

Rising from the floor, I pressed my lips against his. Our blood smeared over each other's faces. His tongue flicked between my lips and into my mouth. His desire overwhelmed him, and he used his weight to push me back to the floor while his tongue probed deeper. I bit down hard. He tried to pull away, but my teeth were clamped around his tongue. He was pinned in place by my needle-sharp jaws. From the corner of my eye, I saw him raise his hand. Too late I remembered he still had my knife. The pain was hot as though a poker had been thrust between my ribs. I shuddered and coughed, letting him go. He scuttled across the floor, his tongue hanging out of his mouth, swollen, and covered in blood. I closed my eyes and let the black heat of my wound carry me away. I smiled as a thought crossed my mind; the word slut wouldn't be formed in his broken mouth for a very long time.

Carmilla Voiez's books are both extraordinarily personal and universally challenging. As Jef Withonef of Houston Press once said - "You do not read her books, you survive them."

4

CLICK BAIT

BY JEF ROUNER

MARCO WAS BORED. BORED AND DRINKING. BORED AND drinking and idly playing with his dick with one hand and his phone with the other. This particular combination of masculine frustration and decadence disappeared after the fall of the Roman emperors only to reappear in the 21st century among the populist masses. With an entire world open to him a man could explore vast expanses of land and knowledge and history without ever leaving his couch, yet the apathy of a small human mind froze ambition except for the most basic of human needs.

In his hand, Marco held a miracle that could unlock the secrets of all human wisdom, and all he really wanted to do with it was to make it serve the tube of flesh in his other hand.

Marco switched back and forth from app to app on his phone. He searched mobile video sites for a pornographic picture or video that might hold his attention long enough to get off. The dings and pings of notifications on social media were too much of a distraction. It was meaningless, but Marco attended to it with the same languid banality with which he was barely pleasuring himself.

Eventually hair, skin, voices and genitals all blended together. There was no meat to it.

His phone went off again and Marco paged over to a profile where a friend of his was having discussion about an upcoming Cowboys game. There was all the usual shit talking of course, mixed here and there with actual discussion on running games and the defense capabilities that had eroded over the last two seasons. His buddy, Patrick, was going back and forth on the new place-kicker with a girl named Carine. Marco's contributions were mainly one-word expressions of support for Danny, but he found himself idly clicking on Carine's profile to get a better look at her.

She was young, with big brown eyes. Her skin was dark and glossy, striking against the Cowboys jersey she wore in her profile picture. She was cheering wildly in a parking lot somewhere, celebrating her team, and Marco liked the look of wild enthusiasm about her.

Skimming through her profile, he liked what he saw. She was a football fan, of course, but also seemed big on beer and car movies. Photos of her over the summer showed that she apparently worked out, and Marco's other hand started to get a little more ambitious as he eyed the way Carine's yellow bikini gripped her ass and clung wetly to her tits.

He clicked "like" on that picture and scrolled through for more. There was nothing else as enticing on her page. Frustrated he scrolled back to the beach and darted his eyes between her body and the laughing smile on her face. On a whim he opened a message box on his phone to her.

Go Cowboys, right!

A small loading icon indicated she was responding.

FUCK AND YEAH!

Pleased that he'd made some contact, Marco considered what to say next. He scrolled back to her picture again and rubbed himself harder.

You're FKN cute. We should get together and watch a game sometime.

The response icon pulled up... then disappeared... and again... and again. Marco was getting impatient waiting for her reply. Couldn't she take a compliment?

Thanks.

That was it, he thought. That's what took her a couple of minutes to come up with? He frowned at the screen wondering what sort of stuck up bitch would just leave him hanging like that.

So, wanna hang out? You look fun to do
LOL
Meant 2B around
Autocorrect

Marco smiled at his flirtation. She was typing again.

Um, no. That's OK. I'm not really dating right now. School's really crazy.

Fucking bitch! She wasn't too busy to argue running stats on Patrick's profile for the last thirty minutes, was she? He started to type something to that effect but began thinking on her picture again. He clicked over and his hand began to really get a workout on his cock. In his head the scenarios involving her had started to evolve. Carine on her knees as he shoved himself down her throat, on all fours with her hands tied receiving him in her ass as she grunted painfully against a gag, his spent seed drying on her face. Marco shook himself out of it. God, he needed to get laid and this was who he wanted at the first opportunity.

O cmon. Didn't say let's get married. School is easier with a friend with drinks. Whatcha studying?

He got up, stumbling a little as he did so. He made his way into the kitchen to open another beer, but the six-pack was empty. Cursing, he opened the freezer and glared at the little bit of vodka he had left, which he topped off with store-brand lemon-lime soda. He halfheartedly swished it around to mix it before taking a big swig. His phone went off again and he fell onto his couch.

Witch hunts. I'm also grading papers for a medieval women's studies class. Taking forever.

He set his drink down.

Sure you don't need a break?

The little icon spun.

Can't, but better luck elsewhere, yeah? Have a nice night.

Un-fucking-believable.

OK, BUT I DON'T THINK I'M GOING TO BE ABLE TO SLEEP WITH AN IMAGE OF YOU RUNNING THROUGH MY HEAD
UR BEAUTIFUL
BEST LOOKING GIRL IVE SEN IN A WHILE
HELLO?

YO
BABY?
FUCK YOUR NIGGER CUNT NE WAY BITCH
UR TITS DROOP AND YOU PROBABLY HAVE AIDS FROM
AFRICA

Marco threw his phone onto the table and slammed his drink down in one gulp. He knew he should probably go to bed but getting up off the couch was a task best suited for the morning. Part of him recognized that even if Carine were to appear naked in his living room like a horny genie it was unlikely that he'd be up to the task of showing her a real man. The rest of his brain compensated by churning the hate in his head like a cocktail in a shaker.

He threw his arm across his face and wondered what the hell was wrong with women these days. Guys used to be able to get somewhere telling them they were pretty. Now they acted like they didn't even owe him the chance. It's a bunch of stuck up nonsense, he thought as a stupor finally calmed him into unconsciousness.

A low ping snapped him awake suddenly a little while later. His head hurt massively. The room was bright, but only because he'd left the lights on when he'd passed out. He picked up his phone and saw that it was only 1:00 AM. There was also a response from Carine.

I WENT AND TOOK A SHOWER TO STAY AWAKE AND GET SOME WORK DONE. THIS IS WHAT YOU SAY TO A WOMAN WHEN SHE DOESN'T RESPOND TO YOU FOR AN HOUR? I THINK YOU'RE A CREEP AND A RACIST.

Marco scrolled back through his responses and for a second couldn't believe that he'd called her the n-word. Shit. She could screen cap that and show people. Guys could lose their jobs if that sort of thing got spread around the right way. He typed...

IF IM RACIST WHY WOULD I WANT TO FUCK YOU? MAYBE YOU DON'T LIK WHITE DICK

That seemed fairly reasonable, he thought.

Don't message me again.

This time, Marco actually said "bitch" out loud. Fuck that, she'd called him a racist and didn't have any right to tell him not to speak to her.

In the back of his mind, an idea was slowly working forward. Carine in the shower soaping herself, letting water trickle down her belly and into the hair between her legs. Marco pictured her, touching herself, thinking about him, wanting a white guy but too stuck up to admit that she really needed a man that wouldn't put up with her bullshit. She needed him, and he had a great way to remind her of that.

Marco shrugged his pants and underwear down, the fastenings still undone from his earlier pawing. His dick was hard as stone and to Marco's mind had never looked more magnificent. He positioned himself with one hand holding it firm and clicked a picture with his phone that made it look huge and thick so close to the lens. Marveling at his own perfect manhood, he hit send.

THIS IS WHAT YOUR MISSING

His fogged mind was a wave of hormonal signals. His phone was able to find him a video of a black girl that looked enough like Carine to Marco's inebriated brain to suffice for release. He timed his strokes with those of the man pounding her over the hood of a car, finally shuddering as a watery orgasm leaked from his member. Marco sat shaking for a minute and finally managed to stand up and wipe himself in the bathroom. He splashed water on his face and decided it was high time for bed.

Padding through the living room he grabbed his phone and put it on the charger. Just as he was turning away, it pinged one last time. He glanced at it.

Won't be me that's missing it.

Whatever, cunt, he thought, and fell into his bed.

THE NEXT MORNING insisted on happening despite Marco's repeated prayers. The hangover in his head felt like a hyperactive child on a bouncy castle and his stomach was filled with poison. He needed water and toast badly. Blinking, he fumbled his way towards the bathroom.

He was still too messed up to urinate while standing so he put the seat down and sat. He filled a rinse cup with water from the sink and sipped from it as he sat with his head dangling low. It took him a while to notice that he couldn't hear any urine. Come to think of it, he didn't really need to go to the bathroom at all. It was just what he did. Weird after how much he'd drank last night.

He stood up, flushed needlessly, and stomped into the bedroom. It wasn't until he passed the bedroom mirror that he realized he no longer had a penis.

His scream was loud enough that his neighbor upstairs started yelling at him to knock it the fuck off. Marco stopped, but only because he'd run out of breath. He looked down at himself and clawed at his face in horror.

There was no blood. No scar. No wound. His belly simply continued down until it met a thatch of pubic hair that ran uninterrupted between his legs. Hands shaking, he ran his fingers through it, feeling nothing. There wasn't a stump or a piss hole or even a crop circle of bare skin where his cock and balls had once been. His crotch was as smooth as a Ken doll.

Marco's breathing was heavy and tremulous. He had absolutely no idea what to do. He wasn't in pain. In a frantic haze, he scrambled to the bedroom and pulled the sheets from the bed, desperately looking for his genitals or, barring that, some blood or sign that they'd ever been there in the first place. The sheets were soaked with sweat but otherwise clean. Nothing rolled out of the shaken sheets and blankets. In a rage, he hurled them at his lamp and knocked it to the floor where the bulb broke.

He must have sat on the floor for hours trying to make sense of it all, but every time he tried to come to terms with reality his mind scuttled away like a cockroach in the light.

He became utterly engrossed in watching the line of light that was slowly crawling through his window as the sun rose in the sky. He told himself that when the light reached that discarded sock, he would get up and figure something out. No, when it reached that stain further on. That's when he'd get up. When it touched his foot for sure.

It was only when it threatened to touch where he once sported his dick that he was able to muster the energy to move.

Marco dressed in a haze. Pulling on clean underwear and jeans felt strange and sick. His stomach lurched from hunger, but he was afraid to eat or drink anything. Where would the water go when it needed to leave his body? It was only the idea of a swollen bladder bursting inside him that finally convinced him to go to a doctor.

Numbly he called his regular physician and complained of a

pain in his... his... all he could mutter was a weak "down there." The nurse chuckled at his prudishness, and her laughter caused him to launch a punch into the plaster wall, leaving a gaping hole. Finally, she told him that there was an open spot in two hours that he eagerly took.

The drive was only fifteen minutes. Marco parked and walked around the building over and over again, not letting any thought find space to exist between the sound of his feet hitting the ground until it was time to go inside.

As he sat waiting, he kept checking his phone. The last message from Carine still burned there.

Won't be me that's missing it.

She'd blocked him from responding after that. Her small profile picture was now just a blank female-shaped head offering nothing. Marco refused to assign any meaning to the message but continued to peek at it like picking at a scab.

Eventually, he found himself in the waiting room and Dr. Baker came in shortly afterward.

"Now what seems to be the problem, Marco?" he asked.

"I'm having some issues... with my... um." Marco didn't really want to come out and say it.

"With your penis?" asked Dr. Baker. "With your testicles? Are you having trouble urinating? Painful discharge? There's no need for shyness, you know. I've seen more than you would ever believe."

"Maybe I should just show you," said Marco.

"Alright," said Dr. Baker, sitting on a stool with his clipboard on his lap. "Let's see what's going on."

Marco hesitantly undid his belt and unbuttoned his jeans. Shutting his eyes tight he hooked his thumbs into his pants and underwear and pushed them down to mid-thigh. Then, he waited for the scream of his doctor.

It never came.

"What am I supposed to be seeing here, Marco?" asked Dr. Baker. "If it's an itch or something I'm going to need to comb through your pubic hair, or maybe get a sample. There's no discharge or redness. Is anything tender to the touch?"

Marco couldn't believe it. He looked down, but he was still smooth and gelded. Dr. Baker reached forward and waved in the air near his crotch, mimicking the act of checking for lumps in his testicles but, as far as Marco could tell, there was nothing there to justify the expression of concentration on Dr. Baker's face. He felt nothing but the air disturbed by the movements.

"You said you had trouble going to the bathroom," said Dr. Baker.

Marco nodded.

"Well, it doesn't look like a blockage in the penis. It could be an obstruction in the bladder possibly. We should do an ultrasound to be sure and soon. Can you stick around?"

Marco nodded again.

An hour later Marco was pulling his pants back on with shaking hands. An ultrasound technician had also failed to remark on his state and the ultrasound showed nothing abnormal. As far as the rest of the world was concerned Marco was whole. Sitting in the car, he stared into the rearview mirror and did his best to convince himself that he was imaging the whole thing. He snaked his hand into his pants and let out an insane scream when he found himself barren there.

MARCO DIDN'T EAT or drink for the next 24 hours. All he did was lie in bed and stare up at the ceiling. He did not go into the bathroom for any reason. As he failed to interact on social media, the chirps on his phone grew fewer and farther between. An apology message to Carine bounced back as undeliverable.

For two straight hours around 2:00 am Marco could not stop laughing. He laughed until his throat burned and bled. He drank his own blood, he had no choice, but he would not drink anything else. His throat felt like a desert.

As the second day edged into the third Marco finally summoned the courage to message Patrick.

Hey man how is your friend Carine?

He sweated the few precious drops of liquid out of his skin waiting on a reply.

Y?

Marco closed his eyes and calmed himself, trying to get his hands still.

We were talking the other night on messenger and she seemed upset.

That was accurate.

The night you called her a NIGGER CUNT?

Oh, fuck.

Yeah. I want to apologize to her.
I was drunk.
It was way out of line.
I cant stop thinking about it.
CAN YOU TELL HER TO UNBLOCK ME OR CALL ME OR
SOMETHING?

The effort of getting even that out in his weakened state made Marco dizzy and he lay back down on the bed. Every few seconds the typing indicator popped up then disappeared as Patrick apparently decided against sending what he was typing. Every time it did Marco let out a sad, childish moan.

Marco?

It wasn't from Patrick. It was from Carine.

I'M SO SORRY
SORRY
PLEASE

The typing indicator. Oh please.

What appeared on the screen was his own dick pic that he'd sent her. The sight made him cringe. Already the image of a cock seemed unnatural and gross. He actually thought he might throw up looking at himself holding his own erection.

This is what you're missing.

Marco typed.

YES

And after a second.

2424 MONTROSE BLVD
10 PM
TONIGHT
COME AROUND THE BACK

Marco let out a low breath. That was only an hour from now.

Just enough time for him to dress and drive over. He started to type an affirmation when his phone pinged again.

BABY

He dropped his phone like it was hot.

IT WAS A CONVENIENCE STORE. Marco didn't know what he was expecting but that was definitely not it. Looking into the clean store, his mouth watered for the images of cold sodas and water and juices. His stomach growled and grumbled for hot dogs on racks and chips in the bins. The first thing he would do, when he got his cock back, was walk in and gorge.

A sidewalk wound behind the building. Hugging the wall, Marco followed it until it opened into a small yard. There was a large shed that might once have been a garage. The rising doors were still there, but they were covered with red curtains. From between them came an electric blue glow.

Marco crept to the window and peaked in. There was a small gap in the curtains, and he was just able to see inside.

There were maybe six women inside. They ranged in age from one teenager to a woman in her late 50s. The walls were lit by glowing crystal lamps that pulsed in an unsynced arrhythmia. The women wore normal clothes, but around each of their necks was a string of blood-colored beads. They seemed to be singing a low song.

"Now you're spying," said a voice behind him. Marco spun.

It was Carine. She was wearing her Cowboys jersey over black leggings. Like the other women she wore a beaded necklace. In her hand she held a loaf of bread from the store and a bottle of water.

"Imsorryimsosorryiwasafraidandimsorryicalledyoua," he began in a twitchy whisper until Carine snapped at him to shut up. He couldn't stop. All he could do was simply mouth the words with his hands in front of him in a pleading gesture. He imagined he looked like a junkie trying to score but no longer cared.

"Get the door," Carine said.

Marco rushed to do just that. Carine walked past him, and he scuttled after her. They moved through a small laundry room and into the blue room beyond. All the women stopped what they were doing and turned to look at him.

After a second, they laughed.

The tiny fraction of Marco, the man that remained, tried very hard to rise through his broken shell to demand that these bitches quit their laughing and pay him the proper respect. It tried to rise, but there were too many broken girders in his soul to safely climb and it tumbled back down into his empty stomach.

The oldest woman and a chubby, short blond in her 30s swooped over to him and grabbed him under the arms. Unresisting, they pulled him to the center of the room and sat on either side of him, cooing and petting him like a puppy. He smelled sage and oak and began to think about witches as they crooned and cackled.

The teenager, with Carine by her side, went to a wall of shelves and grunted as she pulled off a large box with a padlock. Carine helped her steady it and carry it to lay in front of Marco. He was shaking, thinking he knew what he was about to see and being so wrong.

"Marco here has come to say he's sorry," said Carine and the group laughed again.

"Don't they always," said the oldest woman. "It just takes a little lost thing and all of a sudden they can't wait to say they're sorry." More laughter.

"You want your cock back," said the teenager, clearly at an age where she was delighted to be able to say the word in the company of adults. Marco nodded.

"Say please," remarked a thin, grim Hispanic woman in a suit.

"Please," said Marco.

"Say pretty please," said another.

"Pretty please," said Marco.

And with that, they opened the box.

Inside were ten penises. One was the most enormous one he'd ever seen. They weren't just lying there. They inched and crawled like blind worms, dragging heavy balls behind them. They crawled over each other like newborn rats, the urethrae opening and closing like mouths. Incredibly a mewling sound came from each one, the only other sound to be heard save the horrid slick noise of cock flesh writhing against cock flesh.

"Poor things are hungry," said Carine. She reached into the box and pulled out a dark brown cock, stroking it like a kitten as it wriggled in her hand. Obscenely she kissed it murmuring, "Mommy loves you, doesn't she?" If there had been anything in his stomach, Marco would have thrown up.

Carine took a slice of bread from one of the other women and pulled off a small crumb. Marco watched sickly as the penis nipped and bit at the bread, weakly pulling tiny bits into itself through the hole at the tip. Marco watched chunks move down the length as it swallowed.

Another woman poured a small amount of water into her cupped hands and Carine allowed the squirming penis to suck at it until its thirst was apparently sated.

"Now to feed the others," she said.

But instead of picking another from the box, she simply set it down inside. At first the other penises simply waved at her in the air, begging to be held and fed, but Carine did nothing. The full cock lay placidly in the corner, too full to move. One by one the others began moving towards it.

A couple tried to suck crumbs from the penis Carine had fed, but there was nothing there to grab. Ravenous their movements became more and more aggressive and the full cock started to cry out horribly. Red spots appeared in its skin as the other, starving penises wore holes in the flesh like lampreys. They fastened on their box-mate and tied themselves into knots in order to get the leverage to pull off skin and worm their way in deep enough to drink blood. The full cock could only weakly flop and squeal until finally it fell silent.

The other cocks moved off their meal, each fed and watered to their measure and safe from the others. Marco saw his own, laying fat and terrible, in the corner. He wanted to crush it nearly as much as he wanted it back.

"Still want it?" asked Carine.

"Yes," said Marco, crying what few tears he could from dry eyes. This sent another long laugh from the group.

The teenage girl fished her hand into Marco's pocket and retrieved his phone, handing it to Carine. Another woman handed her a cable and charger with strange symbols. She connected it to his phone and reached down to grab his cock. Gripping it in her hand, she drove the prongs of the plug into the skin. It wailed and Marco felt a vague pain. Carine fiddled with his phone and then a horrid sucking sound began. Marco doubled over with pain as his cock was sucked through the narrow cable quickly but painfully. He could feel it pushing out of his crotch and briefly wondered if this was what childbirth felt like. He was nearly unconscious from it until finally it ended, save for a dull ache.

His breathing was slow and shattered. He wrapped his arms around himself. He heard the women talking and was aware that they were leaving. He didn't know how long it was before he found the strength to get up, but he finally did.

Gingerly he felt for his cock and found himself whole and unhurt. He tried to smile but he could feel the still screaming pieces of another man's member writhing inside his own meat. The idea made him sick and he pulled his hand away.

As he left the building, the door shut behind him. The blue glow from the windows went out. He made his way around to the store and guzzled three bottles of water in a row before meekly asking the clerk if he could use the restroom.

In the dirty room, he gingerly voided while sitting down, not trusting himself to stand. When done, he looked in the bowl, expecting to see blood or pus or something, but it was just normal urine. He flushed, washed his hands and left.

As he left and prepared to go home, his phone pinged. The sound made him cringe like it was the roar of a woodland creature at night. It was Carine.

The picture of his dick had been altered in a paint program. The shaft had been colored brown with yellow bristles over his hand. A clip art witch had been pasted above it, with a crescent moon in the upper corner.

LOL

Marco looked at the clerk, idly flipping through a magazine. "Do you guys buy phones," he asked.

Jef Rouner is an award-winning freelance journalist, the author of The **Rook** Circle, *and a member of The Black Math Experiment.*

5

LIBERATION

FIRST PUBLISHED IN PSEUDOPOD (EPISODE 38)

BY KEVIN DAVID ANDERSON

To most people it was just an ordinary Thursday, but to Caroline, today was the day she decided to rid herself of the spiders living in her brain. Even though they pulled only a single spider from that woman in Brazil, there had to be more than one in her brain, living just under the skullcap like lizards burrowed beneath the floorboards.

It had to be more than one. She had so much passion and determination when she was young, it would take several brain-dwelling parasites to eat it all. The spiders lived off impulses of her desire, feeding on her resolve to do the things she really wanted to do.

"That's what the spiders live on," Caroline had said to her roommate exactly one week ago.

From her favorite chair in their small living room, Wendy shook her head. "Please tell me you're joking, Caroline."

Caroline's intensity grew. "It's all right here."

She held out the medical journal, dated July 1986, and pointed to a picture of a woman lying unconscious in an archaic-looking operating room. She slid her finger across to the opposite page to a murky photo of something hideously pale, swollen. The photograph was slightly out of focus like images of Bigfoot and the Loch Ness Monster, but a multi-legged form was discernible.

It had the characteristics of a spider but looked more like some underwater creature – a mutated octopus or alien squid. The arachnid's legs were thick like tentacles, splayed out on a porcelain table. Pools of blood spotted the off-white surface, and a pair of forceps lay next to the spider, providing a sense of scale. The creature's creamy white frame looked to be about four inches in length, reminding Caroline of salamanders discovered deep in subterranean caves, living their lives in darkness; the creatures appeared pasty—sickly.

Wendy traced a finger along the picture's caption. "It says, it didn't have any eyes."

"It doesn't need them," Caroline said, grinning. "It lives in darkness, feeling its way around." Just like the salamanders.

Wendy stood up. "This doesn't prove anything, Caroline. You don't have spiders living in your brain, for God's sake." She put a hand on her hip, sighing deeply. "Okay, let's be logical about this for a second. That woman, whoever the hell she is, lives in Brazil. And I'll admit there are all kinds of freaky shit living in the rainforest that we don't know about yet, but spiders that eat your determination, turning women into breeder cows? Come on! Even if there were, how did they get to Seattle? I don't remember you vacationing in Brazil recently, or ever."

Caroline had anticipated this question, because it had occurred to her as well. She'd never been out of the state of Washington, let alone south of the equator. She'd always wanted to travel, Paris, Rome, Vienna, but when it came down to it, her resolve to make the arrangements seemed to evaporate. Damn spiders!

Caroline slapped the journal closed. "I didn't need to go to Brazil. The spiders were brought to me."

Wendy raised a brow. "What?"

"The rainforest has been harvested and exported for our consumption since the fifties."

"What are you talking about?"

"Where do you think most of our medicines come from? Our birth control, Prozac, Valium? Hell, even our makeup, moisturizers, eye liner, lipstick. You name it. It all comes from the rainforest. Women have been inundated with this stuff for more than fifty years."

"Jeez, you've given this a lot of thought."

"Is it so hard to believe that these parasites could have hitched a ride in our birth control pills or some hair product packaged by men for women?"

Wendy sighed and held out a hand. "Look, I know you've gone through some rough shit. That asshole husband of yours getting custody of your kids – God, I don't know how I could live with that. But it doesn't mean there's anything wrong with you." Wendy stepped forward, her green eyes empathetic. "You've got your life on track now. In a few months we'll both pass our exams and be certified RNs. It's gonna be—"

"I don't even want to be a nurse," Caroline snapped. "That's what I'm talking about. It was my husband's decision. He made all the arrangements. Where we would live. When we would have kids. What kind of career I should have. Why I needed to get a second job to pay for his education. Who he would fuck behind my back." Caroline pictured the unwanted events in her life. "Through everything, I never raised an objection. Didn't complain, not once. My existence is like a movie I'm watching. I didn't want to have kids. I don't think I even wanted to get married. All my life I've wanted to do things, but I've never done them. Not one."

When Caroline looked up again, Wendy had backed away.

"Don't you see?" Caroline gestured to herself. "It's not just me. Why do you think women are second-class citizens? Why do we accept lower pay for the same job done by a man?" Caroline pointed at Wendy. "Why do you sleep with all those guys when you said you really didn't want to?"

Wendy's eyes flashed with anger. "There are no spiders living in our brains, goddamn it. I can't believe I'm even having this conversion."

"That's what they want you to believe."

"The spiders?"

Caroline nodded. "And men."

Wendy quieted for a moment, seeming deep in thought. She blinked and then looked at Caroline. "I've put up with all your craziness, but this... I can't be here right now." She hurried toward the front door of their small high-rise apartment. "Being your friend is just too hard. I'm gonna... I'm gonna just go."

Caroline rushed after her, catching the door as Wendy opened it. "You don't really want to go. It's the spid—"

"Let go of the fucking door," Wendy said, harsh words soaked in fear.

Caroline felt like she'd been doused with a bucket of cold water. She let go of the door.

Wendy moved through the opening, and without looking back said, "Get some help, Caroline. Seriously."

Caroline slammed the door.

That was a week ago and Caroline hadn't seen her since. Two days later Wendy returned to the apartment to get her belongings while Caroline was on duty at the hospital. She must have been in a hurry because she left a couple of things. Knick-knacks mostly, some cookware. Even the note she wrote seemed rushed – echoing her final words to Caroline.

Get some help. Please.

Placing the stainless-steel bit of the cranial drill on the bathroom counter, Caroline surveyed the instruments of her liberation. Scalpel, forceps, sutures and gauze, laid out according to size on the counter. The surface resembled the chalky porcelain table in the medical journal photo of the Brazilian brain spider. She almost laughed but stopped herself—the sutures above her hipbone were still very tender. She'd performed a preliminary procedure on herself earlier in the morning, extracting the few ounces of fat she'd need to plug the hole.

She picked up the forceps and turned them over in her hand. If she used too much pressure, she might tear the legs off, allowing the spider to scurry to the safety and darkness of her gray matter. A soft touch was needed. Her surgical instructor had said the same thing moments before the first brain surgery she'd assisted with. The patient, some man, died on the table, but not before Caroline got an excellent crash course in poking around the human brain.

She set the forceps next to a Tupperware container that held her body fat. She pinned back her auburn hair, exposing the pale patch of scalp she had shaved clean, just an inch above her ear. It glistened with a single bead of sweat in the soft glow of the bathroom light. She tapped the shaved area with her finger.

Numb.

She'd injected herself with a third of the recommended dose of anesthetic for such a procedure—one requiring the patient to remain conscious. A full dose may have made it difficult to stand or keep a clear head. In any case, her partial dose meant there would be some pain. How much?

She stared at her small frame in the mirror. She wore only underwear and an Alanis Morissette concert T-shirt. She hadn't gone to the concert. She'd wanted to but didn't.

The bathroom window was reflected in the mirror. The Seattle skyline bled through, the Space Needle as erect as ever, jutting up from a pubic layer of fog, reminding her who really ran the world.

She wanted privacy, so she turned and drew the curtain. Liberation was often a lone pursuit.

Days before, she began picturing how she would do this. Do it quickly. Do it fast. Don't think about it. Thinking might let the spiders know you're coming.

She picked up the scalpel and touched it to her numb flesh. She'd planned to cut a fast x-shaped incision, but when she pulled the blade back the wound looked more like a bleeding cross. She dabbed it with gauze until the flow of blood subsided, then wiped away the sweat on her brow. Using the scalpel, she cut deeper and peeled back the folds of flesh, exposing her skull. Not much, just enough to touch the drill bit to bone.

No pain yet.

She lifted the drill and inserted the bit in the breach on her scalp. When the stainless-steel point touched her skull, she felt the contact all the way down her spine. The sensation reverberated through her limbs, tapering off like ripples on a liquid surface.

She breathed fast, forcing the air in and out. Her heart raced. She pressed her lips together and gritted her teeth.

Very soon now, she told herself. Liberation.

The sound of the drill coming to life startled her, but not enough to lose focus. She gently pushed the drill inward, keeping her hand steady. Thin bands of smoke laced with ground bone fragments drifted up from the point of contact. Perfectly normal, she told herself. Doing fine.

The drill went deeper, and she kept a close watch on the depth, trying to avoid piercing the meninges—the three layers of membranes protecting the brain. She was amazed at the lack of pain, but as the familiar burning smell reached her nostrils, a blinding white light exploded in her skull.

Agony pulsed like a camera flash going off in her brain. Each flash caused her knees to buckle a little more. She closed her eyes and screamed, reaching for the mirror. Open your eyes, goddamn it, open your eyes. Fight through this.

She opened one eye and then the other. The drill bit wasn't moving. Her finger had come off the button. Damn it. But as she pushed the bit forward, she realized nothing solid was pushing back. She had broken through. She backed the drill out and unfolded the surgical mirror that was rigged to the medicine cabinet.

A clear yellow-tinted liquid dripped from the hole. Oh, shit. Cerebrospinal fluid. She had broken through the middle meningeal layer—the arachnoid. Images from her textbooks depicted this area as a cobweb of thread-like strands attaching to the innermost region. It was where the spiders lived. But the appearance of cerebrospinal fluid meant she had gone below this into the subarachnoid layer. There was only a finite amount of this precious fluid protecting her brain. Losing a little was okay; most people did throughout their lifetime, but losing a lot was deadly.

She tilted her head to keep the fluid from spilling out. She picked up a penlight, clicked it on, then aimed the beam into her exposed brain. The fluid seemed to be stabilizing. Thank God.

Her pain had tapered off, except in regions completely foreign to where all the action was. The muscles around her ribs ached enormously and pulsing pains anchored themselves in the soles of her feet.

She took a deep breath and switched the penlight on and off, aiming the flickering beam into the hole in her skull. Up until this point her plan contained elements of familiar territory. As a surgical RN she had assisted many similar procedures on dozens of patients. The next part of her plan was sheer guesswork.

She hoped that the brain spiders had evolved like other creatures that inhabited the dark. Bottom-dwelling enigmas living in the deepest ocean trenches shared a fascination with the eyeless subterranean salamanders. Although none needed light to survive, they would be drawn to it by an instinctual curiosity. Even creatures without eyes turned toward the light, like a blind man sensing the exact moment someone else entered a room.

Caroline's thumb ached as she continued to flick the light on and off. Rotating the penlight in her hand she tried using her index finger to press the button but found it difficult to aim the light. It occurred to Caroline that she could leave the light on and wave it back and forth over the hole. From the spider's point of view, it would look the same. Why didn't these things occur to her sooner? Maybe the spiders fed on common sense as well. That would explain a lot.

Minutes went by. She started to feel dizzy. I can't do this much longer.

"Come out, come out, wherever you are."

Suddenly, there was movement. Subtle at first. Probing. Just an ivory tip. Then, a white needle-like leg emerged.

Caroline stopped moving the penlight and held her breath.

The thin pasty leg explored the area like a blind person's cane. Then it abruptly stopped. Motionless. It was as if it had suddenly become aware it was being watched.

Caroline reached for the forceps. Her hand fell on an empty counter. She wanted to look for the instrument but was afraid to take her eyes off the tiny leg's reflection in the mirror. If she looked away, it might disappear. She locked her gaze on the arachnid, willing it to stay.

She felt along the counter as the spider's leg investigated the jagged edges of freshly cut bone. Another leg appeared. Then another.

Caroline's fingers grazed the forceps handle. *Thank God.* She lifted them and opened the needle-nose end. She eased the instrument forward, watching her movements in the mirror.

Three legs, almost an inch long, protruded from her skull.

Each one seemed determined to explore a different area of her scalp.

The open forceps hovered over the thickest point of two legs. Caroline swallowed hard. She felt six years old again, playing that silly game, Operation. The similarities were uncanny. Use your tweezers to remove the ghost-white plastic bones without touching the metal edge. A steady hand wins the game; graze the edge and you lose your turn.

More was at stake than losing a turn. If the spider broke free or she tore its legs off, she would lose her one chance to regain her will. Her life.

She clamped the forceps around the spidery appendages and, using a touch so soft and accurate she could have picked up a grain of rice, she began to pull.

The spider didn't come at first. Several other legs appeared, and it looked like they were searching for a way to anchor themselves. Then it began to slip. It slid quickly through the hole like a newborn calf being born. Caroline flicked it into the sink, unclamping the forceps. She glanced down at it, but there was new movement in the mirror.

A second spider had found its way to the hole, its legs probing. How many, she wondered. How many?

Ten minutes later she had her answer. There were three in all. The third seemed to climb through the hole of its own volition, needing very little encouragement from the forceps. Maybe the spiders sought a kind of liberation of their own.

She repaired the meninges and packed the hole in her skull with her own body fat. This should have been surprisingly painful, but it wasn't. She knew that the body's pain receptors could turn themselves off in extreme conditions, but she didn't think that's what was happening. As she sutured her scalp, she glanced at her body in the mirror. She remembered it being so small before, dwarfed in the ceiling-to-countertop glass. But now it looked as if the mirror could barely contain her frame. She felt different. She was different.

Liberated.

The last suture tied she clipped the excess stitching away. As she laid the scissors down, exhaustion hit her. She bent forward, bracing herself on the counter. Her head hung over the sink, hair dangling above the porcelain. She drew slow, deep breaths and took her first opportunity to examine the parasites. She blinked a few times, not immediately registering what was wrong.

Gone.

The sink was empty.

She smiled as she pictured the watery arachnids scurrying down the drain, traversing the miles of plumbing under the city. Liberation, my friends. Liberation.

The air in the bathroom smelled foul so she staggered to the window. She wanted to draw the curtain open, but she ended up pulling it off the rod. Pressing her forehead to the glass, she looked down at the women scurrying on the streets that spun out like a web from downtown. So many women, she told herself. There are more of us than there are men. She felt troubled watching the women rushing to jobs they didn't want, raising families they didn't want, hell, even wearing shoes they didn't want.

There are so many of us. So many women needing liberation. I'm gonna need a lot more drill bits.

There was a tapping at the bathroom door. "Hey Caroline. It's me, Wendy. I know I should have called before coming over like this."

Caroline pushed away from the window.

"Especially after how I left and all. I'm sorry about that. Anyway, I just wanted to come by and pick up my pots and pans. I met this guy and he wants me to cook my famous Italian casserole for him tonight. I know, I know, I hate to cook, but I really like this guy."

Caroline moved over to the counter.

Wendy rapped on the door again. "Are you in there?"

Caroline grinned at her tall and free-willed image in the mirror. She picked up the drill.

Time to start the liberation.

Kevin David Anderson was born in Indiana, and currently lives and writes speculative fiction in Southern California.

6

DELICACY

BY NICKIE JAMISON

THE BASS MUSIC THRUMMED; THE HARD PULSE ALMOST enough to dislodge internal organs. Mike tipped his head back, emptying the last of the Beam and Coke into his mouth, crunching on the mostly melted ice. He pushed his hand through his short auburn locks and smiled at the girl sitting on the bar stool next to him. She looked his type: long blond waves, short skirt, and knee-high black stiletto boots. Her slender fingers wrapped around a short tumbler of scotch on the rocks and her thumb slid back and forth in rhythm with the music across the condensation forming on the glass.

"Hey. I'm Mike. What's your name, beautiful?" he asked.

"Kitt," she said. The smear of gold glitter on her eyelids glinted in the ambient lighting of the bar when she turned to look at him. Kitt crossed her legs and adjusted the hem of her short denim skirt.

Mike glanced down at the exposed strip of milky skin between the lace top of her black thigh-highs and the frayed edge of her skirt. He bit his lip, imagining himself pushing his hand up that slender expanse of warm flesh and exploring beneath her skirt. His fingers tightened on the side of the bar. He leaned closer so that his pectoral muscles brushed her upper arm.

"Well, Kitten, I'd love to make you purr."

"Really?" Kitt's cherry red fingernails combed through her golden tresses, flicking the waves over the bare shoulder side of her off-the-shoulder black sweater. "Mike, I eat boys like you." She grinned, her voluptuous red lips parting to reveal a row of perfect white teeth.

"Good thing I'm sweet," he said.

Kitt's gaze traveled from Mike's face down the tight blue T-shirt that clung to his torso. She paused at his belt line and pursed her lips, seeming to consider something.

"Dance with me," she said.

Mike followed Kitt into the sea of chaotically tangled bodies writhing on the dance floor. He drifted right and left, avoiding waving limbs. As he walked, he watched the hypnotic swing of Kitt's curvy hips and the tight stretch of denim across her pert ass cheeks, admiring how effortlessly she threaded her way through the crowd.

Kitt's white skin glowed blue under the black and neon lights that surrounded the dance floor. Even with the height of her heels, Kitt stood half a head shorter than Mike. Her eyeshadow caught the lights, sparkling with rainbow hues whenever she turned her head.

Mike and Kitt moved together in a slow grind. Kitt's hips swayed back and forth, the round curve of her bottom pressing against the front of Mike's jeans. Mike's cock pulsed at the contact. He placed his hands on her slender waist, letting his thumbs find their way to the bare strip of skin beneath the hem of her sweater, just over her hip bone. He stroked back and forth across the soft curve of her hips and Kitt arched her back, her rear pushing harder against his crotch.

Mike bit into the side of his cheek to keep a total boner at bay.

Kitt reached behind her and threaded her arms around Mike's neck; the cool tips of her slender fingers brushed against the shorter hairs at the nape. They gyrated to the music, lost in the electric thrill of light touches against bare skin that were timed with the pumping heartbeat flow of sound from the speakers.

When Kitt turned to face Mike, he saw the red flush of her cheeks and the glistening sheen of sweat across the ridge of her collarbone. She swung her hips against him, the softness of her belly caressing the denim stretched over his half-hard prick. The friction made him go full-mast.

Mike's hands moved from Kitt's hips to the curve of her backside as he ground harder against her. He felt the heat that radiated from between her thighs on the ends of his fingers when they brushed along the bend of skin where her ass met her creamy white legs.

Kitt smirked and took hold of his wrist. She weaved through the crowd, leading him to the exit.

"Where are we going?" Mike asked.

The coat check kid handed Mike his wool pea coat.

"My place," Kitt said. She slid her arms into a black leather bomber jacket. "It's only a couple of blocks away."

A couple of blocks was more like five. Mike sucked cold winter air into his lungs and watched his breath freeze in front of his face, obscuring his view of the dark city street. He was beginning to consider ditching when Kitt took a sudden sharp left down an alley, reached above her head, and pulled down a rusting fire escape ladder. She began to climb.

"Is that safe?" Mike asked. From his vantage point below the ladder, he could see her lack of underpants and the closely clipped landing strip between her thighs. His dick stiffened again. He adjusted his junk so he could comfortably follow her up the ladder.

Once they both stood on the landing, Kitt pulled the ladder back up. She stuck her hand through a busted-out pane, unfastened the latch, and raised the window. Kitt slid through and looked over her shoulder at Mike.

"Come on," she said.

"Do you actually live here?" Mike asked as he ducked inside the window.

In the dim hallway lights, Mike noticed how the stained wallpaper was ripped and peeling away from crumbling plaster.

"I own the whole building," she said, and took his hand, weaving her fingers together with his. "Inherited it when the old man finally kicked."

She opened an apartment door to the left and breezed through.

"That was nice of him."

Kitt snorted a derisive laugh, her head tipping back and throwing her golden waves across her shoulders. "He used to get his rocks off beating the shit out of me. I was owed."

Mike took a step back, the fine hairs on the back of his neck raising up in goose-pimples. Kitt's lips turned upward in a beautiful, magnetic smile. Mike decided this bitch was crazy; sexy but crazy. Tonight, he was going to make this hook up a dine-and-dash.

She tugged Mike into the apartment's small bedroom. He stared, mouth agape, at a free-standing Saint Andrew's cross perched next to a battered nightstand. The thick black leather cuffs riveted to the cross were scuffed and softened from use and the metal buckles lacked any traces of polished luster. An unframed full-length mirror was mounted on the wall opposite.

"You want me to strap you in?" Mike wiped his palms on his jeans.

Kitt grabbed the top of the cross, tipping the contraption horizontal on the bar running between the two triangular pieces of the base.

"Oh no," she said, and released her hold on the rack then fixed it back into the vertical position, bolting it in place.

Drawing closer, Kitt slipped her hands around Mike's slim waist. She kissed the tender flesh above the collar of his T-shirt, her pink tongue flitting out, tasting the exposed skin.

"I'm going to strap you in." Her teeth grazed along the taught sinews of his warm throat. A bolt of lust shot into Mike's belly and his prick strained hard against the fly of his jeans.

"You'll untie me, right?" His voice cracked as Kitt's fingers wandered under his T-shirt and down into the waistband of his pants.

She popped the metal button open, unzipped his fly, and her cool palm wrapped around his hard shaft. Kitt's hand slipped deeper into Mike's pants. She caressed the crease in his ball sack with her fingertip. Mike moaned as her fingernail skimmed against the delicate skin.

"Of course, once I'm done with you," she said.

Her fingers walked a trail up his torso and under his shirt. Mike pulled the blue cotton over his head and tossed it on the floor.

"Nice," Kitt said, leaning in to kiss the hollow of his throat. Her lips traced a path over his pectoral muscles, down along his six-pack abs, over the spray of dark curls that was his happy trail. She dipped her tongue into his navel and swirled it around.

Mike groaned, resisting the urge to buck his hips. He placed a hand on the top of Kitt's head, urging her soft mouth to go lower.

Kitt stopped just above the waistband of Mike's boxer briefs. "Strip."

Mike toed out of his shoes and leaned against an arm of the

cross to pull his socks off. His cock bobbed when he slid his pants and boxers off and shoved them aside, piling them with his T-shirt.

"Very nice," Kitt said. She pushed Mike back against the cross, securing his hands above his head. Bending down on her knees, she buckled his ankles into place.

Kitt's palm pressed against Mike's inner thigh and braced against him. She nipped at his scrotum as her thumb drew hard circles against his perineum. Mike sucked a hard breath in as the thumb movement morphed into the delicious pressure of her knuckles kneading at the tight flesh behind his balls and the nips gave way to licking and sucking.

With her free hand, she grasped the length of his shaft and stroked slowly up and down. Mike's head rolled back, and he opened his mouth in a deep exhale. He sighed and bucked his hips as much as he could from his restricted position.

Kitt's full red lips touched against the tip of his cock. She sucked him inside, her tongue twirling around the velvety length. She rose up from her knees and bent forward from the waist to keep him in her mouth. She deep-throated him, balls and all, pulled back then moved forward again; over and over.

Mike looked at Kitt's reflection in the mirror. Her bottom was completely visible from his vantage point. The dark curls of her coiffed landing strip stuck along the sides of her pink slit. Her pussy lips glistened with her own arousal. The tips of her slender fingers slid over her opening, two of them pressing inside and pulling out more wetness as they pumped back and forth.

With her other hand, Kitt cupped Mike's testicles. She caressed them, tugging lightly at the skin, her nails tickling the creases. The fingers inside of her tight hole worked in and out, pulling over her g-spot.

Kitt moaned and shuddered with her climax, her knees

wobbling for a brief second. The vibration ran through Mike's pelvis. His balls tightened. His cock pulsed as he emptied jets of hot salty come into her mouth.

Kitt bent and grabbed Mike's T-shirt from the floor. She spat his load onto the blue fabric and wiped the corners of her mouth with the sleeve before balling the shirt up and dropping it back into the pile with the rest of his discarded clothes.

Mike watched her hips swing in the mirror as Kitt opened the top drawer of the nightstand.

"Kitten, you're going to have to give me a minute," he said when he saw a flash of foil packaging.

Kitt stepped up on the bar at the bottom of the cross to give herself more height. Mike felt her warmth through her clothes and the hard peaks of her nipples as they pressed into his chest.

"I don't like that nickname," she said. The tip of her tongue skimmed the edge of his ear. Her teeth grazed the sensitive lobe.

Mike screamed as sudden sharp pain blossomed on the side of his head. His face felt like it was on fire. He hissed, blinking rapidly and trying not to go blind from pain and the rapid collection of tears at the corners of his eyes.

"The fuck?" he barked.

Kitt stopped chewing and swallowed. Mike barely felt the bee sting of the hypodermic needle she jammed into the side of his neck.

Mike fought groggily to regain consciousness. His eyes snapped open when he remembered where he was. He stared at the wide crack in the plaster on Kitt's bedroom ceiling. She must have locked the cross into the horizontal position. He tried to raise his head to look around, but a wide strap across his forehead kept him immobile. His jaw hurt and his mouth tasted like he'd been licking a dirty basketball. Mike groaned with the realization that a ball-gag had been fixed to his face.

He flexed his numb fingers, relishing in the pins and needles in his biceps until the waking nerves triggered the dull ache on the side of his head. Everything below his belly button felt heavy like it had fallen asleep, numbed from lack of blood flow and resting in the same position for – how long? There were no windows in the small bedroom. Mike wasn't entirely sure how long he'd been out.

A lamp clicked on, but its glow did not fully illuminate the room.

"Good morning." Kitt leaned over him, the tips of her blond waves brushed against his chin. She had wiped off her glittery eyeshadow and red lipstick. It took Mike a startled instant to recognize her. She moved away and he turned his eyes, trying to follow her movements.

Kitt sat down at a small folding table beside his head. She picked up a plate of food, took a fried piece of meat and dipped it into a dark red sauce then popped the whole piece in her mouth and hummed as she chewed.

"Oh my god, that *is* good." She savored, her eyes rolling back in ecstasy.

"These are amazing. I fried them in a lighter batter than usual," Kitt said. She dipped another piece and ate, her eyelids fluttering closed in sheer enjoyment.

"I'm sorry. I'm being rude. Would you like some?" she asked, holding a morsel between her fingers.

Mike growled, pushing his fuzzy thick tongue against the back of the ball gag.

"I'll take that as a no." Kitt took another bite from the piece in her hand. "It's funny how people's pallets differ. Some people think Rocky Mountain Oysters are a delicacy and others prefer lobster.

"Lobsters don't really scream when you throw them in the pot. I knew a guy that trapped lobsters for a living. He told me that they're toxic if you don't cook them as soon as you kill them. He was the type that believed in that hokey stuff and I used to believe him. Then, I Googled that shit." Kitt dipped another piece of food in the sauce and ate it.

"What happens is when the lobster dies the process of autolysis starts. The lysosomes in the cells start dumping a digestive enzyme into the cytoplasm. Lobster doesn't become toxic, it just rots faster. Science, bitch." She sucked glistening grease from her fingertips and then wiped her hands on the leg of her too large jeans.

"I dispatched a lobster, once, so I could grill it – split him right down the middle with a cleaver. Half of him took it like a man and lay there cooking, the other half not so much. Motherfucker kept wiggling around, so I had to hold him with the tongs so he wouldn't crawl away.

"I'm not so much a fan of lobster. I'm more of a steak girl. I knew a guy that worked on a ranch. He said the cows he killed tasted different from steaks you buy at the store. He said the big slaughterhouses dope cows up – drug them stupid so they won't know they're about to die and if you show the cow the blade you're gonna slit its throat with - scare it - the adrenaline rush will give the meat a *distinct* flavor. I wonder if he's right."

Kitt pushed her plate away, stood, and grabbed the top of the cross. She released the bolt, letting the cross lurch into the vertical position. Mike's stomach dropped. He felt himself falling. He instinctively tried to move his feet to keep from tumbling to the floor, even though he was strapped in.

Mike screamed around the ball gag when he caught sight of the mirror. His left leg and junk were gone. The thick leather cuff that should have been secured around his ankle held only air. Two jagged suture lines snaked up almost to the middle of his abdomen. He strained against the shackles that held his remaining limbs, his screams filling his head. In the fringe of his vision, Mike saw the contents of Kitt's plate – a deep fried penis and blood red dipping sauce.

He saw the flash of a knife in Kitt's hand just before she slit his throat.

NICKIE JAMISON's stories dabble in and blend many different genres, but she is best known for her LGBTQ+ erotic romances and short fiction.

7

MONKEY SEE, MONKEY DO

FIRST PUBLISHED IN FRI-SCIFI, AKASHIC BOOKS

BY ALICIA HILTON

THE CHIMPANZEE WITH A BANDAGED FOREHEAD grabbed a hypodermic needle.

Michelle smiled and watched Cynthia stab a syringe into the laboratory director's kneecap. The chimp appeared to be making a flower design. The other twelve needles she'd jabbed were arranged around the knee like daisy petals.

Michelle had planned to do the cutting, but the animals that she'd freed wanted to punish the man who'd used them for experiments.

"So...sorry," Michelle's boss sobbed. Harold Wade's pleas for mercy were muffled by the torn sleeve of his tweed jacket that was tied across his mouth in a gag.

A Norwegian rat that was the size of a large cat skittered across the stainless steel table where Harold was trussed. The rat bared his razor-sharp teeth and said, "Sugar, we can't hear you. Can you speak up?"

The biomedical scientist screamed and flailed against the ropes that were tied from his ankles and wrists to the table legs.

The rat glanced at Michelle. She nodded and Ralph locked his jaws over Harold's bare right foot. With one snip, he severed the big toe and the little toe next to it.

The tiny bones made a crunching noise as they were pulverized by the rat's molars.

Ralph jumped from the table to a utility shelf when his victim pissed himself, the gush of yellow fluid soaking the scientist's white boxers and spreading across the table, mixing with scarlet in a swirly pattern that reminded Michelle of a Rorschach inkblot. She wondered what her psychiatrist would say about the gory tableau. Dr. Taylor had encouraged her to express her feelings, but the therapist's advice hadn't worked.

She'd told Harold that his provocative comments about her breasts were offensive, but instead of apologizing, he'd threatened to have her fired. When she'd filed a complaint with HR, her supervisor wasn't reprimanded.

Michelle had returned to the lab on a Saturday so she could clean out her desk before she quit. No one was supposed to be working. She'd been putting her behavioral science books in her bag when Harold came up behind her and grabbed her throat. Remembering what he'd done, Michelle felt a wave of nausea. She swallowed bile and tried to regain control of her emotions.

She felt a tug on her pants leg and glanced down.

A baby chimp danced with excitement, a syringe in his fist.

She lifted Rico. His little teeth jabbered in glee when he sank the needle into Harold's rotund belly.

The scientist's thrashing increased, and his face and chest turned a florid shade that reminded Michelle of sautéed tomatoes.

A gorilla standing by the heart monitor said, "The subject's heart rate has risen to 141 beats per minute."

Michelle set Rico on the floor and addressed the gorilla. "Do you want a turn?"

Amos shook his head and gripped a pencil in his fist, writing in the lab notebook.

Michelle watched tears streaming down her boss's face. She touched her own neck. It was swollen and sore, and she knew she'd be bruised tomorrow. "You shouldn't have raped me."

"Please," he sobbed.

His fear fueled her hate. She held a Bunsen burner to Harold's cheek. The blistering skin made a popping noise and smelled sweet, like grilled pork sausage. Flames engulfed his dyed brown hair, greasy pomade sizzling. The halo of fire spread down his sideburns to the gag.

She stepped back and tossed a beaker of alcohol at his chest.

Now a human torch, his heels beat a timpani against the table. By the time fire burned through the ropes, he'd stopped moving.

The chimps scampered after the gorilla, knocking over a shelf of chemicals as they fled the smoke. She grabbed her purse and followed the rat.

Ralph leapt into the back of her minivan and curled up under a blanket. As she sped down the driveway, away from the conflagration, Michelle glanced in the rearview mirror and saw three figures crossing the pasture that led to the woods. The gorilla's stoop shouldered silhouette reminded her of her dead grandfather.

Alicia is an author, law professor, arbitrator, actor, former FBI Special Agent, scorpio, fueled by green tea and imagination.

8

HOLD ME

BY JASON DYER

THE FOG WAS OVERWHELMING. IT GLOWED SILVER IN the east where the moonlight tried to penetrate its dense veil to light the path of three girls who hurried along the abandoned railway.

"I told you, Vera! I don't like taking this way! It's all nasty, cold and ... and old," Janie cried out in disgust as she attempted to keep up with her friends.

Her cousin, Regina, struggled behind, constantly tripping on her black chiffon skirt.

"Oh deal, it's the quickest way home, and you know it!" Vera shot back, her fiery red hair blew back with the oncoming breeze. "Besides, we aren't gonna encounter anything scarier than what we just saw at Shady's. I swear that opening band. Yech! Especially that way too skinny bass player and his runny eyeliner. I mean, seriously?"

"Don't try and change the subject. It's cold as fuck, Vera!" Janie pulled her flannel in tighter and scrambled to light a cigarette. "You and your damn shortcuts."

Regina cut in with a small protest of her own. "Yeah and I'm starving something ridiculous over here. We could have easily grabbed something at Monique's. I mean, come on, it was right next to Sha-"

All the girls shrieked as four men popped out of nowhere in front of them.

"Oh, what the fuck now?" Janie yelled as they halted.

The leader of the gang couldn't stop giggling. His pale blue eyes barely escaped a faded red beanie that covered matted blonde hair.

"What's going down, gang? Catch some hot and happenin' bands at Shady's tonight?"

Three men stood behind him; the heavyset one gave him a hearty pat on the shoulder as he surveyed the girls. The other two stood back, disguised in their hoodies, hopping with anticipation while cursing the cold.

Trying to get a feel for the situation, Vera stood up in front of her friends. Janie allowed her and sucked in a drag, shivering intensely. Regina did her best to contain her sudden rush of fear but trusted Vera to handle this.

"Yeah, boys. Were you there? Fuck, it was a great show!" She gestured towards Janie. "But I gotta get shit for brains here back home since she's easily frightened of places she's never been before. So, we need to make haste, boys."

With that, Vera signaled to the other two girls and simultaneously advanced but was halted once again.

"Yeah, this place scares the beloved piss outta me," the leader said. "Scares all of us doesn't it guys?"

The whole group laughed until one of the hooded men spoke up. "Yeah, Toni here is petrified."

Vera offered a giggle, but she knew things were about to take a turn for the worse. She swallowed and gazed at her girlfriends with more sincerity than she had the whole night. Eventually, she turned back, reading their true intentions.

"This isn't gonna end well, is it?"

The man with the beanie shrugged and spoke softly, conspiratorially, like a friend. "Well ... I mean I suppose you could run ... I know fat ass here wouldn't catch ya."

One of the hooded men cut him off. "Shit Gabe, forget this. Let's go."

Gabe shot around in an instant burst of fury and pointed at his protester. "I KNEW YOU'D BE THE FIRST TO PUSS OUT OF THIS, TONIO! I FUCKING KNEW IT!"

"Man, I told you to never call me that shit! I didn't want to come here in the first place. You know I don't do this shit to women, fucker! You know I don't!" Antonio yelled.

Vera didn't need any more clues and figured now was as good a time as ever to seize what opportunity the men gave. "GIRLS, RUN!"

They listened, but it didn't take much effort for Gabe to latch onto enough of Vera's hair to yank her back.

Janie leapt forward in an attempt to pry Vera free from Gabe, but the big guy behind him seized her. Regina turned to run but, once again, tripped over her troublesome skirt. The other hooded man jumped on top of her. Antonio merely followed.

Vera's fight was unyielding as she blindly threw fists behind her, but Gabe ducked, filling her head with his maniacal cackling. The best she could do was yank his beanie off. That only made him produce his switchblade to steady her resistance.

"Fucking relax, sweetheart! We just want to play nice."

All three girls were held in place. Antonio was the only one left out, and he was cursing in protest.

"Toni! You're in on this too, bitch!" Gabe yelled then turned his attention to Vera, blade expertly pressed into her throat. "Now you can relax and make this easy, cupcake."

Catching her breath, all Vera had for a response was, "Just don't hurt them. Please. Let them go and I'm yours. For real."

Gabe surveyed his surroundings to assure that his boys had secured the girls.

"Now I can't go that easy. You see how hungry they are?"

Vera shut her eyes, knowing how hopeless the situation was. Janie wailed. Regina cried as her wrists were held in place.

"Just take it easy now, chica," Gabe said as he tried to position himself in front of Vera. "I just want you to hold me. For starters, y'know?"

Vera looked up in shock, but she didn't struggle; she could tell he knew how to use his weapon.

"... Hold me ..." he said as he guided her arm around his waist.

SPRINGING FORWARD from his slumber with the speed of a mousetrap, hands clasped against his eyes, Antonio wailed with the desperation of a toddler. It was one single cry of anguish that left him breathless.

"... Hold me..."

A voice still echoed from his nightmare. Sucking his wind back, the petrified man clutched his sweat drenched forehead, nails digging into flesh in a vain attempt to attack the source of his misery. The tension eased and Antonio's hands slid down his cheeks, pausing briefly to cover his mouth as his gaze raced around his bedroom.

Breathing gradually became easier as Antonio collected himself, spat a few profanities and threw his sheet off to go to the bathroom.

It had been five years to the day...

Antonio knew this had to end, one way or another. He

reached for his cell phone, located the "M" in his contact list and stared at it briefly before making the call.

"Marcus! Toni. Let's do Monique's, man. I'm hungry."

"You're never hungry so why front? And you know I hate eating at Mon-"

The voice on the other end was right, and Antonio ended the call, tossed his cell aside and heaved into the toilet. More grunts followed as he jammed his fist into the side of the decrepit bowl.

Moments later, Antonio had dressed. After pacing about his room, he sat on the edge of his bed, crossing himself. He began a quiet little prayer until it trailed off into a plea to someone else other than The Father or His Begotten Son.

Gazing at the ceiling, Antonio initiated his one-sided conversation. Fear. Anger. Frustration. Guilt. All feelings as routine as his invocation of God Almighty and/or the three women whose rape and execution he'd witnessed.

As his emotions shifted so did his targets. Sometimes he felt he could fully atone for his sins and his involvement in their deaths. Other times he convinced himself that he was supposed to be cursed with visions and nightmares of that night for the rest of his life. Hopelessness shrouded him, but still he denied that he had suffered any mental issues or trauma from the incident.

Antonio shot a look towards the ceiling that could burn a hole into it. "I know you can hear me! You watch me every day! Every night! Every time I take a piss, man! So who's listening to me now, huh? Huh? Is that all you all want to do, fuck with my mind? Because I'm not psycho. I'm no fucking lunatic! I know you're up there! Talk back! No more nightmares and mind-fucks, okay? Just talk back to me! Tell me what you want me to do!"

His cell made him jump when it rang, and he threw himself back to grab it. Flipping it open and pressing it to his ears, he shouted. "Yes! Monique's! I'm on my way, dog, DAMN!"

"I am too, Toni."

It wasn't Marcus who called. It was the last person Antonio ever wanted to hear from, especially during bouts like this.

"Stay your sadistic ass home. Now is not the time," Antonio said and flipped the phone shut once again.

He knew his command would fall on deaf ears. Maybe it was best that they all show up for once. Perhaps then, a solution to all of this madness could be found. Killing Gabe might be the answer he was looking for.

MONIQUE'S WAS a run-down 24-hour dive of a diner on Manhattan's south side. Antonio and his old gang never found trouble hanging around there. They *were* the trouble.

When Antonio arrived, only Marcus waited in the back corner, hiding in his faded blue hoodie, shades still on, his unmistakable ink-covered hand drumming on the table next to his coffee. He looked up as the front door slammed behind Antonio and slowly rose.

"They're both coming, Toni. So, you know this better be worth everybody's time and you know damn well I mean every ... body."

"I should bust that melon of yours for calling him! What the fuck is the matter with you?"

Marcus shrugged. "You're the one that's all about these dramatic reunions. Wantin' to talk about our past as if something can be done about it."

"I just called you this time. I didn't want anyone else!" Antonio calmed himself, knowing his time was extremely limited. "Do you pray? Marcus? Ever?"

Marcus titled his chin and chuckled. "Isn't that where you put your hands together and talk to someone that isn't even in the room?"

"No jokes! I'm for real, man!" Antonio shouted.

"Theologian bullshit is what this is about? Again? Are you fuckin' me, Tonio? I haven't prayed since I was six, man. Yeah, that would be about the first time my ol' man staggered in, drunk off his ass. Now get to your point before I make it for you!"

Antonio's eyes widened as he looked at his old friend for a brief moment. "It's going to go down, Marky. Hardcore, man. I can feel it! We are gonna pay and we are gonna pay dearly and you-"

"Fucking Christ!" Marcus snatched Antonio by his jacket and jerked him forward while simultaneously surveying the diner in hopes that no one was listening.

"What the hell is the matter with you? For real! Why are you talking so damn loud and why here?"

"Because you know how close we are,' Antonio replied, carelessly.

"Oh, fuck you, Holy Roller. Is this why you brought me here? Look. I sleep just fine at night. Each and every single one of them and you know what, it's gonna stay that way. For as long as I say so! It's that simple. We did what we did. It's over. We move on. That shit was five years ago, man."

Antonio managed to crack a smile. "Five years to the very day, old friend."

"Couldn't care less, old friend," Marcus shot back. "I long since snagged my one-way ride to Hades. May as well live it up 'til then, right?"

With that, Antonio broke his clutches, slammed him back into the table, and pushed both back as far as they could go. Marcus grunted when the table caught the wall and jammed into his back. He seized Antonio's throat in an all-out struggle.

"Always starting the party without us aren't ya, ladies?"

Both men froze but maintained their glares at each other, and the voice from behind knew he wasn't being ignored.

"I fucking despise him," Antonio whispered to Marcus.

"He despises you more, preacher man," Marcus returned with a smirk, shades still intact.

Antonio pulled him forward and released him as they turned to face the rest of the group.

The leader, Gabe, was gesturing to the staff and customers at Monique's Diner to remain calm and that everything was going to be okay. He was followed by Trent, the big guy that partook on that fateful night. Trent hovered beside Gabe.

"Haven't either of you found a way to get shot, yet?" Antonio said, coldly.

Gabe seemed unfazed and gave a half-hearted greeting to Marcus.

"I'm sure you would know if you ever learned how to use a gun, princess. That's why we always feel safe around you."

"I didn't ask for you to come."

"You obviously didn't have to. Now let's get serious. I'm here to do you a favor, Tonio. Put your mind at everlasting ease." Gabe smiled that wide puppet smile of his that could never coincide with what was really being conveyed with those eyes. He wasn't fooling anyone, nor did he seem to care. Antonio didn't show the least bit of curiosity, so Gabe continued, his sidekick reverently on standby.

"Well for starters, given the … *nature* of our affair, perhaps it shouldn't take place here."

"No shit," Marcus spoke up with a hint of relief. "Cockwad here likes to wave everything like a fucking banner. I was about to pistol whip the bitch straight."

Antonio ignored him, keeping his attention on Gabe. "What are you talking about?"

"Quit asking when you already know. Let's go."

Gabe shot a look at Trent, and both proceeded to the door. Antonio stared at Marcus, who didn't look back.

"Let it play out, Toni. Dude's crazy as fuck, but do we really have a choice? He shoots you, your problem is solved, man." Marcus tried to lighten things up. "I'll pray for your safe ride to Shangri-La, yeah?"

Antonio made a beeline for the exit.

The four men met up about a quarter mile down from the old diner. Exactly five years ago, they had taken their usual path along the abandoned railway after eating at Monique's.

Antonio's thoughts ran rampant. His skin crawled, and he zipped up his jacket, picking up his pace. Marcus followed diligently alongside him

Could he have helped the three women? It didn't matter. He didn't attack them. And he didn't think to cross Gabe. His hands were washed clean of the entire situation.

As the wind started to pick up, a soft voice glided from the left to the right. Only two words could be understood.

"... Hold me..."

Gabriel had uttered those two disturbing words as he held Vera in his clutches, showing off his new stiletto switchblade. Just as he maintained the peace when the gang entered the diner, he had tried to keep his prey calm by assuring her he meant well.

Once they caught up with the others, Marcus spoke first.

"What's with the tricks? Who was the bitch that just hollered at us? Where is she?"

Gabe shrugged in confusion. "She swallowed and bailed. What the fuck do you mean 'where is she'? We're the only ones here. When you called me earlier, I knew all this paranormal activity bullshit had to end. Plus, you and I both got tired of his mouth. So now what's up? Is the psycho hearin' thangs?"

"I'm not a fucking psycho, you sadistic pile of shit!"

With that, Gabe's hefty sidekick drew his Glock, pointing it straight into Antonio's face.

"End the story, Gabe? Huh? End it? End it now?" Trent lit up with fear and anticipation.

"Not even close. I want to hear him out first."

"Come on, man. This place is already freaking me the hell out. Let's blast this rat and go! You know that fucking mouth of his will land us all in the yard!"

Ignoring them both, Gabe kept his gaze on Antonio.

"What will make you happy, Tonio? I know you've been some sort of bible-thumping fuck of late. So what? Do we say a special prayer? Hail Mary or something? Make those three bitches happy up in heaven? You tell me, Toni."

"You're twisted, man. You couldn't have just let her go. Same goes for the rest of you," Antonio continued, shooting death glares at the others.

Trent's gun didn't budge until Gabe gently pressed a couple fingers against the barrel to push it aside. He withdrew in disbelief as Gabe held Antonio in his cold stare.

"Antonio. Listen to me. What is it going to take to keep you quiet?"

"Fuck it, Gabe! You know this shit won't work! He's gonna talk and roll on us all!"

"Cork it, now, fat ass, or you'll take the nap too! I fucking swear!!"

"... Hold me..."

Trent drew his pistol once again. Marcus joined with a Glock of his own and Gabe drew the same blade that was Vera's undoing.

"You see what I mean now?" Antonio shouted. "It's over guys! We need to pay up and pay good!"

Antonio backed up to illustrate who the worst of this entire outfit were. Pointing at them through the howling wind, he exclaimed. "You three are murderers and rapists, and now it's time to pay the price! His judgment is here, and it's true! May He have mercy on your pathetic-"

Antonio wailed in pain, falling to his knees, as Gabe's stiletto punctured his palm.

As his greasy matted hair frolicked about in the unforgiving winds, Gabe shouted an order to Trent to put Antonio away. The thug was about to comply when he was thrown with inhuman strength.

Gabe only had time to look at Trent's soaring body before he too was seized. He looked into Vera's face in terror.

"Hold me, Gabriel," she demanded with a low demonic tone as she wrapped her arms around his scrawny body and lifted him like a mother scolding a toddler. His face was pressed into her shoulder. Her vibrant hair ablaze and whipping his face without obstructing his front-row view of what was in store for Trent and Marcus.

Antonio fought to pull the blade from his hand.

Trent got up but was tackled back to the ground; Regina sat firmly on his chest. She looked sick with desire as she playfully tugged at her chiffon skirt while it danced about the wind. The same skirt she wore five years ago.

Trent had both hands free, but it didn't matter. He pounded at her, but she easily caught each fist and slid over his chest and onto his throat.

Marcus was frozen with terror, which made it all the easier for Janie to swing an arm around his throat from behind. He screamed in desperation as the woman began sliding her tongue up his cheek, one long passionate lick after the other.

Gabe struggled, but Vera had him secured and didn't want him to miss a thing. Antonio backed himself up against a tree, still tugging at the blade in agony.

Each man was now incapacitated in a unique way as Vera

looked back at her comrades. Gabe's muffled wailing could be heard in the violent winds.

Regina looked up at Vera with a smile as if awaiting a signal of sorts. She positioned her knees around Trent's head, and engulfed it with her skirt as he fought to break free.

Janie continued her aggressive licking and lapping of Marcus's face. Steam or smoke evaporated from his flesh as he shook with agony. As she licked, strips of skin peeled from his face and burnt blood streaked across her mouth.

Antonio and Gabe had no choice but to witness the horror.

Regina rode Trent's head. She released his hands and in the same motion grasped and fondled her own breasts in a display of sexual pleasure. Trent's arms no longer fought, they just shivered outward. Biting her lower lip, the girl reached inside the neck of her blouse to get a better feel. Her other hand stroked the bulge between her legs that shivered and quaked like a bowling ball of Jell-O.

Antonio managed to pull the blade out of his blood-soaked palm. His face glistened with sweat as he let out a small cry. With what little energy he had left, he tossed the stiletto aside and leaned back, ready to faint from the wound. His eyes, however, could not leave the scene before him.

Vera watched Gabe's petrified expression with excitement. She jerked his head back, allowing him to scream.

"OH GOD! FUCK ME! LET ME GO! LET ME GO!" he wailed as she cradled him with one arm.

With her free hand, she strummed his face with her icy fingers until his wails became whimpers.

Regina was having a literal fuck fest with what used to be the block on Trent's shoulders. The round bulge of Jell-O hidden under her skirt began to lose shape. Blood, littered with chunks of flesh and bone, pooled out from under the skirt. The man's arms spasmed at his sides. His feet, no longer kicking, shrank into their respective pant legs as if they were being swallowed by a black hole. The girl smiled in the moonlight; beads of sweat glistened on her forehead, and she looked as if she was about to climax.

Marcus was still alive. Slivers of skin clung to his face as Janie continued to lap up whatever her acidic saliva softened. He buckled to his knees as she shot her tongue into his mouth. His screams were reduced to coughs and gargles as Janie pushed him on his back and continued to dine.

Vera looked ecstatic. Turning her attention back to what was to be her meal, she once again pressed Gabe's face back into her chest. His struggles meant nothing. She slowly and methodically slid her free hand down his torso, over his jeans and unzipped them. His muffled wails returned, and she began, what looked like, a hand job.

"Like that?" Vera asked as she stroked harder in response to his anguish. Gabe's legs thrashed and kicked. Red spread across his groin.

Antonio had no choice but to pray, muttering to The Almighty. "We deserve ... Pay ... You ... Oh, Sweet Lord ... Take flesh ... Save ... Soul?" He continued his chant until a heavy object thwacked the tree behind him. It was what was left of Marcus's skull. As Antonio stared at it, Marcus's shades landed behind his skull.

Soft cooing and moaning radiated from Regina, who was still on her knees enjoying the orgasm her hellish feast upon Trent produced. Gabe slumped over Vera's arm when she jerked him back by the head and held his lifeless body up like a rag doll. His pants were drenched with blood. A chewed out a hole the size of a football where his crotch area once was. Vera let out a snicker and dropped the gang leader to the ground. Janie rose from Marcus's decapitated body. Regina's skirt covered her long legs.

It was only as she stepped away that the shriveled pile of blood and slime-soaked clothing was exposed.

Antonio looked at what was left of his gang. The girls were nowhere to be seen. He didn't know whether he should cry with relief or grief. Fat tears fell, and he swallowed deeply.

Looking down at the hole in his hand, he mumbled to himself. "This ... This is my payment. Forever scarred for my cowardice on that night. The Lord has spoken. Passed ... judgment ... and spoken."

After another pause, he crossed himself with his bloodied hand then bowed his head. "May their souls be at peace with you now, Great Savior. Amen."

Slow claps. Antonio stared at the ground with another rush of terror.

"Hey. That sounds good in theory, doesn't it babe?" said one voice. "We get to go to heaven now?" asked another. "Cool, I hope my wings look badass!" said the third.

Antonio looked up and saw the three girls closing in on him. His fear gave way to anguish and sorrow as he began to weep.

"Oh please, no! I'm so sorry. I don't deserve what they did. Certainly there's mercy! THERE'S MERCY!"

Vera put a finger to her nose as if in thought. The finger belonged to the same hand that sealed Gabe's fate.

"Y'know, you may have a point. Since you didn't touch any of us and well... you did do a lot of praying... we have something EXTRA special for you, Toni!"

She whipped her hand, palm outward, as she and the other three drew closer to Antonio.

Her hand revealed a gaping mouth at the center layered inward with rows of teeth. The base of each finger contained a smaller version of each. All were chomping desperately for their next meal.

Vera began to lean forward. Janie did the same as she stuck

her tongue out as far as it could stretch. Regina was already tugging up her chiffon as Antonio shouted his longest cry of the night.

"I WANT TO SEE HIM. Just once," Pamela demanded to Dr. Hampton, the director of operations at Grobe's Institution for the Criminally Insane.

After a pause, Dr. Hampton said, "Pamela. You have to understand something. This individual never attacked your sister. When they recovered the bodies, each one had DNA samples that matched their assailants and nothing more. We... recovered their remains. It was an animal attack, that's the best I can say. In fact, that's all I will say with regards to the deaths of those... assailants. But what you must understand is none of Antonio Rodriguez's DNA was found on any of the victims. Not even a thread of clothing or hair. So, what I can tell you, off the record, is I don't think he harmed your sister or either of the other women that night."

Pamela held her stance. "I want to see him. Just one look."

The doctor sighed then nodded at an assistant. "Come this way, ma'am."

As she walked down the hallway, Pamela heard the wails, moans and cries of the other patients, but it didn't bother her. All she wanted was one glance, for closure, of the last surviving witness of that fateful night.

"Here he is," said an orderly as he slid open the small door to the observation port of Antonio's room.

"I don't know if he's the nuttiest, but he's for damn sure the loudest," the orderly said as he waited impatiently for Pamela to look in.

In the corner sat the final member of the gang who brutally raped and killed Pamela's sister, Janie. He was thrashing about in his straitjacket and appeared to have long since eliminated any food and drink in his system. Wailing turned to sobbing. Then the sobbing went back to wailing.

One thing was for certain, and that was Antonio despised the unforgiving confines of his own attire.

... HOLD ME?...

———————

Jason Dyer will have you know that he enjoys listening to Missing Persons.

9

AX TO GRIND

BY SHANNON GRANT

THE NEW BLADE WAS SHINY AND SMOOTH. NEXT CAME the test.

Alice dropped a sheet of paper on top of the ax, the way she had seen in martial arts movies when the hero was testing a new sword for defeating the big bad. The sheet fell on top of the blade, silently splitting in two as Alice's stomach flip-flopped, this time in a good way. She remembered when Elton had started making her stomach butterflies turn into giant moths, churning and whirling inside her gullet, rising into her throat.

Ghosts of memories echoed inside Alice's head. Things she'd been trying to forget throughout the winter, from the first dusting of snow until the damp heat of summer. Tears had been shed; the last ounces of love she'd felt for him were gone. Everything had been replaced by a stinging, biting rage. It gave her a strange sense of energy that kept her alive after months of wallowing in depression.

Hence, the desire to go out and buy an ax and finally confront Elton.

She found the old blue dress in the back corner of her closet behind various shirts, skirts and dresses. The forgotten outfit. Alice felt like wearing it again. It was time.

She stripped out of her jeans and t-shirt then donned the blue dress with a white apron. The rusty stains remained from the last time she wore it. Her black patent leather shoes were still in the box along with long white stockings. She smoothed her choppy bleach-blonde hair before she pushed it back with a black hairband, completing the look.

Her reflection stared back with creepy pale blue eyes. Her alternate self was returning, the self that was braver, more confident.

Her new ax leaned against the wall. She let her inner Alice take over.

Down the rabbit hole she went, looking for what she needed to find.

"Drink me," the bottle on the table read.

No, she thought. She'd done that before and became small. Helpless. Someone she didn't want to be in this strange world. This time she avoided the bottle but took the silver key.

The house shifted. The ceiling became the floor and the door grew large enough to accommodate her.

I knew it, she thought, reaching for the upside-down door. *I didn't have to shrink myself down to size after all.*

The key in her hand fit perfectly in the lock. It turned and swung open, revealing a dark garden that beckoned to Alice.

Flowers bloomed around her. She followed the path to a staircase that led to a second level. The stairs creaked. Vines grew and flowers blossomed under her feet. A beautiful fresh smell pursued her. The night sky twinkled, letting her know everything had changed.

She remembered the last time her inner Alice had come out, and the last man who had made her turn to Wonderland. That time she'd used a knife. The man became another card in the Queen of Hearts' deck. Cut.

Now it was Elton's turn. As she reached the top of the stairs, his door appeared as if by magic. Alice turned the knob, hoping she wouldn't need a different key.

The door squeaked as it swung open, but not loudly enough to fear being heard. The full moon beamed through the window onto Elton and the new girl he had fed his pile of lies to. He lay like a flat card cut from the Queen's deck. The last one had become the Six of Spades. Elton was the Jack of Hearts.

White hot rage seared up inside Alice.

"Elton," she whispered, acid in her voice.

She nudged him with the blade. He stirred, eyes fluttering then opened wide. His arm stretched around the woman, but all Alice saw was her mass of dark hair. Alice wouldn't touch a hair on the woman's head. This was between her and Elton.

"Hi, Elton. Remember me?" Alice said, raising the ax.

"Alice!" he shouted.

It was his last word before she brought down the ax. The sound of a playing card being ripped apart echoed through the room. She smashed the ax in the middle of the card again. The Jack on Elton's chest stared back at her, bloody.

A high-pitched scream. Elton's latest victim had woken up and witnessed everything. Reality returned slowly to Alice. Elton's flat body morphed into the familiar one Alice had loved. He lay unconscious, dead, as she backed away from the scene. She went home and washed the dress. It would return to the back of her closet, waiting for the next time.

Shannon Grant is a horror writer living in upstate New York. She wrote this story for fun and catharsis.

10

WOULD YOU LIKE BLOOD WITH YOUR COFFEE?

BY ELISABETH POPOLOW

I WAS COLD. SO COLD. AND WET. AND STICKY. THIN bars of pale sunlight slanted through the window blinds as I lay on the hardwood floor in a mangled mess. My whole body ached and throbbed as I struggled to drag myself to the door, but my limbs just wouldn't budge. An opaque darkness smothered my vision. I meekly lifted myself up then pitifully collapsed. Fresh blood made a sickening suction-like gurgle against my torso.

"Raped, stabbed twenty-seven times and throat slit." A man's voice shattered through the silence, and I quivered in terror as I thought, *No, not him!*

Black boots stepped in front of me. He crouched and lowered his face to mine. It wasn't *him*, thank God. It was someone else. Maybe someone just as dangerous.

"There's no need to fear me," he said, quietly. "I'm here to help you live. Wouldn't you like to live? Perhaps take revenge on the person who murdered your daughter and attempted to kill you?"

Crimson eyes like burning embers, full cherry lips and a pallid complexion made him seem almost angelic. His hair was long and tumbled to his waist in golden waves as he gazed at me with those red orbs. I opened my mouth to speak but nothing came out. I whimpered as pain gripped hold of me once more.

He caressed my head with a slender hand. "If you want to live, I can grant you a new life, but you must promise to murder the man who did this to you. Understood? Nod if you agree."

It took all my strength to nod my head up and down as hot tears spilled across my cheeks. Who was this man and how was he going to save me? I was already dead, wasn't I? He was the angel that came to take my soul to heaven.

"I'm no angel." He laughed. "But I will tell you that there are other people out there, other potential victims of the monster who wronged you. Will you let him do as he pleases or put a stop to his cruel ways?"

I choked. "I-I wanna see that fucker burn in Hell."

The man grinned; his canines were a bright pearly luster, very sharp and strangely elongated. "This will only hurt for a second then your pain will be relieved."

His cool breath ghosted along my neck. He stretched his jaw wide and struck me like a viper. A tiny cry escaped my lips as his fangs pierced my flesh, and he cradled my head with one hand as the other supported my back. He sucked long and hard, drawing the remainder of my blood into his throat.

The pain faded into a sheer tingling ecstasy that surged through me like a tidal wave and vanquished all the hurt. I felt my strength returning, my body reviving quicker than modern medicine could ever accomplish. He yanked his mouth from my throat and pricked his wrist with his nails.

"You must drink this," he commanded and placed his arm to my lips.

Tangy, coppery blood filled my mouth. I swallowed a few gulps before he took his arm away and smoothed the bangs from my eyes.

"Sleep now, little one. When you wake, you will have a craving for blood, and I shall be right here waiting for you. Rest now and let your body heal."

As if his words were a lullaby, I closed my eyes and let sleep embrace me.

DAVID CONNOR WAS FORTY-FIVE, built like a tank, and visited the coffee shop on Main every weekday from six to seven in the morning. He had already gone bald, and his teeth were rotting and yellow from a lifetime of neglect and chain smoking. His eyes were a vacant brown and his thin lips were cracked from the cold.

It was the middle of winter in Ontario, and the weather had not spared the little town of Woodbury. Two feet of snow blanketed the land. Icy winds hurtled through at breakneck speeds. Because he couldn't get his '97 Plymouth out of the driveway to travel fifteen miles to work at a construction site, David simply pulled on a layer of sweaters and walked two blocks to get a cup of half-and-half coffee, a glazed donut, and the daily news at the local coffee place, The Sleepy Dragon.

I watched from across the street as he stood up from his seat and went to the counter, ordered a jelly donut and a vanilla latte, and slid into a booth opposite a young mother and her tiny daughter. I closed my eyes and focused on hearing, enhanced since the change. From across the road, I could hear them talking as if they were right beside me.

"Did you have the day off school today because of the bad weather?" David asked the girl. Her brunette hair was tied into high braided pigtails, and an oversized pink coat flared over her small hands as she munched daintily on a donut.

The mother replied. "Yeah, she has a snow day today, but we

woke up early for school, so I thought, why not take her out for breakfast?"

David bobbed his head like he was listening intently. "Snow days are always fun. I couldn't get the car out of the driveway to get to work so I jogged two blocks to get my favorite morning treat."

The mother patted her daughter's head affectionately. My stomach knotted at the sight, and my chest tightened and clenched at the memory of Amy's smiling face and the gaps in her teeth, cheeks rosy from the cold.

"Hey, are you okay?" a woman who was sitting at the table behind me asked. I blinked a few times and realized I had crushed my coffee cup in my hand. Hot liquid was splattering all over the table and onto my lap.

"Oh, I'm fine. Just tired," I said despondently and wiped the coffee with a pile of napkins. My hands shook as I composed myself and tuned into the coffee shop again.

"I can help you with your driveway if you want. I already missed work so I can take some time and shovel for you," David offered.

The mother paused for a moment then smiled warmly. "That'd be great, um-"

"Dave."

"Dave. Then I won't have to pay twenty dollars for the neighbor boy to do it."

"Great! Do you just want me to go home with you then?"

She sipped her latte. "Yeah, that'd be easiest." She turned to her daughter. "Shannon, are you done with your donut?"

Shannon nodded, her face plastered in strawberry jelly and powdered sugar. Her mom sighed and dabbed at it with a wet wipe then the two exited the store. Dave deposited the tray on his way out. I shrugged into my jacket, left my hiding place and sprinted after them. I kept my presence hidden behind cars, people and streetlights as I pursued my prey to Shannon and her mother's quaint blue townhouse, watching as they trudged through the snow.

The mother carried Shannon in her arms; as she made it to the door, she called back to Dave. "The shovel's in the garage! Thanks so much!" Then shut the front door.

Dave whistled a familiar tune, *Mary had a Little Lamb,* as he grasped the shovel and started digging. I staggered as a distant memory crashed into me – Amy and me playing in the yard throwing snowballs at each other as we giggled and grinned. After we went inside to steaming cups of hot chocolate and brownies.

A pair of men walked past me. One held an envelope, trying to rip it open, grazing his finger on the edge. Tiny drops of blood dripped from his hand, and my insides panged as hunger awoke and roared in heated desire.

I ran in front of the two men and faced them. "You won't remember me. You, the one not bleeding, go home and take a shower. The other one stays." Their pupils dilated; one man walked away while the other stayed stiff as a board. "Take me to your car," I commanded.

Five minutes later and dealing the best I could with a snarling stomach, we hopped into the back seat of his little red Mazda. I hastily ripped his turtle-neck sweater from his body and licked the blood on his hand. He threw his head back and moaned in delight as my venom inflicted its enticing magic. I brushed my lips against his chest, his collarbone and to his neck where I clicked out my fangs and plunged them into him. A gasp tore from his throat as I buried my fangs deep inside and began to pull at his sweet, salty sustenance. He relaxed completely. When I felt full and refreshed, I retracted my fangs and gave him a quick peck on the forehead.

"Drive home and take a nap. You never saw me, never met me. Understand?"

"Yes."

I hurried out of the car and dashed back to Dave, who was still busy shoveling the driveway. I exhaled in relief and decided it was time to finally make my move. Dave had moved from Pennsylvania to Canada. He had been clever and used a special type of glove to null the chances of the police finding any prints on Amy's body. He had washed her thoroughly before shoving her inside a metal box and dumping it into his family's privately-owned lake in the Catskills. I had left it alone. I *would* get my revenge, involving the police would only hinder me.

My hands clenched into fists as I strode to where Dave was resting against the garage door. I used my most innocent voice. "Hey, what are you doing at my sister's house, cutie?"

I had cut my hair, dyed it a fake shade of red, and worked out so that my body was much leaner and fitter than before. I wore a long, cream sweater dress that showed lots of delicious cleavage. His mouth gaped as he stared at me, shovel falling from his hands. I noticed the wicked gleam in his disgusting eyes.

"Oh, well, she needed help with the driveway so I said I'd do it for free. So, you're her sister, huh?" He licked his lips.

I flipped my hair. "Yeah, Paula," I replied, seductively. "Maybe when you're done, you'd like to come to my house, and we can ... talk?"

His gaze widened. "I'd love to! Here, just wait five minutes and I'll be done. Why don't you wait inside while I finish up?"

"No, I'm okay. The cold doesn't really bother me. I'll just wait right here."

"If you say so." He shrugged and shoveled faster.

I chuckled, watching him stumble over his feet to get finished as quickly as possible. When he finally finished, he jogged back to me and set the shovel back in the garage.

"Ready?" he asked.

"Aren't you gonna tell Liz that you're done with her driveway?"

"I'll just leave a note." He scribbled on a yellow sticky-note and pasted it onto the front door then joined me on the sidewalk.

"So, where do you live, Paula?" He was like a dog in heat, and I could smell the hormones pouring off him.

"Just at the next block. I like to be close to Liz and Shannon."

"Ah, that's nice. I have a brother in New York. I wish I lived closer."

"Why don't you?"

"Oh, I like it here much better." He sniffled. "I prefer cold temperatures."

I nodded. "Uh-huh. Oh, look! We're here." I skipped to the door, unlocked it and ushered him inside.

As he crossed the threshold, I locked the door and threw the key in the furnace. Every window blind was drawn, and the house was black as night.

"Where's the lights?" he inquired, shakily.

"Let's go into the kitchen, and I'll make some tea," I said, ignoring his question.

He followed me like a lost puppy to the kitchen where I flicked on the lights. He got a full view of the metal table with leather straps attached. His gaze slid from the table to me then he lunged. He pulled a knife from his pants, thrust its blade into my back, and punched me in the face. I pretended to fall to the floor and made the perfect pained grunt.

"You crazy bitch!" he hollered. "What are you, a fucking serial killer?" He kicked me.

I laughed as I rose from the floor and cracked my neck to the side with a smirk. "The question, dear David, is what are *you*?" I padded toward him.

He struck me with a flurry of fists and kicks. I felt nothing.

"What the fuck do you mean? I thought we were gonna have a good time!" His voice shook in confusion.

"We are gonna have a good time, David. Mainly me, though." I darted at him. In a split-second, I'd pinned him to the table and was tying the straps tightly around his wrists, ankles and neck.

"How did you-? When did this-?" He attempted to move but he was secured well to the table, and the table was nailed twice to the floor.

"I can't believe you can't see through me, David. After all we've been through. After you proposed to me and took Amy to school and read bedtime stories to her and bought her a kitten. After you fucked me in the shower and told all your friends at work then paraded me like some expensive trophy wife. After you raped and murdered my daughter, dumped her body in a lake and left me for dead. Huh! Do you fucking remember now, you goddamn mother-fucking prick?"

Horror crossed his features as he realized who I really was. That I was, somehow, alive and had tricked him. Beaten him at his own twisted game.

"Jennifer," he uttered in pure terror and struggled and thrashed wildly against his bonds.

"That's right, Jennifer; the woman you screwed over! The woman whose daughter you took away forever! The woman you raped and stabbed and left to die a lonely death! Well, guess what, David, I came back from Hell exclusively to punish you! Isn't this just a peachy reunion?"

"No! No! Someone help! Help! Help!" He screamed and writhed against the leather straps that kept him in place.

"No one can hear you, you fuck," I whispered in his ear. "These walls are soundproof, and everyone went home earlier to sleep like I told them."

"What the fuck are you?" He sobbed. "What in the fucking hell are you? How can you just tell people to stay inside and sleep the whole day? That's some crazy shit medicine you been using?"

I laughed loud and high and it felt good, wonderful. "No, you little shit." I elongated my fangs and hissed. "This is what I am. What you would call a vampire. Like it, *honey?*"

He yelped as I raked my nails against his sweaters and yanked them and his pants off him in one quick motion.

"Whiney bitch," I growled and injected a high dose of Novocain into both wrists. He instantly stopped squirming, and his body became numb as I whistled *Mary Had a Little Lamb*. I showed him a hammer, a tiny kitchen knife, and a pair of pliers. His whole face was contorted in horror as I gripped the hammer and swung right between his legs. Again and again. Blood spurted from him and painted his naked body and the table crimson, his muted shrieks a soothing melody to my ears. When I could no longer see that part of his body for blood, I set the hammer down and used the pliers on each finger, each stubby toe, clamped as hard and painfully as I could. His limbs flailed pathetically as I snapped each digit off and let it roll to the floor. Blood streamed from his mangled stumps, and I set the pliers down and grabbed the knife. He whimpered and sobbed quietly as I stabbed him again and again and again, on his shoulders, on his arms, his legs, his chest, his face. I giggled crazily as I stared in awe at the pain warping his face, quirking his lips, screwing his eyes shut in total agony.

He moved his mouth, but no sound came as I stuck my hand into his chest and ripped out his pumping heart. I bit into it as the life drained from his eyes and his body went as limp as a doll. After devouring his heart; I slammed my fists into his chest cavity again and again until a gory, tangled mess slid from his body onto the table and the floor.

When my throat was hoarse from laughing, I walked into the bathroom and peered at myself in the mirror. My face and clothes were stained scarlet, hair wild and frizzy, an evil gleam burning in my eyes.

The vampire who changed me wrapped his arm around my chest, and a fiery hole opened in the floor. I laughed all the more as I plummeted down into my eternal prison.

I decided to visit David first.

Elisabeth Popolow mainly writes paranormal romance, but she writes the occasional poem and fantasy short story.

UNHEARD VOICES

BY SANDRA WILTJER

THE DINING ROOM TABLE SCREECHED ACROSS THE tiled floor. She ran into it knowing full well it was there, but unable to avoid it. The impact hurt. Blood dripped on its surface and to the floor as Mei tried to steady herself. She pressed down on her arm to try and stop the bleeding. The make-shift bandage was already saturated. When her life was on the line, she did what she had to do to survive.

With her teeth clenched, she took a few steps into the space she called home. It wasn't big, but it was enough. Her vision was blurred, and the blood loss began to play its part. It made her feel faint and light-headed, blacking out on occasion. The only light came from a lamp burning in the small living room; its dimness made it harder to navigate, and Mei cursed when she collided with the couch.

Still, the relief of being home flooded her system. No longer able to bear the fatigue, her feet gave way. She lost her balance and collapsed, her agonized scream echoing through the room. A pair of arms kept her from hitting the floor and pulled her back to her feet.

"Geez, Mei, what have you done now?"

Macchan sounded worried. He inspected her bleeding arm while holding her close to his lean body. It took her a moment to see what he was doing. He was protecting her. It was a position she hated. Mei pulled her arm out of his grasp and stepped aside, almost falling again. She held herself upright by leaning against the back of the couch.

"I did what I had to." Her voice was cranky from the pain, and she felt annoyed that he still tried to protect her. After all this time he should know better.

By the state of his hair, she knew she'd woken him. It stood every way possible, defying the laws of gravity. He wore slacks but nothing on top. He was not bad to look at. Mei had to give him some credit for looking wide awake and alert. He stared at her with a grin like he was guessing her thoughts. Mei wore her black camouflage clothes, her hair as wild as his. Flashy purple dyed locks in her black mane. Her clothes didn't leave much to the imagination. She'd had a rough night.

"Stop staring at me," Mei told him coldly, and he looked away, still smiling. Macchan was a good and loyal friend, but Mei didn't care much for friends; they were a liability in her line of work, never knowing who to trust or who would stab her in the back. He was caring and positive, a ray of sunshine, and it annoyed the heck out of her.

Macchan could act like a complete lunatic. He would say things without reason, often misplaced and missing the mark, but he also had moments of sheer brilliance. Such moments were rare but brilliant enough for Mei to keep him around. He had friends all over town. Friends whom Mei used as she saw fit. He didn't seem to care that he was selling them out. He just wanted to please her and see her smile.

With another look at her bleeding arm, he shrugged. "Right, I'll go wake Nino up, then."

The chain around his ankle jangled as he walked towards their joined bedroom. Nino was jokingly referred to as their resident chemist. He made the untraceable poisons that Mei used on certain jobs. He also had a range of homemade cleaning lotions. He was gifted in his work, but his main job was to patch Mei up when needed.

Her unwilling house guest emerged from the bedroom. Nino walked in front of Macchan who was showing a slight bruise on his cheek. The look on Nino's face was dark and stormy. He had trouble sleeping so waking him up was generally a bad idea. Mei smiled. Nino was a prime example of how she made Macchan use his friends. He'd been a chemist in a small lab and, when Mei needed poison for a job, Macchan had no trouble introducing her to Nino. The men's friendship had taken a serious blow when Nino found out he wouldn't be leaving any time soon.

Macchan was pacing. He watched her, looking worried, then looked away again. His usually tanned skin looked pale, making his dark auburn hair stand out more.

"You okay?" Mei asked, smiling sweetly.

Nino unwrapped the makeshift bandages on her arm.

Macchan nodded. "Okay! I'm okay!" He sounded like he didn't believe it himself. Mei couldn't contain her smirk.

Nino was almost done unraveling the cloth she had used to stop the bleeding. The cut was deep.

"Are you okay?" Macchan stopped pacing and watched as his friend uncovered the damage on her arm. Both Nino and Mei looked up at him in mock surprise as he stood between them. They knew full well how this was going to end.

"Yeah, I'm peachy." Mei laughed.

The last part of the removal would sting like hell. Nino wasn't here to help patch her up the easy way. She knew he made her suffer on purpose. It was his revenge for being locked up in *the dungeon* as Nino referred to her house. They lived on the outskirts of Tokyo. Mei didn't mind his rebellion. She was intrigued by how he worked. Plus, Nino was a constant puzzle. Whenever she thought she'd figured him out, he'd show some other side of his personality. He had changed himself so much and so often that Mei had the sneaking suspicion that even Nino didn't know who he was anymore.

As Nino pulled away the last part of blood-soaked cloth, he looked briefly up at his friend. "This is the time to look away, Macchan."

Mei clenched her teeth. She tried to keep herself from reacting to the pain, not wanting to give Nino the satisfaction. Removing the bandage enticed the bleeding to begin again in full force. Macchan's breath caught. With a secret smile, she eyed Nino and counted back from three. Macchan fainted as blood dripped down Mei's arm.

"He never listens," Nino said, half laughing while arranging the chemicals he used to disinfect her wounds. "Dumbass."

The blood dripped on the ground between Nino's legs as he examined her wound. He wasn't a doctor, but he knew enough about chemicals and medicines to know what treatment might be needed. And so far, she was still alive. Nino poured some homemade lotion on her arm. It stung as he cleaned the wound roughly, making it bleed more. Mei kept her lips clenched together and glared at him. Her eyes conveyed what she would do to him if he kept hurting her. Nino knew her well enough not to feel threatened by that dangerous look, but he didn't feel brave enough to smile.

He cleaned her arm efficiently and poured another liquid on the wound to make the blood bubble, stall and dry. He removed the dried blood and stared her in the eyes for a second. She offered a masochistic smile. There was no easy way to do this. Nino kept quiet as he took his glasses and a needle and thread.

"Go for it. I know you want to," Mei joked, ignoring his desire to make her miserable.

He returned her smile with one of his own. Even numbed it hurt when he pushed the needle into her skin. She kept staring at Nino and watched him work. He wore glasses for the stitching. To drown out the pain, she focused on her chemist. His hair was darker than Macchan's, but tussled just the same, standing out in every direction. He wore an oversized shirt, pajama bottoms and a chain around his ankle to prevent him from leaving.

"How did this happen?" Nino inquired, filling the silence while he stitched her arm. He surprised her with both the question and the tone of his voice. He actually sounded interested.

"You really want to know?" Small talk wasn't something they did. It weirded her out that he wanted to know.

"No. Not particularly."

Honesty was something Mei appreciated most about him. Nino became silent again. Mei sighed, staring at the cut in her arm. The scar would be a constant reminder of what had happened.

MEI LOOKED at her reflection in the bathroom mirror. Dark eyes stared back at her; the actual color was a shade of dark green. They formed a striking contrast with the bright purple highlights in her black hair. The mirror was fogging up fast with steam from the hot running water. She took off her gloves and laid them on the edge of the sink. A trace of blood ran down the basin. She watched it mix with the water.

Mei congratulated herself, smiling at a job well done. Looking in the mirror as it fogged, she ran a few fingers through her hair.

Something about the silence in this small luxurious bathroom felt good. A bit of serenity. She spent most of the time working with people who yelled at her; this felt almost peaceful. Not that she minded the screaming. Mei was the first to admit it was kind of fun to hear their meaningless pleas for mercy. She rinsed her expensive custom-made gloves in the running water, taking her time. After all, Makoto-san wasn't going anywhere anytime soon.

The black combat clothes she wore were practical. Her trusted backpack was stained and patched up countless times. It stood on the bathroom counter, waiting. Mei took a cleaning solution and a cloth from it and started to clean the weapons she'd used; her precious throwing stars, her short swords and bow staff. Her set of throwing stars were incomplete. Some were still in the living room. She cleaned her dagger last and put it back in the sheath hanging from her belt. She wiped the sink and rinsed the cloth, drenching it with more lotion while she listened for sounds coming from the living room. There were none. Mei decided it was a good sign. She put the stars in her backpack and some in the holder on her belt. The swords she put in their sheaths on her back.

Her bow staff was a weapon she usually carried, even though it had a holder on her back between the swords. The staff was shorter than regular ones, custom made for her with retractable blades. It was by far her favorite weapon, but not always practical.

It was quiet in the living room, apart from the sounds of the fake fire on the white plasma TV screen. It looked clinical, for want of a better description. It was white; the walls, the floor, the furniture, everything. It almost hurt her eyes and felt cold and eerie. Another part of the room was darker in tone and served as a dining or conference room. In one corner was some sort of security set up with two screens displaying the entrances to the house. She had seen more cameras through the house.

Makoto wasn't just some small-time guy. He needed the security.

There was a large dining table on which she had spread out photos. Near the table was a huge window that offered a view of the garden and a pond with a small fountain. Mei put on some relaxing classical music. The sounds of old Japan came to life, and as she stared out of the window, she could almost feel herself at peace. Sadly, work came first.

The smaller coffee table had photos of children on it. They were all disheveled and beaten up. It made her blood run cold every time she laid eyes on them. It was part of the reason Mei loved this assignment. Vengeance was her line of business. The lack of rules was what made this job that much more fun. She would've taken this job, regardless of the pay it offered, because, as much as this was business, it was kind of personal as well. Not long ago she had lost her sister in much the same way as Makoto and his partners had disposed of their under-age victims.

Taking her cleaning cloth, Mei set to work. She wiped every surface that she had touched as she danced between the furniture and the bodies of a few of Makoto's bodyguards. Mei hummed along with the music, the sounds becoming darker as time passed.

She paid no attention to the silent man anchored to the wall, his feet hanging above the marble floor. He stared at her like a madman, the life-threatening fear clear in his eyes. Mei felt no compassion for him nor his family. The guy had three children and a wife; they should be thankful Mei was disposing of him. She felt satisfaction as she heard him break his silence. Small, meaningless, terrified sounds crossed his bleeding lips, his voice already hoarse and broken from screams. He wasn't dead; and he wouldn't be soon if she had any say in the matter. His end would be painful and prolonged, as much as he could endure.

With the cleaning done, Mei took a good look at Makoto. She

crossed her arms, head a little tilted. He looked like he had been squashed by a giant flyswatter on his nice white wall. Blood was smeared around him, making the effect that much better. The idea made her laugh out loud. It sounded playful and sweet and echoed through the room. She had literally nailed him to the wall with throwing stars. She had pressed them into his arms and chest, carefully avoiding the major organs and arteries. Blood seeped from countless small wounds and dripped in a growing pool beneath his feet.

Her gaze left his body and settled on the iron pole she had brought along for the occasion. The pole was thick and had a blunt point. She looked up to Makoto and noticed he had followed her gaze. He asked her what it was meant for. She left him in the dark, smiling deviously. Blood ran from his lips over his chin, dripping on his smudged shirt, making a deep red stain which slowly grew. She needed to hurry this along. She needed him alive and aware to experience her special treat.

"Just a little more patience, Makoto-san."

His eyes grew big in terror as she stepped toward him. She was good at her job.

"Don't panic, Makato-san. This will hurt me less than it will hurt you. Besides, this is nothing compared to what I'm about to do next."

Her eyes wandered back to the pole with a devious smirk. He tried to kick her but lacked the strength. Mei took his right leg; it felt heavy. She stared at him for a moment longer then pressed two stars into his thigh. He screamed as loudly as his lungs and voice could manage. All kinds of profanities crossed his lips to which she shook her head in disappointment.

"Now now, Makato-san," she told him, grabbing his other leg and mirroring his right. "No need to say such things. Besides, you took such great care to soundproof this room for exactly this reason, didn't you?"

Her smirk turned hard and cold. Those poor children whose pictures lay on the table never had a chance to defend themselves once they ended up in this room. She pressed the last of her stars in his flesh with a hard but triumphant look. Makoto now resembled an old-fashioned jumping jack doll with his legs unnaturally pulled up. His eyes were almost popping out of his head from pain. His voice had broken, and he could no longer scream. Had he become immune to the pain? She backed away, viewing her work and took hold of the pole, twirling it between her fingers like she did her bow staff. His eyes followed every move.

There was a flicker in his eyes, barely noticeable, but one she saw nonetheless. Turning around Mei noticed the flashing light near one of the security monitors. The look in Makoto's eyes changed from terrified to triumphant.

"Smile you, lowlife creep, it will be the last pleasure you have," Mei remarked, stuffing a piece of his own clothing into his mouth so he couldn't alert anyone to her presence. She couldn't see how many entered but there were at least two. Mei had already chosen a spot to hide. It was a bit lame, but behind the door was a good option. Often not the first place people would check.

As the door opened, Mei was hidden. Two guys entered. The first one looked around and called for his boss. He wore a black suit with sneakers. He noticed his comrades' bodies on the floor then spotted his boss on the wall. His companion was about to shout to their buddies in the hall. Mei stepped out of hiding, dagger drawn, cutting his throat before he could utter a sound. She held on to the body as Sneaker Guy pulled out a gun and took aim. She slammed the door shut when she heard footsteps but didn't take her eyes off the gun. The gunslinger took his shot. Mei dodged behind his friend as she pushed the body forward. She retrieved her throwing stars as she rolled over the floor. Another shot echoed and the door opened. Two more people poured into the room, trying to assess the danger. Her throwing stars sailed through the air, hitting her opponent and slicing one of his hands.

"Guns are for cheaters," Mei called, making him fire once more as she ran into the path of one of his two friends.

She shifted out of the way and the bullet hit his friend in the shoulder, near his neck. He collapsed to the ground, gripping his wound, gurgling. Dodging the bullets, she ran toward the table where her bow staff lay. Frustration made the gunslinger fire more until she heard empty clicking. Just before she reached the table, she felt a stinging pain in her side. The fabric was torn. She looked up with a hateful glance. Not taking the time to assess the damage, she reacted. She swung her staff with ease, keeping her assailants at bay. It was more like twirling as she swung it left to right, over her head and back again. It didn't matter that she wasn't cutting anyone. She was just showing off, playing with her toy like a cat with a mouse. She made a few mock moves and struck the gunslinger's wrists with the blades. His hands fell to the ground still holding the weapon. He stared in silence at the horror before screaming.

"Just shut up already!" Mei called out to him. "They are just hands!"

Blood squirted all around as she looked for the other two. They backed up, hands half up in a pleading way, but she was in this line of business for vengeance and vengeance alone. Mercy was not something in her vocabulary. This was her calling, her legacy. It didn't matter who crossed her path. If the price was good and the cause was even better, she would rain holy hell on those deserving of it.

"You didn't bring any of your toys to my little party, did you?" She sneered at the two.

"No, ma'am," the one with the blond hair said, hands still raised.

"Too bad!" she said, walking up to them to take them out.

Makoto made a small sound that tipped her off, as well as the reflection she saw in the blond guy's eyes. A familiar samurai sword was raised high above her head. She dropped her staff just in time to fetch her short swords and crossed them above her. The impact was hard, and the edge of his blade broke through her hold, skimming her scalp as she tried to block his attack. Kicking backward, she turned to face her opponent.

Her eyes went wide in shock as she stared at the man in front of her, Takaya.

Seeing him confused her. Memories of her sister flashed through her mind.

"Mei," Takaya said, cheerfully watching the emotions play out on her face.

"I knew you were working this case the moment I saw your handiwork at Taizo's. Very well done, very artistic. How nice of you to come and pay Makoto-Chan a visit too. It saves me the trouble of cleaning his mess up."

Mei's mind reeled. Takaya had been the one responsible for taking down her sister, and Mei blamed herself for being too late to save her. The memory of her sister's body cradled in her arms caused her to tear up in angry rage. She had longed to take down Takaya ever since but never got close enough to have a fair shot at him. And now here he was. The question why didn't matter. This could be the first real shot she had at getting revenge.

Takaya watched her with gleaming eyes, grinning ear to ear. He wore one of his famous dark suits and pinstriped shirts. His necktie was loose. Hair combed neatly back.

"Come on, sweetie-pie," Takaya offered. He looked smug. "You aren't really surprised to see me here, are you?"

She was. Mei knew he worked for a secret government

division, one that wasn't in the books, that didn't deal with legal stuff. Her sister Zoe had been undercover within his organization. It was a classic tale of sisters ending up on opposite sides of the law.

The memory hurt and Mei looked up at Takaya, teary-eyed and full of rage. She wanted to taste his blood on her blade.

"What did she do to you, Takaya? You didn't have to kill her." Mei kept her distance from his samurai sword.

Takaya laughed. "Come on, Mei. Zoe was nothing more than a lousy pest. You should be glad it ended the way it did. I actually intended on sending you bits and pieces. So smile, damn it! I did you a favor!"

He wanted her to be angry, to make mistakes. She knew it and yet she was unable to shake the effect of his words.

"You did me a freaking favor? By killing her?"

She couldn't stop reliving that moment; the darkness, then spotting a single light from a lamp, half obscured by the boxes and crates, which surrounded her sister.

Before entering the warehouse, Mei had already taken her short swords. Swinging them in a protective manner, she had walked slowly towards the light. Suspended by chains from the ceiling, hung Zoe, naked and covered in blood, which dripped on the stone floor. The drips echoed in the room. Her head hung forward; her long dark hair draped over her body.

"Zoe!" Mei had shouted, forgetting her surroundings and hurrying over. The skin of her sister was cold to the touch as Mei shook her. "Zoe! Talk to me!" She shook her some more. The swords fell to the ground as she kept repeating her sister's name.

"Wake up, wake up!" Mei whispered again and again. She lifted Zoe, taking the chains off a hook then falling to her knees with the body in her arms. Immense dread was replaced by an all-consuming anger. This couldn't be happening! Zoe couldn't be dead! She just couldn't be.

Don't lose it, Mei, she told herself, trying to focus on her opponent rather than the memory. Takaya was sizing her up, smiling at her grief.

Hatred burned in her veins.

"So how does this work, Takaya? Are you going to send your men up against me now? You want to wear me out because you can't take me one on one?"

"Ha!" He countered, following her steps as they measured each other up. "Like I need my men to take care of the likes of you. Maybe you should call one of your little friends to come and help you! Oh, wait, they can't! I guess you like your men chained up, huh?"

He was trying to distract her, and it was working. The reference to her friends being chained up was proof enough he had been watching her house. It made her even more on edge.

She reacted in anger: thrusting forwards, swinging one of her blades, the other following the movement. Their weapons clashed and echoed into the room.

"You will die here, Takaya!"

"I would like to see you try," he shot back, kicking her away and making a sweep with his sword. His blade sliced into her right arm as she stumbled backward. Mei tried to keep up with his movements as he chased her. Blood ran from the wound on her arm and over her blade before hitting the floor. The cut burned like crazy. As much as she tried to ignore the pain, it was enough to make her almost forget she was fighting a skilled opponent. His blade came at her full force. Diving to the ground, she evaded it. With a neat roll, she got back to her feet.

They stared at each other. Time ticked by. She needed to find an opening. Any opening, to deal with him once and for all. As she charged again, she made a fake move and got what she was after. A clean swipe over his torso and one on his back as she twisted her body around. But with the gunshot wound in her side, it was not as perfectly executed as she had hoped. He countered her attack with another kick which sent her flying. As he came after her, she took a few stars from her belt, leaving her sword on the ground. Turning toward him, she threw the stars with all her might, aiming for his throat. His blade blocked some as others missed their mark completely.

"Is that all the tricks you've got, little girl? Can't you do any better?" he taunted, watching her get to her feet.

She swung her swords in a circular motion to have something to do while she thought out a strategy. Any strategy. There was no way she would let him leave alive. She had to kill him or die trying.

Mei held her swords tighter. Takaya smiled and waved his one sword about like she was a meaningless insect he could crush at any given time. They circled each other. From the corner of her eyes, she saw one of the remaining guys come at her.

The blond guy had found her dagger and obviously planned to use it. Effortlessly she side-stepped, slicing him open in one smooth motion before he had a chance to react. It was an automated defensive move, one she made so often it happened without thinking. She watched Takaya make a sudden move, but not towards her. He slid onto the ground and stabbed the other person in the heart with minute precision. Mei used this opportunity for all it was worth, never taking her eyes off him. After all, Takaya knew how this game was played.

Both her swords flanked his neck as he pulled his katana out of his victim.

"Mei! Come on, I just defended you," he said amused, looking up to her from his half kneeling position. His mock astonishment to find her swords against his skin didn't fool her. "Weren't you the one talking about a one on one fight earlier?"

"You thought I would let you go if you saved me?" Mei retorted, looking down at him. Takaya didn't look quite as terrified with her blades on his flesh as she had hoped. "You killed Zoe. You cut her open and left her to die for nothing." Her voice sounded cool enough. She wanted him to believe she was cool and collected. She didn't want to express the inner turmoil she was feeling. Takaya shrugged as much as he could.

"It was necessary to protect my business. I did what I had to." He smiled sweetly. That infernal smile.

"So do I," she countered. A bitter smile of her own crossed her lips as she cut the skin on his neck. Blood rushed out as he stayed on his knees, smiling away at her. Rage filled her, overriding the desire to see him suffer. With one move she sliced his throat, kicked his body over and stabbed it for effect with one of her swords. "Stop smiling, damn it!"

Stumbling to her feet, Mei looked around. Her head was pounding, and her arm hurt worse than anything she had experienced before, but mostly her pride was wounded. Her mind kept reeling, and Mei could barely collect herself to take care of pending business.

Makoto still had to pay for breaking one of the honored codes. You never, ever touch children. It was a code she lived by. It made her hate towards him that much stronger. Made her eyes shine feverishly. She had uncovered photos and videos of poor kids in all kinds of states. He and his friends were going to pay. Makoto was one of the last ones to pay by her hand. This creep deserved what he was going to get.

She stood in front of him again. The pole in her hand, she swung the blunt edge in front of him. She let the metal hit his chest and slid it slowly down between his legs. She pushed upwards a few times, leaving no room to misinterpret her plan. Mei clenched her teeth. Her arm stung, but this was going to be worth it! The pole finally tore the fabric of his pants; Makoto was screaming, trying to move away but to no avail.

"Scream little piggy!" She moved the pole again, looking up at the man who had destroyed so many lives. "Did you enjoy doing this to children? Did you enjoy the power it gave you?" Her eyes mirrored all the hate she felt towards him. "Did you really think you could get away with this? That no one would find you? That no one would care?"

She pointed behind her to the table with the pictures, stabbing him again. The pole shot up through his flesh. His body twitched and froze. Blood streamed over her hands as she stabbed further, inching her way through his body. Makoto squealed like a little piggy in a slaughterhouse.

"It will take a moment for you to bleed out. Enjoy the experience!" Her voice was intense with rage. She yanked the pole upwards in a fluent motion and heard bones crack. The end of the pole jutted out his neck. His body shook, twitched slightly. "See you in hell!"

———————

MEI STARED UP AT NINO.

"How did this happen?" he inquired, stitching her arm.

"You really want to know?" Eyebrow raised, she looked at him, questioningly.

"No. Not particularly." The honesty was something Mei appreciated most about her unwilling friend. Macchan and Nino knew nothing about her sister, and she liked to keep it that way. She gave him a half-hearted smile.

"Let's just say I got the job done."

———————

Sandra Wiltjer is a Dutch redhead, kept busy with terrarium gardening and learning Japanese.

MONSTERS AND ICE CREAM

BY ASTRID ADDAMS

IT WAS A GLORIOUS DAY, THE KIND OF DAY WHERE THE sun beams down through your windscreen and tries to turn you into another traffic accident statistic. Danny squinted through sunglasses as he sat behind the wheel of his old but clean Ford. He'd spent the day before making sure it was spotless. Megan had left him to it, emerging from their house every so often to offer a supportive smile, drink or ice cream. She'd offered to accompany him today, but he couldn't allow that. Danny believed firmly in compartmentalizing. Megan and his job and the life they had built together belonged in one compartment; his childhood and the family he never mentioned in another.

The day might be glorious, but it was also joyless, and he was in no mood to enjoy the drive through the verdant countryside. His shirt collar and tie were loosened; he'd folded his black jacket on the back seat next to the wreath, which he'd finally chosen and collected, only to discover he couldn't look at the blasted thing, just like this beaming summer day.

He drove carefully through winding country roads and postcard-perfect villages, thinking about his grandmother. He'd been eight when he met her. The memory lingered: the old house and the tall pale woman with dead eyes, so thin she appeared sharp. She answered the door and peered down at him through wire glasses as if he was a particularly ugly insect that had been foolish enough to land on her doorstep. He'd feared the sharp old battle ax on sight, recoiling from her, sensing her revulsion at the chubby little grandson who'd only ever known love and kindness from his family. As much as she repulsed him, his grandmother fascinated Danny and he resolved to do all he could to please the old witch and get on her good side. If she had one.

She was his mom's mother and she had never approved of his mom, or so Mom had told him. She'd approved even less of her daughter marrying Danny's dad. He hadn't known what that had meant until he'd stood before her under a gaze that made his cheeks flush. Mom and Grandmother had not spoken to one another for the duration of his parents' nine-year marriage.

When his mom and dad got divorced, Mom, who had always stayed at home, was forced to go back to work. Danny remembered how confused he'd been at the time and how much he'd missed his dad, 'the two-timing waste of space' whose rejection still burned its scar into Danny's psyche like a branding iron, even as an adult.

When Danny's mom had been forced to work, it had been his grandmother who'd stepped in to look after him over the summer holidays. There had been no one else, his mom had assured him of that when she dropped him off at the malevolent front door between the snarling gargoyles. Danny hadn't known when his mom and grandmother had got back in touch; now he never would.

THROUGHOUT THE SUMMER HOLIDAY, his mom dropped him off at the creepy house every morning on her way to work, then picked him up again on her way home. When his mom or grandmother handed him over, the two women barely spoke, nor exchanged any affection. Something was missing and Danny sensed Mom's unease, her fear of the old woman and her house. Grandmother's house was an extension of her, tall and severe with sharp edges, dark colors and long crooked shadows. He dared not run his fingers over the hard stone of the gargoyles, though he itched to feel the rough stone.

The days were long, and he'd wander uncomfortably through spotless rooms full of stuffed animals, old furniture, dark paintings, and black and white photographs. If the weather was fine, his Grandmother would allow him to explore her immaculate back garden where he would play on his mom's old swing. The swing creaked and sang as it climbed higher and higher. The wind swept through his fine hair and he wanted to whoop as the sky became his world, and he feared he would swing around the top bar. Grandmother would never allow such giddiness, such folly, but the swing wasn't afraid of Grandmother. He heard it in its song as he held his tongue. No one else whooped in front of Grandmother and everything was done under his grandmother's hawk-like, mainly silent gaze.

She sat on an iron bench a large hat impaled to her head by a small spear his mom said was a hat pin. She'd sit as if her spine was an iron bar and she was made of stone, a disapproving look carved onto her face.

On the rare occasions she decided he was too restless she would take him to the park. There too, she watched him incessantly, only occasionally distracted by glaring at the other children and chastising the odd parent she didn't think was disciplining their child correctly. Most people avoided her and him by association. Whenever they entered the park it would start to empty until it was just the two of them. No one sat on her bench, not even at the farthest end. Not that Grandmother seemed to notice as she sat and stared at him, waiting for him to do something wrong.

He didn't dare *play* in her house. Instead, he sat quietly under her witch-like gaze and read or drew pictures. She'd read too sometimes, but mainly she sat at her sewing table beside a box full of needles, pins and far too sharp scissors. There she'd mutilate pieces of fabric and sew them back together again or do some hand sewing or embroidery, forcing needles and pins into and out of fabric. He saw how it assaulted her wizened fingers, how she struggled to force the needles through and how they stabbed her bones, not that a little pain would stop Grandmother. She rarely spoke, content to watch him with pursed lips and dead gray eyes. After a week, he was convinced the dead eyes could see him even in his bedroom at home. If he was drawing, she would ask to see his work. Embarrassed, he would show her.

"Your colors are too bright," or "that watercolor is messy," she'd say, and he'd try again, but she would never be satisfied.

The worst part was lunch time when they'd sit together in the dining room, eating dainty sandwiches and drinking tea, and his grandmother would ask him about school. She asked him about school on the very first day he had spent at her house, and witnessing his discomfort, was determined to get to the bottom of it. Every lunch time became an interrogation. There Danny had sat, beside a giant painting of the libertines and their eternal torment, trying to fend off the old woman's relentless and increasingly cunning questions. The painting, his grandmother told him, giving him a look that made him blush to his socks, was called *Desgranges Hellish Passions*. She'd had it painted especially for her dining room and its subject matter was so unpleasant and agonizing that he avoided looking at it.

For two weeks Danny managed to hold his tongue. Then, one particularly brilliant, bright, hot day, his grandmother impaled her hat on her head and announced that they were going out. Even in the blistering heat that covered him and everyone else in a thin film of sweat, his grandmother wore a long black coat over her black jumper and skirt as they walked to the new Beetle parked in the drive. He didn't want to get in. He had never seen his grandmother drive, but she walked with a stick and he still didn't trust her not to swing it at him if he didn't do as she asked. So he got into the passenger seat beside her and she drove them into town.

To Danny's surprise she parked the car opposite the new ice cream parlor. It had only been open for a week and it had one big window through which Danny glimpsed shining silver tables, the long silver bar and gleaming red plastic booths with bar stools. At the counter were what seemed like hundreds of different bright-colored, delicious-looking flavors. It was the coolest place on Earth, and he yearned to be taken there so much that it hurt. Ice cream was Danny's favorite food, especially in the summer. Kids who were being taken out by their parents for a summer treat, or old enough to go themselves swarmed the shop. Some of them Danny knew or recognized from school.

He envied their happy care-free summer as well as the delicious ice cream that made his mouth water. Sitting in the Beetle, he hated them as well as Mom and Dad. He should be in there, eating strawberry and chocolate ice cream, not forced to spend a miserable summer with his grandmother. He must have done something wrong. She'd brought him here to torture him.

Danny had begged his mom to take him to the ice cream parlor, but each time he asked she looked at her hands and blushed, mumbling that maybe, at the end of the holidays, they could go. Danny guessed what that meant, and his heart sank enough to make him stamp his feet and cry in anger and frustration. Worse still, he knew his dad would have taken him; before he'd moved away.

"Daniel, stop staring."

"Sorry, Grandmother." Danny turned to look at her.

She smiled and his heart felt like a brick in his chest.

"Well, Daniel, as you know, I want to know why you do not like your school. I am prepared to make a deal with you."

Danny tried to keep his face blank, wondering what she would offer him. Sweat drenched his skin and he wanted an ice cream even more.

"If you tell me why you don't like school, the true reason, I will know if you are lying, I will take you to this gaudy establishment and buy you whichever ghastly concoction your heart desires."

"School's okay, really."

"Is whoever you are protecting worth not getting ice cream, Daniel?"

Danny studied the witch's face and knew there was only one way to get what he wanted.

"Well, Mr. James, he..." Danny hesitated then began to talk in a staccato manner.

His grandmother listened, the smile fading from her face. Her lips tightened, and her skin became pale and waxy beneath the hat. She looked like a witch before; now, she looked more like a vampire. When he finished, he stared at Grandmother, self-conscious and anxious in the ensuing heavy silence. Mr. James had said that no one would believe him and that everyone would hate him for being a liar. Mr. James had never met his grandmother who hated him anyway and who could tell when anybody was lying, even the Prime Minister.

"Are you telling me the truth, Daniel?" Grandmother asked at last, her voice sounding funny.

"Yeah," Danny murmured, blushing under her hawk-like gaze.

"Say yes, Daniel, not yeah,"

"Sorry, Grandmother."

To Danny's dismay, Grandmother started the car, turned around and drove right past ice cream heaven. After a couple of minutes, Danny realized they were driving towards Mr. James's house. A black monster of fear gnawed at him. Mr. James had been right, no one would believe him. His grandmother was going to tell Mr. James what he'd said, and he'd be punished. Danny shrank himself into as small a ball as possible in the passenger seat, tears streaming down his face and his entire body shaking. He thought about jumping out of the car and making a run for it, but he was too scared to move.

As if no time had passed, Grandmother pulled up outside Mr. James's house. She clambered out, retrieved her stick from the boot, and ordered Danny out of the car. Taking his hand, Grandmother led him towards Mr. James's house and its towering front door. She slammed the stick against the wood and Danny flinched. Then they waited. Mr. James opened the door and, before he could react, Grandmother barged past him into the house, dragging Danny with her.

"Danny, what the hell is going on? Oi, love! That's my front room! What the hell are you doing here?" Mr. James demanded as Grandmother positioned herself on a rug. Mr. James wore jeans and a t-shirt instead of his normal suit and tie. He barely looked like Mr. James at all, but Danny could hear it was him; the voice made his flesh crawl, and he could smell it in the sickening sweat that created dark circles beneath the man's arms.

Danny wanted to throw up as Grandmother spun around to face Mr. James. "Mr. Jason James, I presume?"

Danny stared at his shoes, but he heard the smile in Grandmother's soft voice.

"Yes. Who are you? What are you doing here?"

"Oh dear, did I forget to introduce myself? I am Daniel's grandmother, Miss Iris De Sade. I believe Daniel is in your class at school, is that correct?"

"Yes."

"And is it also correct that during breaks, or whenever you can think of an excuse to give him detention, you have Daniel remove his clothes?"

"What! Of course not."

"And that you take photographic images of my grandson's body?"

"Bullshit! I..."

"And that you have him touch your own lustful flesh?"

"No!"

"That you have taken him here to show him secret areas of your..."

"He's lying! Of course, I'd never do that. I'd never touch a child like that. It's sick and I'm a teacher and..."

"As I suspected, thank you for confirming my suspicions, Mr. James. Daniel, please go outside and wait for me by the car. I won't be long." Grandmother was still smiling. She didn't even sound angry, but that didn't fool Danny. He ran from the house as fast as he could and crouched by the car, waiting for her return, trying not to think about what they were planning to do to him.

They'd tell his mom he was a liar. He knew they would, and Mom would apologize to Mr. James, and Mr. James would say it was okay, but it wouldn't be...and next time Mr. James would hurt him badly. Like he'd hurt Willis who'd sworn at Mr. James when he'd told him to take his trousers down. Danny had been there at the time, serving yet another detention, huddled at his desk, hoping Mr. James wouldn't pick on him. He hadn't. Willis had made sure of that. The rest of the detention was dismissed, only Willis was kept behind. Willis hadn't returned to school for about a week. When he did, he wasn't the same, jumping at his own shadow, wetting himself at loud noises and crying in the toilets. Now whatever happened to Willis would happen to Danny.

His best chance was to run away and join the circus, Danny reasoned. Grandmother would never find him there. She hated the circus more than she hated anything else. She wouldn't be seen dead at a circus, he knew that, just as he knew vampires couldn't step out in the sunlight. Before Danny could propel his legs into action, Grandmother stepped out of the front door and made her way towards him and the car. She seemed to be leaning heavily on the stick and it took her a long time to reach him. When she got close enough, Danny saw that she was sweating. Grandmother never sweated, no matter how hot it got. Without speaking a word, she unlocked the car and struggled into the driver's seat, then leaned across and opened the passenger door. Frightened and confused, Danny got into his seat. They sat together in silence for a moment.

"A liar as well as a pedophile, what is education coming to?" his grandmother said at last, offering a tight smile. "I'm sorry I brought you here, Daniel, but the fiends of this world must be challenged."

His grandmother drove in silence. Danny barely dared to believe that he'd got away with telling on Mr. James. Grandmother drove them back into town and pulled up under the shade of a giant ice cream that was lit up at night. She fixed her hat by pulling the hair pin out and reinserting it firmly. As she lifted it, Danny spotted a flash of red in Grandmother's white hair.

"We have not been to see Mr. James today, have we, Daniel?"

"No, Grandmother."

"We spent the day cleaning out my attic."

"Yes, Grandmother."

"And now I am taking you into this gaudy monstrosity for whichever elaborate ice cream you choose to reward you for your hard work."

"Really?"

"What do you say, Daniel?"

"Yes, Grandmother."

"Good boy."

She'd never praised him before. They went into the ice cream bar, and true to her word, she let Danny order the ice cream of his dreams. A tower of ice cream and whipped cream barely contained in a tall glass. The flavors melted in his mouth as he savored every spoonful. It was just as wonderful as he'd imagined it would be. Sitting opposite him in the red booth, his grandmother daintily ate a small dish of vanilla drizzled in red sauce and for the first time ever, seemed almost human.

When his mom dropped him off the next morning, Grandmother was not herself. She limped, leaning heavily on the stick. While he drew his pictures, she lay on an old sofa and slept. The next day Grandmother was more alert and watchful, but winced when she moved. Danny watched her anxiously, guilty that his confession was responsible for the change. To his relief, Grandmother was her usual sharp self by the third day, mutilating a pair of jeans as he painted a picture.

The rest of the holidays were uneventful, and Danny felt more relaxed. Grandmother's gaze no longer seemed harsh and disapproving. Her criticism felt more like gentle suggestions.

When Danny returned to school, Mr. James was not there. He hadn't really expected him to be. His grandmother made a point of visiting him and Mom every other Sunday. His mom hated it, but Danny didn't mind.

They'd sit at the dinner table eating the Sunday dinner his mom spent hours sweating, swearing, and crying over and

Grandmother would ask his mom questions. Then she'd ask Danny questions. Normally the same or similar questions, but you had to keep on guard because every so often she'd slip in a new one. She would sternly ask him how school was, and he'd tell her that it was okay. She'd peer at him for a few seconds, then nod and ask Mom how work was going. By the next summer, his mom had gotten a job as a school administrator, giving her school holidays off. Danny was spared from spending another summer at Grandmother's house.

He'd not been back there since that summer, even though he'd visited Mr. James's house five years ago. Leaving his new life and new girlfriend, traveling five hours on the bus and hitchhiking for two more before reaching it and finding it just like he'd seen it on the news, surrounded by police tape, flashing lights and onlookers. That was also the last time he'd seen his grandmother, who still looked older and sharper than the earth, if smaller than he remembered.

She'd insisted on taking him to the ice cream bar that no longer gleamed. The bright colors looked cheap and tacky to his older eyes. She bought him an ice cream, given him a lift to his mom's house, and insisted he take the cane she'd carried that day.

"It belonged to my mother, and her mother before her. Take it, I have a new stick."

IT WAS ONLY by accident later, in his old bedroom sitting among his childhood toys, that he discovered the cane concealed a long, thin, razor sharp sword of the kind used in dueling. The police had identified Mr. James's victims from pornographic images, all boys from Mr. James's various classes. One boy named Danny as another victim. He denied he'd been abused but shared his memories of Willis. Danny suspected why no images of him had been found and kept his grandmother's secret.

At the inquest, it was revealed that Mr James had been tortured, stabbed over a hundred times by a long thin blade, barely thicker than a needle. The same blade had been forced up the man's penis, through his urethra, as far as the bladder neck then ripped free, effectively filleting Mr. James's penis. Something long and substantially thicker had been forced into his anus, as far as the rectum and used to destroy the rectum wall. Excrement was found fermenting in Mr James's stomach. The medical examiner, looking decidedly green, said there was evidence that Mr. James had been forced to swallow the contents of his rectum. The murderer left Mr James to bleed out and mummify in a secret sound-proofed cellar alongside his child pornography. It was a big scandal. Former classmates came forward, among them Willis who had developed substance abuse problems, but was now clean and training to be a chemist. The murderer was never caught and that was fine with all concerned.

———

DANNY DROVE along bright leafy streets, circling twice before locating the old house that had held such foreboding for him as a boy. As a man, he saw it was an attractive, large house with all the original features. It was probably worth a fortune by now. The gargoyles were still there, as menacing as ever. This time he promised to run his hands over the stone before he left. Grandmother's latest Beetle was in the drive; she liked to get a new one every five years or so. Danny retrieved the wreath and walked towards the front door, noticing that the iron bench had been placed beside it. Sitting ramrod straight on the bench was his grandmother, watching his approach. She wore the same black hat, probably with the same hat pin. Beside her, on her left, was another wreath. Danny's spelled out the name, MOM, in yellow roses. Grandmother's spelled out ROSE in white.

His grandmother attempted to stand. She managed it, using the light metal stick that had replaced the cane. She was smaller than she had been five years before. Danny noticed she'd been crying. Her claw-like hand took his and squeezed. He squeezed back. The bench was large enough for Danny to sit beside his grandmother without disturbing the wreaths. Her bones and joints creaked as she sat back down. How she got Mr. James into the cellar he didn't know. He suspected the cane had something to do with it, but he'd never know, and it didn't matter; it had never mattered. Together, hand in hand, they waited for the hearse to arrive.

Astrid Addams is a British author who likes to write and read horror stories. Her novella *The Haunting of Hacket House* can be found at amxn.to/2RHmG9K
Her charity short story *Zombie Santa Claus: Axe Murderer Edition* can be found at
http://mybook.to/ZombieSantaClaus

IF I EVER LAY MY LINGERING BLUE EYES ON YOU...

EDITED BY MICHELE DUTCHER

BY SERGIO "ENTE PER ENTE" PALUMBO

It was a perfect day
For sowing; just
As sweet and dry was the ground
As tobacco-dust.

I tasted deep the hour
Between the far
Owl's chuckling first soft cry
And the first star.

A long-stretched hour it was;
Nothing undone
Remained; the early seeds
All safely sown.

And now, hark at the rain,
Windless and light,
Half a kiss, half a tear,
Saying good night.

Sowing by Edward Thomas

IT WAS A COMMON PRACTICE AMONG VILLAGERS TO light torches along the main street in preparation for a night of feasting and to warn people that dancing and singing would soon begin. Six large tents and four small ones had been put up, serving beverages, warm food and sweets. The town square had been crowded since just after noon.

Ilsa couldn't wish for anything better. She always made the most of the festivals. The twenty-year-old woman loved to put on her hip-length delicate blue jacket with pleated cuffs that brought out the color of her eyes. The outfit was practical and comfortable, made of cotton, fully lined and laced in front. The close-fitting garment had an intoxicating effect on all the men who saw her walking, which was well-suited for her current goal.

She folded a plain white fichu to form a triangular neckerchief to keep her warm when the temperature fell. The ruffled petticoat with fitted waistband buttons was dyed in vegetable colors, with a drawn waist, hoop flounce and an unfinished hem. It was, in a way, a skirt beneath a skirt: the under-petticoat was made of a white sheet material, while the outer petticoat, or real skirt, looked like a tablecloth. All of this was in accordance with tradition.

Ilsa didn't wear the laced coifs or full caps that other ladies would commonly put on to temporarily cover their hairstyle; she was blessed with beautiful long curls and she loved to show them off. It was all part of her plan to get the upper-hand on whomever would become her new partner (or partners...) for the night.

The small village of Chmielno, with a population of about 1,800, lay approximately 22 miles west of the much bigger town of Gdańsk. It had only been a short time since the plague had devastated the area, following trade, travel and army routes that crossed the entire region during the Great Northern War. People were just beginning to forget the turmoil, trying to lead calm and ordinary lives again. It was a confused period and no less problematic for the village itself, which was otherwise adorned with traditionally painted houses and many verdant places.

After the Treaty of Frederiksborg in 1720, Old Western Pomerania had been given to Prussia while the other portion of the region continued to be called Swedish Pomerania. Battles over land had completely destroyed the rich farms and soil was generally poor. Its ponds were frequently full of dirty water or filled with sand, the same went for the meandering rivers and streams.

So, the citizens and the peasants didn't lose any chance to have fun and forget their worries, and the festivities that day seemed to be the right time to leave it all behind. They were happy to enjoy the dances and fresh food available in the main square. The young women wore their most beautiful dresses to draw the interest of the young men. The male inhabitants did the same thing. Nobody wanted to waste time, especially the younger people – everything was ready for merrymaking and happy revelry.

The place was already busy when late evening came, and many people were intoxicated before dinner time was even close. Ksawery, the present partner of Ilsa, who she had just lovingly eyed and danced with a few hours before, seemed to be one of those already drunk, even if he didn't show the effects of the excess alcohol that flowed through his well-muscled body. The young woman knew he was drunk enough; there was no way to deceive her blue eyes.

Ksawery was no older than twenty-two, or so Isla thought. He had the peculiar traits of someone who was of Kaschuben ancestry. His eyes were neither the icy blue of a man from the north, nor the clear hue of the place where the sky meets the sea, but simply a tint that was somewhere in the middle. His long, fair hair complemented his short beard of the same color, and he had on a simple but refined outfit: a yellow embroidered shirt under a dark blue heavy cloth coat and a pair of traditional trousers. The dark hat he wore had a reddish band. Most of the local male population wore something close to this costume.

Kaschuben, also known as the Kashubs, were a West Slavic ethnic group in north-central Poland. Descending from the old Pomeranian tribes that had settled in the region during ancient times, they had been subjects to Polish and Danish men of power at various times. And while most of the Slavic populations were assimilated during the medieval German settlement of the area, some had kept and developed their own customs and way of life.

Many men and women attended the feast, and the main square had already become a very busy place, showcasing several stages with continuous singing and music. Between all of those food vendors, they served close to 200 different dishes. It was impossible to carve a straight path through the huge crowd that covered the three main streets.

Pushed together in the crowd, Ksawery looked into Ilsa's eyes and took her hand. She nodded in silent agreement, and they moved away, leaving the main square full of noises, boasts, and passionate chants. They left all the lit torches behind, as they walked to the outskirts of the village. Then, when they were far enough from the last houses, the young woman laughed and turned to the man, challenging him to run with her to the verdant hills that stood in the distance, if he was able.

Ksawery tried to catch up. Reaching the young woman didn't prove to be an easy accomplishment; she swiftly outdistanced him with her slender, skinny legs that looked more like the ones of a strong mountain man than of a girl her age. He pushed himself harder as they battled for first place until they got to the top of the first of the hills that covered that part of the land, just in front of the woods.

It was there that Ilsa finally stopped running and let her body drop to the ground, apparently worn out and completely bereft of energy. She stayed there silently – as if to regain her strength. She looked weak, powerless before the young Ksawery, but the smirk on her face made it understood that she was ready to abandon herself to his desire.

Her hair was disheveled, with long blonde curls that dropped down to her sensual bare shoulders. The young man regretted that it was already getting dark; he protested that he wanted to see her splendid figure in full light and admire her wondrous body. They had no bed at their disposal, nor some soft blanket on which they could comfortably stretch out, but they made the most of the present moment, there was nothing else to do.

"Well," a mischievous Ilsa said, cleverly smiling. "Aren't you going to tell me how pretty I look?"

Staring at her fair skin, that the refined jacket displayed, enraptured by her beautiful face, small chin, thin nose, narrow cheeks and her wonderful full lips, and her sculpted legs, highlighted by the removal of a wide portion of her heavy skirt, he exclaimed and kissed her wildly.

"You're unbelievable! I love you!"

The woman looked at him and grinned back, but she didn't say anything. The sleeved waistcoat that he wore over the yellowish shirt and knee-breeches endowed with buckles attached to the hems at the knee, and the pant leg that covered the end of the stocking made him appear very vigorous. He looked handsome, Ilsa considered, and his desire could not possibly be denied. In a way what was going to happen next was a pity, but she had to respond to a more passionate call, unknown to that man, and act accordingly. She told herself there was no way to change her behavior and nor did she regret it, at all...

The back of a hand that seemed a bit too rough, touched her shoulder. The young woman gave ground and let him go on. The other followed the curve of her body, down to the soft breasts still covered by her jacket, and stroked her skin, feeling her slender body in his strong hands. He was moving too quickly, impatiently, perhaps he wasn't experienced at dealing with moments like this, with someone like her.

"I'll carve your name somewhere in these woods!" Ksawery announced, keeping his head close to her body. "So that everyone knows I loved you here tonight..."

She laughed at those words.

"Don't you believe me?" the man retorted, in a surprised tone. "In my heart, I am sincere...just let me show you that I'm serious, and you'll see!"

"That will not be necessary, my dear..." Ilsa replied, glancing at his handsome features. When he was upset, or under stress, Ksawery opened his mouth in a peculiar way that made him look comical. But what was going to happen soon wouldn't amuse him.

"But I promise you! You make me so very happy..." Ksawery insisted.

He promised her? What a dear lover he was, it didn't change anything, however. Their relationship wasn't going to follow a natural path, even though at present her partner thought they would never be parted.

She fully opened her blouse, revealing pale skin beneath.

"I have never seen such a wondrous woman's naked breast..." Ksawery told her, and kept moving his fingers under her wide skirt, trying to find his way.

Their lips met passionately, and soon after they did it once more, and it was a slower, more controlled, sensual kiss. Their tongues investigated the distant corners of each other's mouths. As they became increasingly immersed in the kiss, their hands undressed each other. The young woman's soft hands expertly unbuttoned the man's clothes then she reached around to stroke his muscled back. Ksawery did likewise and with passionate movements, he savored her breasts and nipples.

"Do you want me, Ksawery?" Ilsa whispered and pulled her skirt up still further.

"Yes, I want you, I want you…" he said.

As Ilsa continued to stimulate her partner, provocatively swaying her hips, the young man reached with his tongue toward her pussy lips before moving up slightly and running it slowly around her womanliness, trying to tease out her love bud. Soon after, he stopped his circling and very gently licked across her in the hollow of her thighs, producing another moan and a shudder from the body he was pleasuring.

Oh, my handsome lover, go on and just fuck me, baby, Ilsa groaned in her mind.

As if in response to her silent request, Ksawery lowered himself until her breast pressed against his chest. She took a deep breath and prepared herself for orgasm which struck like the opening of a bottle within a matter of seconds. Some moments of rest followed, in silence.

They made love just once, a heated act that left the young man nervous, but not without some charm. As Ksawery finally stopped maneuvering beneath the woman's clothes, she said, "I'm ready for what is to come next…"

"Uhm? What's next… what do you mean, my darling?" he asked, in an uncertain tone.

"You'll see my enthusiastic lover…"

At first, the man didn't understand. Then, he thought she was referring to what might still happen between them, as the night was still young, and so he smirked... but Ilsa displayed a strange smile.

He bowed to reach her lips but, while he was kissing her, a strange sound filled the air, a noise of bone fragments and ripped skin, knitting themselves together. A shadowy, tall female figure rose to its feet and appeared behind them.

There was nothing better than the fresh blood of a strong, healthy man who had just made love, full of epinephrine and norepinephrine, two separate but related substances secreted by the adrenal glands. Everything had been done precisely in the way that the new unearthly presence liked most and needed to satisfy her taste and drain the life energies she longed for.

The vampire made her move and threw herself at the young man. In seconds, she covered the distance between them and was upon her human prey, her pointed teeth ready to savor the precious blood from the living body that she had taken off-guard. As she pierced his neck, poor Ksawery floundered and tried to move away, wriggled for a while, but it was useless. The end result was always the same. The blood pumped out of the man, unstoppable, fatal...

As the cruel feeding process ended, the presence stood upright, displaying her considerable height, and turned to the woman, whose long blonde curls dropped languidly down to her bare breast.

"It's about time..." Ilsa said. "I thought you weren't going to rise tonight..."

"Uhm?" The naked vampire stopped for a moment, staring at the woman's eyes with a dubious look. Long, dark hair outlined her cold but incredibly attractive pale features, which ended with an eagle-like nose and two greenish irises that glimmered on her unearthly face. "What did you say?"

"You heard me, Maryla," Ilsa replied. Her deep blue eyes

looked at the vampire's traits again, the ones she had not been able to admire for an entire year.

The Nachzehrer, as the German-speaking people living in the area called her, was a sort of female vampire. The term translated as "afterward (nach) devourer of energy (zehrer)". It was reputed, or so legends recounted, to be created from a suicidal event or, sometimes, an accidental death. What had killed Maryla was not an accident or plague. Ilsa's house had been surrounded at night by those who wished to set her on fire, which was how angered villagers usually dealt with ones charged with sorcery or involved in some forbidden love affair with another woman.

The local peasants, armed with deadly mauls and other weapons, were searching for Ilsa; she was the true witch they wanted to find and seize. However, they stumbled upon her lover. No escape was possible, so Maryla ended her own life.

The raging crowd had entered the residence and carried Maryla's corpse to a secluded place in the hills. There, in the deep woods, they buried her remains and treated her body as was common when they feared that some evil dead woman might come back from the afterlife.

Ilsa had watched everything from afar, although nobody in the group of the madmen had noticed her. The young woman regretted that she was not at home to protect her lover, but she understood that her absence had been a good thing. She was able to put into action a plan to help her beloved partner, and to revive her, in the end.

Ilsa returned to the burial place the following night, and although shrubs and branches concealed the exact point, she found it. She started digging until she saw the corpse lying beneath the surface. The entire forest was silent with snow, but it wasn't asleep yet; many wild beasts and winged predators were already hunting somewhere in the surroundings.

When her eyes spotted the seductive features of her woman

under the feeble light of the oil lamp – her beautiful face turned cold, her lips lifeless, her arms and chest still half-covered and dirty with dust and soil, a great sorrow unsettled her mind and a feeling of powerful hatred seized her. After removing Maryla from the ground with much difficulty, Ilsa loaded the body on a wooden cart and brought the remains to another location where she could perform her forbidden rites and apply the most unholy preparations that she had at her disposal in order to achieve the desired result.

They would be allowed to stay together and love again, even though in such a cursed way that no one on earth would accept nor forgive. Who cared? Her passion was too deep and her affection too strong to be overwhelmed even by death...

The process had not caused any suspicion, nor attracted undesired attention, so far. People commonly disappeared in the woods or along the roads; it had always happened, and it was going to continue to happen. Unending wars, the plagues, and all the dangers commonly implied in traveling: going up steep, sloped hills to reach lonely and insidious places. The locals become accustomed to such occurrences, and no one noticed too much if a young man suddenly disappeared here and there.

Single men were the perfect target. Young women were chosen from time to time, in order to accomplish her bloody rite and join her dead lover again. Even if it only lasted for twelve hours during the Night of the Dead, not one minute less or longer. She would remember their brief time together for the rest of the year until that moment would come again, and she would be ready to do it another time.

This night, as usual, she had been very cautious. She always cast her blue eyes on an unlucky, lonely man, just like that poor villager named Ksawery whose blood Ilsa needed so much. In the end, he had not found the love he was searching for, but he had done her a great favor.

There was no fear that the Nachzehrer's feeding might turn other corpses into a creature like herself. A person didn't become such a peculiar vampire simply by being bitten or scratched: the transformation only happened after death, if you knew the proper substances to use. Most of all, a person needed the fresh blood of a sacrificed lover, and the correct ritual to perform.

Isla relocated Maryla's remains every single time, to a different location, not too deep under the ground. The intended victim must be willing to follow to that place. But Ilsa's beauty, experience and the proper festive dress easily attracted new partners. They followed more eagerly than a person might think...

"How long will this keep going on?" Maryla asked.

"As long you wish, my darling..." Ilsa replied, cracking a smile. "I'll always do my best to find a new lover every year, on this date, so I can bring him before you, and let you feed on him to be revived to full strength again, even if only for a short time. You know I really loved you, and I still love you now, and that love will be forever... I can't stop growing older, but I'm an accomplished witch, and I know how to slow or hide my aging process."

The other stared at her, in silence, looking thoughtful and estranged.

"I'll never stop doing this, despite all the poor young men that I'll entice to your remains, who'll be used to give you their life energy. After all, what are they, compared to us? What is the brief act of love they would give me in comparison with your deep, true passion?" Ilsa continued.

"But you'll age, sooner or later, even if at a slower pace than any other human, no matter how capable you are at performing your rites. And certainly, with the passing of time you'll not be able to do it anymore. Our existence together will be lost..." Maryla argued.

"I look like I'm still in my twenties. I'm still young and breathtakingly beautiful, according to the men in the villages around. I'll be able to provide you with fresh energy for many long years more before I grow too old. You can be sure I'll do my best to find all the ones I can and bring them before you. I'm good at this, you know it well..."

"So, you'll be with perhaps a hundred other men over the course of the years, before I take the energy out of their bodies to revive me..."

"Are you jealous, darling? I'll do it all only for you..."

"Maybe I should be. But that's just something I'll have to learn to accept, after all..." The female vampire nodded.

"Give me a passionate kiss, and let's make the most of this night. We still have some hours before dawn, and these are only for us!"

"I'm not going to disappoint you..."

"It will be a long year before we meet again, so don't waste our time..." Ilsa added.

"I'll always be here to satisfy you..." the aroused Nachzehrer whispered.

Sergio Palumbo"Sergio 'ente per ente' Palumbo, an Italian public servant who
published a Fantasy RolePlaying illustrated Manual, WarBlades, and has some of his short- stories
published in numerous American, British and Canadian anthologies.

14

DARK TUNNEL OF LOVE

BY N.M. BROWN

I SEE HER BEFORE SHE SEES ME. HER BODY'S SMALL... thin, but thick in the right places. You know what I mean? She stands alone outside the Tunnel of Love like a lost soul. This'll be too damn easy.

"Hey love! What's a pretty thing like you so sad for? And outside the tunnel of love no less. Surely there are blokes lined up round the block to take a ride with a gal like you."

Her cheeks burn the color of a Florida sunset, but she doesn't respond; she continues gazing at her feet.

"Well...seeing as I happen to also find myself without a partner; fancy a ride?" I extend my arm towards her gently. "Name's Thomas; what's yours?"

"Amanda...and I'd love to take a ride with you." Her gaze meets mine. Huge green eyes sparkle under the full moon of the evening; a dainty mouth, pursed like a bow.

This girl takes my breath away. Too bad that's the very same fate that I have planned for her. A pleased grin blisters across my lips. I'm even more satisfied to see that we're the only ones waiting for the ride. It'll be no problem to ditch her body inside.

No one will think twice about me coming out alone. They'll figure some lonely pervert just took a ride solo for jollies.

I help Amanda into the boat like a gentleman and take my place beside her. It takes all the inner strength that I can muster to feign shyness. All I want is to feel her blood run through my fingers. Homicidal hunger courses through my veins like an undeniable itch. My knuckles are numb from my grip on the knife in the pocket of my jacket.

"Amanda...you wanna have some fun?" I grin.

"I thought you'd never ask," she answers.

Jumping on me faster than I can react, her lips nibble mine hungrily as she pulls my hand to her chest. Her velvet kisses trail from my lips to my cheekbones then down the length of my neck. I become dizzy and release my grip on the knife.

Her once tiny mouth unhinges wider than a snake's. Fangs extend from her beautiful canines and sink into my jugular vein. I'm too intoxicated to push her away.

Amanda comes out at the end of the Tunnel of Love *alone*; wiping the corners of her mouth.

And no one thinks twice about it.

N.M Brown is a happily married mother who sheds light on the dark corners of the mind that we like to keep hidden.

15

WORDS

BY AMDI SILVESTRI

YOU WANT ORIGINALITY? WELL THERE'S NOTHING original about this setup. It's a chair. You're in it. By now you've probably realized that your hands are bound. No need to guess. It's an extension cord. In my experience it works like a charm if you tie it nice and firm. It gets slippery when wet. Sweat, tears, sperm. Doesn't matter. The wetter, the tighter, right. All the things you like. Believe me, this is as tight as it gets.

I've listened to you a lot. You like to hear your own voice. I must admit, it is a nice voice. What a shame that you use it for evil. All those nasty and belittling words. You cage people in slurs and anachronisms, podcasting your views on the world web. You boast and challenge anyone and everyone. I have taken you at your word. Challenge accepted. You speak sounds. I speak metal.

Simple contraption that gag. You'll find one at any dentists. Keeps the jaw from closing, gives access to the oral cavity. Almost sounds like a jingle. The ratchet mechanism rag. You blink quite a lot. You can't blink this away. I'm as real as it gets, baby. Isn't that your go-to-statement? Where have all the real women gone?

Your tongue looks like a shaved hamster. So vulnerable. Feels all convulsive-y. Your spit rises like a tidal wave. I know what you want to do. You want to yell at me. You want to call me the b-word, the c-word and especially the n-word. Better put a stop to that. Trussing needles work well. One. Two. Three. Four. I declare a thumb war and press the fifth needle through the sweet spot.

Oh my, what a big boy. Blood gushes and sprinkles the inside of your teeth and my pretty face. You gargle and gurgle, spit, wince and whine. Don't you know that boys don't cry? You said that yourself. Now now, there there, mommy will make all the bad things come to life.

Some view money or muscle as the greatest force. We both know that it's the human tongue, that erudite flesh machine. It can lash and soothe and command and execute, all with the tiniest coiling of tissue. If you press the tip of the tongue to that place right behind the incisors, you produce the t and the d-sound in the beginning of words like tomboy or dumpy. Roll it all the way back and you make the g of girl and the k-sound of, well, that c-word you like so much.

Shh. Don't interrupt me with your sounds. I'm talking. A woman's place is in the home, right? You make the word home sound like the word prison. Quite the phonetic artistry. I like the home. I like the tools of the home. The traditional tools of women. The carry-bag, the sewing needle and of course the scissors. Snip, snip go the scissors. Can you feel it? Can you feel how deep I go?

How that tiny tip of your tongue curls and dances. Dodging, weaving, and then, snap, it's caught in metal jaws. Then snip, and it tumbles down your face hole. Those t's and d's dissolving in your stomach. You scream like a beast while your wounded clit-licker whips from side to side, spraying red paint on my face. Do you like that, baby? I made myself pretty for you.

I wipe and suck the blood from your teeth. Spit it out. No swallowing. You hurt yourself with all that bobbing. Those needles tear. Lie still. It'll be over soon. The tip went easily. I hardly had to press the handles together. The next part demands strength. Muscle power. As a weak and frail woman, I won't be able to make this quick. The tongue is quite sturdy, but I won't take everything. Only the parts you use to make those bad and hurtful words.

But then again, you know so many, many words.

Amdi Silvestri has 17 books published in Danish. He has recently begun writing in English.

16

TEMPTRESS OF THE NIGHT

BY SAMIE SANDS

VIVIEN SHOOK HER HIPS LIGHTLY FROM SIDE TO SIDE in time with the music, perfectly aware that everyone was looking at her and always conscious of the effect she was having on the occupants of the room, but the bored expression never left her face, even for a second.

Jeffrey was practically salivating at the sight of this mysterious brunette on the dance floor. He'd been coming to this bar for many years and had never ever encountered such a classy beauty. If he was honest with himself, the only thing that kept him coming to this dingy place, complete with sticky floors, was the copious amounts of slutty women that came through here like a revolving door system. It didn't seem to matter to those young, drunk, eager girls how old he got, they kept throwing themselves at him with vigor.

But this one.. wow. Her dark, curled hair fell slightly above her tiny waist. Her curves and voluptuous breasts excited him in a way he hadn't felt for many years. He'd become bored by the game; a few drinks, maybe a dance, meaningless sex and then the ignored seven or eight phone calls until he was ready to try again. But those red pouting lips ignited a passion that he knew needed quenching. He needed her. He had to have her, but how to go about it?

His usual flirtatious banter was not going to work. She was obviously highly intelligent and barely intoxicated. Two immediate dampeners on his plays. He needed to try something different.

He dragged his eyes away from the magnificent creature. The longer he watched her, the harder he found it to concentrate. It was like a magical spell that fried his brain and turned him into a blubbering mess.

Alcohol: always the answer. He downed two more whiskeys, trying to steady his nerves. He kept glancing over to the woman, just to check that no one else had swooped in there first, but every time he spotted her she was still alone, still swaying seductively.

He took a deep breath to calm his labored breathing. If he didn't move now, he never would, and he might never forgive himself if this wonderful opportunity slipped through his fingers. He'd never sleep again knowing he'd been so close to perfection and let her get away.

The booze had an unwelcome effect as he stood up. His head buzzed, his heart raced and his feet couldn't get a decent grip on the ground. Jeffrey wished he could still smoke indoors, just to give him something to do with his hands.

Vivien became aware that someone was shuffling towards her, concentrating deeply on each and every step. She forced herself not to laugh at the pathetic being. They were all the same, these men. Unable to accept that a woman could possibly be way out of their reach. They had to give it a go, just in case; a quality she wasn't sure whether to admire or despise. She readied herself for his inevitable ridiculous chat up line, knowing exactly how she was going to respond.

Jeffrey's lips moved, but the words wouldn't form. He'd been gearing himself up, prepping his speech the whole way over, but as soon as his eyes locked with the woman's, terror consumed him.

Vivien grabbed hold of the fat, slightly balding man's pudgy hand and brought his fingers up to her lips. Tantalizingly, she ran her tongue up and down his index finger before clamping her teeth tightly around it. Arousal gave way to fright as Jeffrey sensed danger. Suddenly, she was much more startling than she was sexy.

However, this didn't stop him from following her out from the bar. He didn't pull his hand away as she entwined her fingers with his. Instead, he marveled at her porcelain skin. He knew he was going to get lucky with the most stunning human he'd ever had the pleasure of laying his eyes on, and that overruled the alarm bells that rang violently inside his mind.

Before he'd taken full stock of the situation, they were alone inside a brilliantly white hotel room and the woman was already half-way naked. She was moving way too fast, he wanted to be able to savor every moment, but instead of saying anything, his weak-willed nature just got swept away with the flurry of activity.

An odd sensation squatted in the pit of Jeffrey's stomach. Something was wrong. Something was *really* wrong. The woman's eyes had changed from a deep hazelnut color to a hollow, dead black. Jeffrey recoiled, wanting to get as far away from her as possible. As he pushed himself against the headboard, other things began to change.

The woman morphed into a much younger body; a girl barely into her twenties, shedding dark curls and leaving behind a short blond bob. Jeffrey looked on in shock and amazement as the form before him slowly became more recognizable.

Dread shot through him so violently that he lost control of

his bladder. The strange beast before him bellowed with laughter. He couldn't grasp what he was seeing. He knew it must be real because he was right there, witnessing it, but it didn't make the situation any less bizarre or any easier to digest.

The gorgeous woman from the bar had become Sarah – a girl he'd met on a night out when he started college. He'd been trying to impress his brand-new friends; he wanted them to think he was cool. He wanted to finally fit in after having such a rough time at school.

The dares started off little; drink this, kiss her, jump off that. But as the night wore on and the girls became more intoxicated and willing to play along, the dares became more stupid, more risqué. Jeffrey had been watching Sarah from a distance since the beginning of the night and was disappointed when she passed out just outside the boy's residence. Everyone ignored her, stepped over her. None of them were friends who cared enough to sacrifice a night of drinking and frolics in order to help someone who had over-consumed.

He didn't want to go along with it when the rest of the group told him he should have sex with her anyway. He did fancy her, but their goading confused his moral conscience.

As the memory flooded back, he was filled with shame. He remembered acting on the dare as the others watched and cheered. He recalled Sarah's confused expression as she woke up, bleary-eyed, right in the middle of it all and the tear that rolled down her cheek, but he didn't stop, not wanting to let anyone down.

The saddest thing was none of the others respected him after that. He was still an outsider, tolerated rather than liked. He'd ruined his chance with a wonderful girl for nothing. In fact, he'd ruined everything for her because two days later she was found hanging in her room.

He never admitted to anything, preferring to let her parents believe that she'd struggled with depression which they'd just never noticed. He'd carried on his life regardless; building a successful career and the group of friends he'd spent so much time desiring, but he'd never settled down. Instead he played with women's feelings. His guilt over Sarah might be the reason he never fell in love. Maybe he'd never truly let go of what had happened.

As this revelation hit, so did a fist. He was thrown against a wall with such a force that plaster fell to the floor around him. Jeffrey blinked in shock. Sarah was a waif of a girl. There was no way she could possess that kind of strength.

But of course, this wasn't really Sarah.

Jeffrey tried to stand, but a searing scratch down his leg made him yell out in agony and crumple back to the floor. Blood seeped from the wound and dribbled down his foot.

"Wha...who... what..?" he stuttered. The first words he'd spoken since meeting this woman.

She gripped his bottom lip, seductively stroking his chin, before yanking down with great force, completely removing his jaw from his body.

Tears fell down his cheeks not because of the pain, he was far too numbed by shock for that, but because he finally understood. This was karma. He wasn't being taught a harsh life lesson; he wasn't learning where his fear of commitment came from; he was going to die. This beautiful woman was going to murder him, and he'd brought it on himself. He hadn't felt enough remorse for his actions, and now it was too late.

Vivien reached forward, knowing the end was near. Now Jeffrey understood all that was happening, she only had the final act to carry out. If she was human, she might have felt a myriad of emotions: sorrow, remorse or even happiness at the justice that she was about to serve, but she felt nothing. This was her duty; this is what she'd been put on this earth for. To complete His work.

As she touched Jeffrey's chest, feeling his heart pound erratically, she paused for just a second, before tearing through his skin and bones and plunging. Gripping on to the offending organ, she tore it out; entrails followed, and lust finally ignited within her. This was why she did all of this, this was her reward.

Jeffrey's eyes opened wide as he saw her rip a chunk from his heart with her teeth. He watched in a bemused silence as it continued to pump, forcing droplets of blood to cascade down her chin and make their way to her cleavage. She'd returned to her previous form, and her heavy breasts heaved with each breath, making the action strangely sensual.

He ignored the roaring sound behind him, the tearing of ground as a fiery hole opened. Deep down he knew what was coming; he was aware that his soul had been condemned to the eternal pits of Hell and despite the fact that this very woman had sent him here early, had cut his life short, he still couldn't drag his eyes away from her.

Then a falling sensation and he knew everything was over. An all-encompassing blackness swallowed him forever.

Vivien stared at the lifeless body that lay at her feet. She knew she'd eat him, the hunger burned inside her, but that didn't mean that she liked the vile beasts she was forced to consume. They were terrible human beings, who'd committed despicable acts; murder, conspiracy or rape like this pathetic Jeffrey. It tainted the taste of them as if the evil poisoned their blood. Just for once, Vivien wanted to feast upon something pure, someone wholesome.

But of course, that defied her purpose.

After the last scrap of Jeffrey was gone, leaving only stains, Vivien stepped into the shower. Cleansing was essential before moving on to the next victim.

Other sirens had given in to the cardinal sin of slaughtering an innocent, driven by the same lust, and found themselves thrown into the worst corners of Hell to endure torture for all eternity. She didn't want that to be her, as much as she'd like to give in, she couldn't. A moment of satisfaction could never be worth an eternity of nightmares.

People assumed that the devil's work was evil; that his minions preyed on the human race, but the only people they targeted were the truly malevolent, the ones who'd done harm unto others and who deserved to die violently before descending into Hell forever.

Vivien fixed her lipstick. Throughout history, the laws of attraction had changed as had the desired appearance, but the voluptuous vixen look never went out of style. Men would always desire her, no matter what. Especially the sort of men she hunted.

Donning her highest heels and little black dress, Vivien stalked down the dark road. She had nothing to fear even when wandering alone through dangerous alleys. She'd been attacked, but the aggressors always ended up much worse for wear. Going after her would invariably be their final act.

Loud music reached her eardrums, and she flinched. This new style of thumping bass aggravated her. Vivien had a soft spot for jazz. The thought that it had long ago gone out of style, disappointed her to no end. She spotted the next bar she'd enter, complete with nasty neon lights and women dressed in hot pants and low-cut tops where the worst kind of men hung out in a desperate attempt to pick up some skanky stranger. She wouldn't even have to try to be the most attractive woman there.

As she stepped towards the bar a martini was placed into her hand. Vivien had never had to queue or pay for a drink in her life. Her magic captured the barmen quickly, which was extremely useful to her work. It left her more time to focus on selecting her next target.

Her eyes flitted around the bar and, as expected, almost everyone stared back at her. Usually, she picked up an immediate vibe from a shady corner and wouldn't need to search, but there didn't seem to be any obvious evil in here, which made a change.

Letting out a deep sigh, Vivien gave up and was ready to move on when someone captured her eye. A boy in his mid-twenties, laughing and slowly creeping his arms around a younger, innocent beautiful girl. He was a sociopath; Vivien sensed it emanating from him. A compulsive liar, a cheat, a manipulative pig, but unbearably charming so that girls fell under his spell. This young girl would be his next victim. She was about to lose all of her self-confidence, cry more tears than she knew possible and sever ties with everyone until she became a shell of her former self, just for this idiot.

Vivien couldn't bear it. Boys who would never grow up to be men capable of seeing the trail of destruction they left behind. She studied the young girl whose bright eyes shone with lust and laughter, and a strange emptiness sat in Vivien's stomach.

She narrowed her eyes and furrowed her brows. The guy would end up in Hell, but his crimes weren't significant enough to require immediate retribution. He'd already emotionally destroyed a few girls, and Vivien didn't want it to happen again. There was something about this young girl that made Vivien want to protect her.

Decision made before Vivien was even aware of it, she made her way toward him. The closer she got, the more apparent his unpleasant nature became. Screwing up her nose, Vivien composed herself for her next move. True evil was something she was used to, but this was entirely different.

Her hips began to sway; her lips started to pout. She slipped into the familiar game with ease, but he paid her no mind. He was good, Vivien realized. He'd mastered his play well. He knew that he had to give this girl his entire attention, just for one night, to capture her forever. Ready to pick up and put down as he pleased. Vivien was going to have to pull out all the stops. She would need to get much closer and do more of the chasing than she was comfortable with. She preferred to keep her distance, allowing the men to feel like they were the ones in control.

Then it became a waiting game.

BENJAMIN SCANNED the room over the top of Tori's head. His last conquest had finally wised up to his games and he needed a new girlfriend, one to sit at home and wait for him to decide he was bored enough to hang around with her. He hated being single. Sure, having a girlfriend hindered his pulling ability slightly, but having no one left him uneasy. What would he do on those lonely nights when he couldn't be bothered with the flirting routine, when he just wanted it to be easy? He'd never been completely alone, and he certainly didn't intend to start now.

Tori was a great target: no relationship experience and sweet enough to believe each and every one of his lies. He was lucky to have stumbled across her. Despite this, he couldn't help looking at the unbelievably sexy, older woman. Her come hither eyes were irresistible, and he felt an unexpected hardening in his pants. He'd always wanted to bag an older woman but had never mastered the right way to pick one up. It was a game he hadn't got the right skill set for.

But now his chance was here, staring him in the face. Literally.

What to do? Should he sacrifice the perfect girl for the chance of great sex with his fantasy woman? Would that be wise?

Unfortunately, his body was making the decision for him. His feet moved against the logical arguments of his brain. The mystery woman's hips had him under some sort of spell, and he couldn't break free. He felt uncharacteristically nervous, unsure of what he was going to say, but it seemed that didn't matter because their lips collided before he could begin to form words.

VIVIEN WINKED at the young girl as she kissed the sociopath. As soon as she'd managed to capture his eyes, he was hers. He was pitifully easy, worse than any of the others. He'd literally left his date in the cold, unsure of where his comforting arms had gone. Vivien didn't enjoy inflicting the pain that marred the girl's expression, but a little discomfort now would save her a whole world of hurt.

Grabbing Benjamin's hand and leaning in close, she let him breathe in her musky scent, the same one that had worked wonders for centuries and whispered in his ear, knowing that it didn't matter a jot what she said.

"Come with me," she whispered, huskily, adding an Irish lilt to her tone, certain this would send him wild.

It did. He followed like a sheep, just the same as every other. Vivien felt strange about this one. Usually, she'd feel excited at the prospect of feeding her hunger, but now she knew that she was ultimately doing wrong. This boy wasn't one she really should be killing. She'd already saved the young girl from him. After blatantly rejecting her like that in public, there was no way she'd go back to him now. Vivien could realistically just leave him here, job done and get on with her real work.

But she couldn't let him go.

What about all the other women he'd go on to hurt? What about his future children that would be forced to endure miserable childhoods because of their deadbeat, unreliable dad? If she let him go now, he would just be free to continue his destructive pattern, and that wouldn't do at all.

However, if she went through with this, if she killed him just for being a bastard, she'd be condemned. Would she be able to talk her way around this one? She wasn't convinced that she could. After all, He wasn't exactly what you'd call a reasonable boss.

Even as these thoughts ran through her brain, Vivien didn't stop. She just couldn't. Something inside her needed to do this, needed to defend her gender or at least the gender she portrayed. She was sick of the inequality she'd witnessed for centuries. Women were stronger these days, but they still managed to get sucked into these tangled messy webs, which could be completely avoided if men weren't so obsessed with sowing their wild oats. Deep down Vivien knew that she was tarnishing half the population with the same unfair brush, but she was on a rampage and couldn't see beyond the aura Benjamin gave off. All the dissatisfaction that had been bubbling away for longer than she could remember exploded like a volcano and a snarl of human-like rage burst through her lips.

They entered a bland hotel room. Benjamin's excitement seemed to be reaching boiling point. He needed to calm down. He plonked down on the edge of the bed

Vivien paced the room. Normally she'd already be naked, or at least down to her red lacy underwear, but this time she needed to pause. She heard the boy's arduous breathing in the background and knew she didn't need to worry about him losing interest anytime soon. She needed to think, to make a rational decision, not one fueled by abhorrence. She wanted to do this only if it was the right thing. Then the boy opened his mouth, making the choice obvious.

"Come here beautiful, let's make this night special."

His words disgusted her. It was so rehearsed. A line that always got his targets to shed their clothes. She growled lightly, anger flooding in front of her like a blinding curtain. She leapt.

IT WORKED! Benjamin couldn't believe his luck. He never realized how easy it would be to get an older woman into bed. If he'd known, he would have done this much, much sooner. Her lips crashed against his and an involuntary moan escaped his throat as he started to lose himself in the passion of the moment.

Pleasure rapidly became pain. Vivien bit down on his bottom lip. Sensually at first, but soon hard enough to draw blood.

Benjamin became pale, unsure of what was going on. It happened too quickly for him to notice the transition between pleasure and the dizzying nightmare he now endured. His vision became blurred, and the room started to spin. He knew he was drunk, he so often was, but this was a whole new level of sensation.

SHE ENJOYED THE TASTE. His blood was toxic, as she knew it would be, but nowhere near as vile as the stuff she normally consumed. She lost control and realized how easy it was to break the code. She sucked hard, draining his body.

His body slumped to the hard floor, and Vivien pushed herself across the room, forcing herself to take a break. She needed to gather her wits. Her self-control was a point of personal pride, but something had changed, and she was rapidly becoming unrecognizable even to herself. She slapped her palm against her forehead, trying to think. If she stopped now, before he died, she might escape her terrible fate. He'd probably learn his lesson, and she wouldn't have to be damned.

She stepped tentatively towards the door. She'd have to flee town or change her appearance. She couldn't be traced by fingerprints, she didn't have any, but she was sure the boy would remember her and want her captured. That was a hassle she didn't need.

She made the mistake of turning back; just to have one last glance at him before vacating the premises and her feet became frozen to the spot. He lay on the floor, tempting her, luring her in. She moved unwittingly towards him, sucked in by his scent. Was this how men felt when they saw her?

Benjamin began to stir and mumble. He smiled serenely, pleased to witness Vivien's beauty. The smile never left his face even as she clawed violently at his chest, shredding his skin, even as she bit into his jugular, spraying blood. He smiled as the remainder of his life ebbed away.

DARKNESS.

Why was it so dark? Benjamin blinked, trying to figure out where he was. A figure moved towards him, and he rubbed his eyes, trying to get a better picture of who it could be. A woman, a beautiful, curvaceous woman.

A memory!

The older woman, the fantasy, the one he was about to have amazing sex with. What happened? He racked his brains. Why weren't they doing it already? As he looked closer, he realized she was crying. She was red faced and snotty. Any allure that she'd held before was long gone. Now she repulsed him. Urgh, why was he going to sleep with her? Surely, he could find someone better to fulfill his needs. There were plenty of hot older Mrs. Robinson types about. Why did he even consider picking this one?

VIVIEN COULDN'T REGAIN CONTROL; she couldn't stop weeping. Why had she done it? One moment of satisfaction for this? Now she was stuck with the bastard for eternity. His punishment for her.

She'd gone off course. Maybe that young girl wouldn't have been sucked in by the boy; maybe she did all this for nothing. And now she would be stuck with the horny, pathetic bastard forever.

She tore into him over and over, knowing this was the only way she could spend eternity without descending into madness. She may not be able to continue her mission, but at least she could enjoy making this idiot pay over and over again. She was determined to enjoy herself. She wouldn't let men control her, not this boy or Him.

He wanted her to be miserable, and she wasn't going to let that happen. She was going to be the exception to the rule and enjoy Hell, whatever was thrown at her.

Samie Sands is the author of the AM13 Outbreak series, published by Limitless Publishing. She's also had short stories included in Amazon best-selling anthologies and work featured on Wattpad.

17

TWO-PART HARMONY

BY EMILY C. SKAFTUN

THE SUN GOES DOWN AND YOU GET ON THE TRAIN. IT is winter now, which makes you happy. You love the way winter sounds; the way each coin dropped sings its song, clear in the cold air.

The train hurtles through the night sky, lit so the vulgar world outside fades away. Passengers pry scarves and hats from their faces, adjusting to the heated capsule. They reveal faces, and you want to look at them. It is hard to choose based on a hat, a coat, a handbag. The shape of a hip or a shoulder as it walks away. But looking begets looking, draws eye contact like a magnet.

You do not wish to be seen, only heard.

So, you look at their shoes. Your favorites are thick, dark. With a heel. It's rare that a heel is silent on the street; usually they speak volumes, broadcasting her life story in a language like Morse code.

You've learned not to choose too soon. The first time you were too rash. She lived just down the block from you. Tonight, you wander far before you pick her: cowboy boots, orange. It's dangerous to go after such a bright color, but you can't resist.

She gets off the train at Damen and so do you. She takes off walking and you follow, drinking in the clump of her boots on the cracked pavement. It's no prim melody, no high-toned click of upper-class heels. These are low, broad sounds, almost hollow, as if they echo all the way through her body. She walks quickly, but you close the gap until you're just a few feet behind her. Your own shoes are rubber-soled, silent as you step and almost skip over the sidewalk's unlucky cracks.

You wait until you're right behind her, then you start to whistle. The even pace of her steps sets the tempo, *vivace*, and her brightness inspires your choice of song: *I'm Walking on Sunshine*. It's one of your favorites.

Usually they startle, showing surprise if not fear. But she keeps steady, betraying nothing yet. She will, though. You've only just left the crowded brightness of the El station; these streets are public, and she thinks nothing of a man walking behind her. As she walks on, twisting and turning toward her home, narrowing your possible destinations down to only one location, she'll start to wonder. She might think your whistling a courtesy, a passive way to let her know where you are. She might think it intimidation. By the time you reach her street she'll fidget. When she reaches her home, she'll be afraid and consider going around the block, hoping to lose you or to find you out. She won't. As you whistle past, tipping her a wave, she'll sigh out loud.

She'll laugh at herself for having let her imagination run away with her. She'll tell her roommate—or husband or cat—about the man walking behind her, and how silly she was. If she lives alone, she'll just shake her head.

You'll be watching at the window. And when you creep up behind her she won't expect it, won't even know it's happening.

You'll slip a length of piano wire out of a pocket, wrap it around your gloved hands, and not a sound will escape.

They're so beautiful, those moments, that it's hard for you to remember your life without them. The old job, your little diurnal life. Were you really once like all the other zombies on the train, bouncing back and forth between the same two stops, making the same walk home every night? You hardly ever felt like whistling back then.

You're excited, lost in imagination, so it is a moment before you realize that the tapping of orange cowboy boots has stopped. You almost reach her by the time you notice, almost trip right over her. The notes fall out of your mouth, skidding to a halt on the ground between the two of you. Flustered, you stop.

You've walked several blocks, left the lights and bustle of commercial streets for the eerie calm of a residential neighborhood. A breeze waves skeletal branches past sodium streetlights, giving you the strange sensation of being underwater. But it is the silence that kills you. She has stopped, and you have stopped, and you feel like the two of you are onstage under these yellow lights, and you've forgotten your lines. Forgotten, even, what play you're in.

She turns around, swiveling on one heel. You expect confrontation, anger, maybe pepper spray. Your shoulders hunch, sinking inward like a dog awaiting a kick.

"What's your name?" Her voice is low but clear, tones neither sharp nor flat. They hang in the air between you as though an unseen foot rests heavy on the sustain pedal.

Disarmed by her voice, you look up into her face. It's a flat face, smooth and just a little chubby in a charming way. She's smiling, and one side of her face smiles more strongly than the other, revealing a deep dimple on the left and a shallow one on the right. Heat rises in your face. You miss the sting of the winter wind. And you have forgotten how long it's been since she asked your name, but her smile is starting to change. There isn't time to lie.

"Dwayne," you say.

"Dwayne," she repeats, looking you up and down as if checking you against a definition of the name Dwayne. You don't know if you've passed her test, but she moves on. "You live around here, Dwayne?"

Now you remember to lie. "Yeah, just up ahead." You wave a gloved hand vaguely down the street, trying not to indicate any particular building.

"Well, Dwayne," she says. "You don't have to walk behind me if you see me 'round the neighborhood. Shall we?"

She extends her arm toward you like she wants to link elbows and skip down the street. What is this, the yellow-brick road? It may as well be, because you feel like the scarecrow, the tin man, and the lion all rolled into one, missing your brain, heart, and courage. You stand where you are until she puts her arm down and starts, away from you, down the block.

You've made your escape without even meaning to. She's walking away and you're free to go back to the train, start over or just go home. Have a drink and hunt again tomorrow. Instead you find your feet moving after her.

"So," you say, scrambling to catch up. "What's your name?"

She spins around, still smiling. You think you might be smiling too.

"I'm Harmony," she says, extending her bare right hand toward you in a gesture you're more comfortable with. You take her pale little hand in yours to shake, thinking *you sure are*.

At the end of the block Harmony stops again, gesturing at the houses and small apartment buildings. "Which one's yours?"

You look around, knowing you're caught. Nobody who lived here would have to think so hard about it. Your mouth hangs open, letting the cold night air onto your teeth. "It's..."

"Oh my god," she interrupts, laughing. It's almost a giggle. "I'm sorry to ask that. We only just met a couple minutes ago; of course, you don't want to show me where you live."

You try not to let your jaw drop, try to laugh along with her, nodding like that's what you were thinking all along.

"It's just... look, I know this is super-fast, but do you want to have a drink with me? We'll go to my place."

She's smiling at you again, that lopsided smile with its uneven dimples. You look all the way at her for the first time, all the way into her eyes. It's too dark here, in-between street-lights, to tell what color they are. They just seem radiant, like fire.

You don't even manage to get out a *yes*. You just nod, thickly, on a neck of rusty metal, a neck stuffed with straw.

You hurry to her apartment, on the top floor of a small brick complex. It would have been difficult to secretly follow her up the narrow creaking stairs. Somehow, she just leads you inside, holding the door for you like you're friends. It's warm inside, almost too warm. No roommate, no husband. Just a cat, a little black ball of fuzz that circles around your ankles. Harmony takes your coat and invites you to sit on her plaid sofa, and you've already moved before you remember the bad luck. The black cat that crossed all of your possible paths.

Too late now. "What's your cat's name?" you ask, trying to sound interested rather than disgusted or terrified.

Harmony reaches down and picks it up, holding the cat in front of her chest. "Oh, this is Omen. She's so black I just had to give her a spooky name."

She shrugs, and you notice that her beautiful long hair is the same shade of black as Omen's fur. You try not to shudder as she drops the cat back on the floor and turns toward the kitchen.

"What do you like to drink? I've got beer, wine, and maybe some whiskey or something."

"Wine's good," you say, watching her go.

She turns her back to you so easily, boots still thumping against the hardwood floor of her apartment. You stand, slowly, listening to the movement of the floor under your weight. It's quiet in her apartment, no noisy neighbors moving around, no traffic sounds coming in through the walls. The only real sound is the clinking and hiss of a leaky radiator. It's not enough to cover the creak of your body as you move across the floorboards, but you don't have to be silent this time, do you? She knows you're here and, apparently, she trusts you.

Your gloved fingers reach for the piano wire. The loudest thing in the world is your heart, knocking about in your chest like a rock tumbling down a hillside.

You stop, push the wire farther down into your trouser pocket, pull off your gloves, and push them in after. When she returns, two glasses of red wine in her hands, she finds you standing in the middle of the room, looking as turned around as a blindfolded kid with a donkey's tail in his hand.

"I really like this art," you say, waving your arm to the wall. It is a painting of a bare tree in an alley, saturated with unnatural colors, and actually you do not like it at all. "Did you paint it?"

She shakes her head. "No, I stole it."

You look at her, unsure if she's joking. Harmony presses a glass into your hand. She's so close your bodies almost touch. Without her winter coat you see how slight she is, small. If she wasn't looking up at you, you'd be gazing down at the top of her shimmery, black-haired head.

"To chance encounters," she says, "and new friends."

You clink glasses, and drink.

YOUR EYELIDS FEEL like sandpaper as you force them open; your head aches. The world is bright, and warm—too warm—and something is wrong. The floor is hard under your face, and a blurry dark figure slowly resolves in front of your eyes. A cat. A black one. An Omen.

You try to sit up and find that your arms are pinned together behind your back. You pull on them and it hurts; whatever binds them is tight and sharp. Your legs seem to be stuck together. You can't separate them to get them under you, but by squirming around like an inchworm you get them in front, and eventually you sit up, leaning like a rag doll against the wall. The cat watches you struggle with what you take for disdain then saunters off into another room. Her work here is done, you think.

"You're awake," says a voice. It is low but clear, with tones neither sharp nor flat. She sounds pleased, and when you look up at her, goddammit, she's smiling a crooked smile. She sits on the plaid couch, cradling a glass of red wine in both hands.

You wonder how long you've been out and look frantically around for clues. You see your wine glass, broken on the floor in a puddle of red wine. You see Harmony's orange boots neatly lined up against the wall with a jumble of other shoes—sneakers and snow boots all rubber-soled. Your own feet are tied with a length of twine. It's not long before the movement of your looking makes your head start to throb.

"Piano wire," she says, shaking her head slightly. "I love it. It's classic. Effective and ironic: using an instrument of sound to bring about a silent death. Especially after all that whistling." She pauses to sip her wine, and you try to keep up with her. "How long have you been a killer?" she asks.

You don't know what to say, so you are silent. You've often thought of the day someone would find you out. For all your crimes—you don't even know anymore how many—you knew there would someday be a reckoning. But you imagined cops, squad cars, handcuffs. And then, probably, the chair. Not this woman who looks like an angel. Maybe she is an angel, you think, judging you.

"You don't have to play dumb with me," says Harmony, scooting down off the sofa to face you. "How long?"

It's nice that she thinks you're playing. You sigh. "Couple years."

"So, you follow people home. That seems risky. You never know where you're going or what'll be inside. You must be so brave."

You shrug, tugging downward on your lips to keep from smiling.

"Especially in Chicago," she continues. "These apartments seem like they'd be hard to sneak into. Like this one. How would you have done it?"

You shrug again. "They've all got back entrances, don't they? Hooray for the fire code."

Harmony looks past you, presumably toward her apartment's back entrance.

"Okay," she says. "But what if there's somebody else in the house? You can't strangle them both at once."

"That's true," you say, nodding.

"So, what do you do?" She leans forward, one hand under her chin, like a kid waiting to hear her favorite story.

"It's instinct, I guess. Sometimes that means it's time to quit. But often they'll be in separate rooms, or they'll turn their backs on each other. Sometimes that's all it takes."

"Huh," she says. "And how do you select your victims? For example, how did you choose me?"

You close your eyes. Your head feels light, thinking about her walking ahead of you, the flash of orange and the even thump that propelled her along. Even if you wanted to answer, you couldn't, and you shake your head as you feel the color rising on your face. It dawns on you that you are talking to a person. A person who knows you kill.

"Who are you?" you ask.

"Wow," she says, eyes widening. They're blue. You see that now. "That took you a really long time. What if I said I was FBI?"

You nod, looking away from her. It figures. But then you hear her laugh, a sound like sparkling water. You look back to see her shaking her head.

"I'm not FBI. You know, maybe I misjudged you. It became clear to me almost a year ago that there was another killer operating in the area. I assumed the other killer would also be aware of me. Does this mean you don't keep up on missing persons reports?"

You shake your head, *no*. The thought never even occurred to you.

Harmony groans, and even in this sound you hear music. "I can't believe you just told me all that. What am I gonna do with you?"

You feel a tingle run through you like electricity. She said *another* killer. And she doesn't know what to do with you. If she's a killer, then killing you is a possibility. How do you keep that from happening? You know you have to say something smart. Something charming, maybe. Various possibilities occur to you, things like *why don't you let me go?* and *what do you want with me?* But none of them seem quite right.

You shrug. With your arms pinned behind your back it's one of the only gestures available to you. At least your head is starting to clear.

"How 'bout another glass of wine?" you say, raising an eyebrow in what you hope she'll take for mock-sexy. "I think I could really get into this scene after a couple of drinks."

Harmony tilts her head. "You know, that's just what I was starting to think. But I'm not sure you can hold your liquor." She pokes you in the shoulder with one slender finger, and you can see that she didn't find your suggestion smart or charming. "Look what happened to you after only a sip. And what I gave you isn't half as strong as the wine my visitors normally get."

You nod. "Poison. So, you lure men in here and poison them."

She nods, smiling innocently. A killer. Since that first day when you lost your temper and doubled back around, slipping across the line, you've dreamed of meeting another killer. You figured one day you'd meet scores of them in prison, but even there you suspect that few kill the way you do. You're not interested in those who commit crimes of passion or opportunity. Nor do gangbangers hold any appeal. But apparently you are now in the presence of the real thing. There are so many things you've wanted to ask.

"You must go through a lot of wine glasses," you say, nodding toward the broken one on the floor.

She sighs. It sounds disgusted. "I get a bulk discount."

"So, every time it's pretty much the same?"

"Pretty much." She sips her wine but doesn't look at you now. Apparently, she finds the bookshelves far more interesting.

"Is it presumptuous of me to assume that tonight is somewhat different? I'd guess you don't usually bother to tie us up for a little chat."

"True," she says, smiling grimly. "And I'm beginning to see why."

It hits you like a slap in the face: she's going to kill you, and there's nothing you can do about it. You should have killed her when you had the chance. Your mind spins back to that moment when she turned her back to you, and now you imagine stepping behind her, pulling that wire down over her head and wrapping it tight. There'd have been a squeak, you imagine, or a gasp, before her body went tense and then finally let go.

"Okay," you say, trying to pull yourself together. "So that was different. Do you always turn your back on your visitors like you did, or was that different too?"

Her voice is a whisper. "I love those moments the best."

You nod. "So, there's your element of danger. Combined with the safety of a proven routine. It seems there are some advantages to doing it in your own home."

"There are." She swirls her wine, coating the insides of the glass with a pinkish film.

You continue. "But there are disadvantages too, aren't there? I'd guess your range is pretty limited; that most of the people you kill are from your own neighborhood."

Harmony lifts one dark eyebrow, the right one. Finally, she nods, sighing. "I guess you're a little more insightful than you seem. It's true. My missing persons reports are suspiciously local."

"How do mine look?" You regret the question once it's out of your mouth.

You don't want to call attention to your ignorance. Harmony raises her glass in front of her face, but it doesn't hide the pinkness gathering on her chubby cheeks.

"Actually," she says, "I couldn't tell *exactly* which ones were yours. I only knew for sure you were out there because of the numbers. Eventually I isolated patterns based on some of the neighbors' statements." She smiles with a downward tug, a smile that tries to hide itself. "Your pattern seemed so clean; I knew I wanted to meet you."

For a moment you feel strong, more powerful than ever. Better, even, than during those moments of death. You think, as always, of the first time. She lived between you and the train station. You'd seen her all over the neighborhood, waved to her, once you even stopped to chat about the weather for a few minutes. But if you happened to be behind her on the way home, she gripped her purse more tightly, walked more quickly. You told yourself it was only natural. A woman walking alone at night was bound to feel threatened by a man walking behind her. But her fear burned you. You didn't deserve it.

Until one day you did.

Even thinking about it makes you angry; your hands tighten into fists that strain against their bonds. Your eyes narrow. Then they look up and see Harmony and soften again.

She sighs. "But now I have, and it all seems so accidental."

"You were hoping for some kind of evil genius?" You mean it as a joke, but you realize it's true. She'd been expecting something. You could never have so thoroughly disappointed her if she hadn't.

"I guess I just thought you'd be harder to catch."

"I could've killed you."

"But you didn't."

"Neither did you," you point out, but she just looks at you. There is no smile on her face now.

"My turn's not over yet," she says. Very slowly, she drains the last of her wine.

With one deliberate movement she pushes you over. You fall ungracefully onto your face. Hers is impassive as she disappears into the kitchen. You know she usually poisons her victims, and poison isn't such a bad way to die. Will she just force it down your throat? Or does she have a backup plan? Maybe she's gone to get the butcher's knife.

In a moment she's back, and you crane around to see what she's carrying. Two wine glasses, half-filled with a red substance that looks to you like blood. She sets both of them down on the floor in front of you, and you see the knife. It's not a butcher's knife, but it looks sharp, and as she steps around behind you, you know this is it. You should pray, you think, but you don't know how. So all you do is whistle, the first thing that comes to your head. It's the tune from *The Wizard of Oz,* pouring out too fast, too high, and sloppy with extra notes. "We're off to see the Wizard," you think, and almost lose the tune when you start to laugh.

Harmony slices with the knife, and you're so tense you don't feel it at all, don't know what's going on. Then you find that your arms are free, and your legs; you wave them around as blood resumes its normal pathways. You sit up, stretching, no longer whistling.

"Keep going," she says. "I like that song."

She sits back down on the floor, spilled wine like the red sea stretching between you. She picks up one of the half-filled glasses and sips from it. "Will you join me for one more glass before you go?" she asks. "You don't have to; your coat is hanging right there by the door."

You look from her to the wine to your coat and over again. Is it poisoned? Maybe. Probably. The smart thing to do is to stand up, put on your coat, and leave. Never to look back. Never again to be seduced by a pair of flashy boots on an otherwise sneaker-wearing woman.

You can't say why you pick up the wineglass. It occurs to you to spill it, wine for wine on the floor. You even think of throwing it in her lovely round face. But you don't. You clink glasses. It's only as you bring your lips to the rim that you finally realize why: you just have to know.

You sip, savoring the wine's rich, wintery taste.

Emily C. Skaftun's tales of flying tigers, space squids, and evil garden gnomes have appeared in Clarkesworld, Beneath Ceaseless Skies, Asimov's, Daily Science Fiction, Strange Horizons, *and more.*

18

DRUG COUNT

BY JOE DICICCO

"REPORT, ACQUILANO."

The Knight-Scoutsman stepped forward. On his black uniform, he bore the crest of House Antino. On his belt was sheathed the longsword gifted to him by the Count. In his gloved hand, he held firm the heavy steel chain.

"Only one, Signor Antino."

The Count scowled from his throne. "One? Have the Wastes truly become just that?"

Acquilano bowed his head. "The villages are mostly deserted these Suns and Moons, I fear. The outposts keep their females heavily guarded. But I believe you will be satisfied with this one, Signor Count. This one has the beauty of ten females."

"Is that so?" The Count sat in silence for a moment, bathed in red neon light from the high chamber walls.

"Very well. Bring it in."

Knight-Scoutsman Acquilano tugged hard on the long chain. From the darkness came a young woman into the blood-neon of the high chamber. The Count gasped and raised an ancient bony hand to his lips. She wore a ragged dress that had once been white but was now deeply stained. Her pale face was lowered, and over it hung locks of ebony silk, wild as they poured well past her shoulders. She was small, but well developed in her feminine form. Her bosom appeared supple enough, pale and smooth as cream above her torn blouse. Her hips were wide, very womanly.

The Count leered. "What is its age?"

"Seventeen, by her padre's own admission."

"Acquilano, you will command it to look at me, but don't you dare strike it. Keep your grip firm on the chain, but do not yank."

The Knight-Scoutsman turned, scowled down at the girl.

"Raise your gaze in the presence of Signor Count Antino."

The girl did, slowly. Her gaze met that of the Count. Her face was young, as fair as virgin snow. Her features were so beautifully feminine that the Count could not stop himself gasping.

But her eyes. They were so dark as to be nearly black. They stared at him with a hot intensity. The Count smiled.

"You are to be commended, Acquilano. You have brought me the shining diamond of the Wastes. I am amazed we did not find this one sooner. I knew her father could not hold out forever. Every man has his price."

The Count studied the gorgeous young creature for another moment before speaking. "What is your name?"

The girl did not reply, only continued to glare at him with those black eyes.

Acquilano tugged on the chain. The collar around the girl's neck tightened.

"Acquilano!" the Count barked. "Did I not just tell you? Do not yank the chain."

He returned his gaze to this strange, enticing female. "What is your name, child?"

"Sienna. My name is Sienna Alligretto."

The Count considered. "Alligretto, a peasant name. Which Noble House does your father owe his allegiance to? Speak, child!"

She did not. She lowered her gaze back to the steel tiled floor of the chamber.

The Count twisted his ancient lips into a smile. "We know the answer to that, do we not, Del Razzo?" He lifted his bejeweled right hand to the great hulk of a man standing beside him.

The massive Knight-Guardsman, Del Razzo, bowed his head. "That we do, Signor Count. As you so wisely said, every man has his price, and the peasant's price was exceptionally cheap."

The Count began to laugh a deep, chortling sound that belched forth from his throat. He drew back his lips to reveal greasy green teeth.

"I would have paid that peasant ten times his asking price for this little angel. But it seems your father was willing to part with you for nothing more than a few credits to cover bread and swill wine for the next few months. Drunken fool. If he was a smarter man, he might use those credits to head for Milano or Berlin. Instead, he'll squander what pittance we paid for his girl-child and starve to death in the Wastes."

Sienna raised her face, burning intensity in her dark eyes. Those eyes did not swell with tears. Her small red lips did not quiver into a frown.

"You lie. My father would never sell me for any price."

The Count saw the face of his Knight-Scoutsman twist, and the dark gloved hand squeezed the chain.

"Acquilano, if you yank on that chain, I promise I'll have your cock cut off. You'll never shiver with ecstasy as you drain those balls of yours into the cunt-silk of one my angels again!"

Acquilano eased his grip and snapped to attention.

The Count glared at him for another moment then shifted his gaze to the female.

"How could I lie to such a lovely angel as you? I'm just an old man. I have no reason to lie. Your father is Vittorio Alligretto, is he not? He was a farmer. Before the war broke out."

Now, the Count was satisfied to see, the girl's fiery eyes welled up with tears. She lowered her gaze once more.

"Don't be too angry at him, my sweet little piece. It took us weeks to finally convince him. But in the end, he saw reason."

The girl said nothing. She stood in her rags, her head lowered. The Count listened carefully for the beautiful sounds of her weeping and became irritated when he heard none.

"You see, dear child, I have built up quite an empire here with my acquisition of young cunt. Sometimes my men steal them away from their nasty little homes in the Wastes. Always by night. Sometimes, as in your case, I will purchase a young female. I have more than enough funds to do so. Females have become quite rare these days, and that is doubly true in the Wastes. Quite the commodity. Most of your kind are owned and heavily guarded, usually by men of wealth, men of power. Men like me. But an angel such as yourself … What a find!"

The Count waved his bony hands above his head, jewelry catching the neon blood-light.

"I am a businessman, after all. My business is fresh, young cunt. Buying … or taking what I will. I sell for ten times the credit. I have quite the collection as you'll see, child. Men of noble blood, men such as myself, must carry on our line. We are the ones who can afford to sire young. It is us who must repopulate this world, after all."

"You're a dirty old man!" She finally spoke out. "You call yourself a Count? You're nothing more than a pimp. My brother Massimo will come for me. He is a rivoluzionario out of L'Aquila. He will come for me. You have made a terrible mistake, Count."

"Ah, yes. Lieutenant Massimo Alligretto." The Count radiated with wicked joy. "A brave rivoluzionario. Del Razzo?" He waved his hand to the burly Knight-Guardsman.

Del Razzo swiveled and bent to reach behind the throne. The lock of a mesh crate could be heard clicking open. The Knight-Guardsman turned back then, a wicked smile coming over his homely face.

In his massive gloved hand, he held the severed head of Massimo Alligretto.

"You see, child, I do not believe the rivoluzionari will be any more bother. Not one of them was spared, save their Capitano. He's still out in those hills somewhere. But all alone I do not believe he will be hard for my men to locate."

Sienna could no longer fight back the tears. They rolled, hot, down her cheeks. The face of her brother, Massimo, five years her elder, had once been so handsome. Now it was beaten black and blue, eyes closed forever, mouth slightly agape. Bits of jagged, torn flesh hung from the severed neck. He had been such a good man, an honest man. An idealist. He had fought for what was right. One of the few who still dared to fight. This brutal death, this was how a good man was rewarded for his courage.

Del Razzo tossed the head forward. It landed on the steel floor at her feet.

"Don't be too broken of heart, little angel," the Count said, relishing every word. "He died a warrior's death. That's all a peasant can really hope for in these decaying days."

She was able to bring herself to speak now. "But how? How did you find them? Massimo was a guerillo. He and his men knew these hills."

"Yes, yes I suppose they did. But you see, child, my knights know the hills of the Wastes even better. Some may say even intimately. They are trained to seek little cockroaches like your fratello here, and to burn them out. Burn them out and squash them. You should be proud he held out as long as he did.

She did not raise her gaze, but her voice was firm when she spoke. The Count furled his brow, slightly shocked.

"I will never be obedient to you. I will cut myself. I will slash my pretty face to ribbons! No one will want me. I will find a way to escape."

"Yes, yes. You and all the others, correct? My little angel, I have safeguards against such liabilities."

Again, he raised his hand. Del Razzo stepped forward. From the satchel on his belt, he produced a syringe. A long needle jutted out from its tip.

Sienna stepped back, right into the waiting arms of Acquilano. She squirmed, but he held firm.

"Don't struggle, tease. In a moment, you will understand. You will understand why my females are all so content here."

"No!" Sienna screamed and tried desperately to escape the grasp of the Knight-Scoutsman. She felt the prick jut into the soft flesh in the crook of her elbow.

The Count had been right.

She no longer cared. No longer cared that her brother was dead, that her own father had sold her to this monster of a man. A wave of exquisite euphoria washed over her, bristling in its intensity. It coursed through her veins, warming her body. She felt it roll up through her chest like sunshine. It poured down her legs and curled each of her toes. She could do nothing to stop the moan of ecstasy that escaped her mouth.

"Yes, yes! Such sweet nectar for my little angel! The nectar of the gods! How easily the will of the female breaks under the power of the Nectar! I don't think you'll be going very far out into the cold now, even if you were to escape! And believe me, you wouldn't dream of it. Here you'll have all the sweet, sweet Nectar you can dream of."

The Count waved his jewel-clad hand. "Now take her away. Put her with the others."

The Knight-Scoutsman walked her toward the door. Suddenly the Count called out to Acquilano.

"Wait! Do not put this one with the others. No, not this little angel. Give her separate quarters."

"As you wish, Signor Count."

The Count watched them go. After another moment, he spoke. "That will be all, Del Razzo. I wish to be alone now. But inform Acquilano to prepare a special meal tonight. And ready the dining hall."

Del Razzo bowed low. "As you wish, Signor Count."

The Knight-Scoutsman dragged Sienna by the chain down many flights of stairs, deep beneath the sprawling complex. She was led down a dusky hall; the only light, seeping in from the grates in the walls far above was gray and soft like warm wool. It was damp, and the earthen stench of mold filled her nostrils. She smiled in spite of this. She felt warm, pulsing with life. A whimsical sigh escaped her lips as she reached out to run her fingers along the wall where the light touched. She felt the light as it entered her fingertips, coursed through her arm, and spread across her chest.

Acquilano inserted the crest key into the lock. A deep boom thundered down the hall as the door cranked open. He put his gloved hand on her arm and guided her into the cell. It was a tiny room, heavy with mold. A flimsy cot sat in one corner, a toilet hole in the dank floor on the other. Far, very far, up the wall a grate let in long beams of light and painted bright bars across the floor of the cell. She stood for a moment, smiling up at the skylight high above.

Acquilano removed the choke-collar, gently. She turned to smile at him as he did. He seemed to hesitate, studying her from under a furled brow, then he smiled back.

She heard a strange noise, a sort of crackling, like from a warm fire. The raspy voice of the Count seemed to be coming from the Knight-Scoutsman's belt.

"Don't you so much as dream of it, Acquilano! Unless you desire to part with that cock of yours! Drain your balls in one of the other pieces down in the common cell, but don't you dare touch my little angel! That is unless you want to deal with Del Razzo."

Acquilano's smile turned to a frown. He took the collar and began rolling the heavy chain in loops around his arm. In another moment he was out in the hall, pushing the heavy door shut. Sienna felt the vibration deep in her chest as the lock crashed into place.

She was alone. She liked the way the bars of light sparkled across the floor and sat down on them.

She heard a voice, disembodied as the Count's had been. It seemed to come from all around her, and echo off the high walls of the cell. This voice was young, wispy, female. It came from a grate in the wall beside the cot. She could not see through it, the bars were too narrow, too close together, but she heard the girl loud and clear.

"What is your name? Where did they steal you from?"

Sienna stood to face the grate. "I am Sienna Alligretto, from L'Aquila. Who are you?"

"My name is Santina. My peasant name is Coltani. I am not from a Noble House. And I assume neither are you."

Sienna stepped closer to the grate. "Where are you? Why can't I see you?"

"I'm in the cell next to yours. A few of us are alone in cells, but most of the girls are in one big room all together. The prigione."

"How many girls are there?"

"Many. He collects us, you know. We are... We are his

property. Signor Count Antino's property. Some of us, like me... he keeps us around. He really likes us. Most of the girls, though, get sold off. Sold to other lords in other castles. Girls leave all the time, but also new girls are coming in all the time. How did they catch you? Those two awful men. More like demons than men! They chased me through the hills. They chased me for so long; a few times I thought for sure I had lost them. I ran for so long, as long as I could. But they finally caught me. That's why I'm here."

Sienna sat down on the little cot. "They didn't catch me. My father sold me."

Silence from the grate, until finally: "How could your own padre sell you? What kind of a man is he?"

Sienna felt colder. "The man, the one called Acquilano, came and took me away in a collar. A collar around my neck. Just like an animal."

From behind the grate: "That's how they took me. That's how they took all of us, I imagine."

"How long have you been here?"

"I'm not sure. Time is funny down here. A year? Two? Some of the girls have been here for many years. At least they think they have. It's hard to tell."

Sienna looked up at the skylight through the grate. The light looked colder now. "Has anyone ever gotten out?"

Hesitation from the grate, then: "I'm not sure what you mean."

"Escaped. Broken free. From this place."

"No, no, not since I've been here. Where would you go? You won't make it very long in the Wastes, all by yourself. Here at least we have food and shelter, plenty of clean acqua and... the Nectar. Signor Count has let you taste of the Nectar, yes?"

The syringe. The long needle. That sweet honey-brown liquid she had seen, had felt being pumped into her veins.

"Yes. He has."

"Beautiful, is it not? He has so much of it. He lets us taste it, you know. Whenever we want. But only if we're good. Only if we behave. And believe me, you won't dream of escaping once you've tasted the sweet Nectar. You might not be hooked yet, but you will be soon. We need it, Sienna. We need it to live. Just as much as we need food and water, we need Nectar. And he gives it to us. Don't worry, in time, you'll forget all about escaping."

Sienna lowered her gaze. "They murdered my fratello Massimo. They showed me his head. He was a brave man. He was a rivoluzionario."

"Rivoluzionari! They would not dare try to fight Signor Count Antino if only they knew! If only they knew just how sweet his Nectar is. Take my advice, Sienna. Forget your past. Forget your famiglia. Your fratello is dead, and your padre didn't want you. If he did, he would not have sold you. You are here now, and Signor Count will take care of you. If you are alone in a cell, that means you are special to him. He likes you very much. He won't sell you to another lord, no, not if he's put you alone in a cell. It means he'll keep you. He'll give you all the Nectar you want! Three, four, five times a day even. Sometimes... Sometimes Acquilano will want to have his way with our bodies. It's terrible at first, it was for me too. But with the Nectar, it gets easier."

The Nectar was wearing off, and Sienna felt tears well up behind her eyes. She felt cold. Raising her eyes to the sky-grate, she saw that the light no longer sparkled. Now it looked the way it always had; greasy and polluted, and it was beginning to darken.

She wanted more. Already, she wanted more. She began to sob.

From the grate: "Don't worry. If you're in that cell, Signor Count likes you. You will see him soon, very soon. He will give you more."

Sienna did not reply. She lay down on the cot, which stank of filth and mold, and shivered. She pulled her legs up under her ragged dress.

She dreamed. She dreamed of her father. She saw him sitting there in his chair where he always sat, staring into the generator-stove as it cranked out heat. When she called out to him, he did not turn, seemed not to hear her. She saw her brother, Massimo, smiling, happy. He was walking over to her, to save her, to take her away. But then a claw, a terrible black claw, came out of nowhere and swallowed him up. And then there was only darkness.

It was the thunder of the door lock that woke her.

She was shrouded in darkness. No light came in through the sky-grate above. She heard someone enter the room. A beam-torch burst to life, flooding the cell in neon blue. She saw a small man behind it, the one the Count had called Acquilano. He stepped forward, holding something in his hand. It was the choke-collar. She did not fight as he put it around her neck.

She was led into that long, damp hallway, up many flights of stairs. Acquilano did not speak a word to her. At the top of the stairs, he led her down another hall. This one was brightly lit by orange beam-torches. He led her into another small room, but this one did not appear to be a cell. It was much cleaner than the one she had been in below and was lit by a golden beam-torch. She saw in this room not a cot, but an actual bed; the sheets appeared fresh. On it lay the gaudiest outfit she had ever laid eyes upon. It was a cheap, tacky-looking thing, covered in what appeared to be gold frills and white ribbons. To her, it looked hideous. Beside it sat a pair of painfully-sloped yellow heels.

Acquilano stepped into the doorway behind her. "Signor Count Antino has ordered you to bathe yourself."

He pointed to a water spigot in one corner of the room. "Use as much acqua as you need to thoroughly clean yourself. You are to wash every part of your body. Signor Count wants you fresh.

You will then put on the dress and shoes Signor Count has so generously provided. Do you understand?"

She did not answer. She continued to stare at the dress, more of a costume, really.

Acquilano shut the door and stepped quickly in front of her. "I asked you a question, you little sow. Do you understand?" He grabbed her bare arm, squeezed.

She raised her gaze to meet his and held it. "Yes."

He smiled. "You truly are a wonder in flesh. So smooth. How did I not find you sooner? You are a gift to us."

She continued to hold his eyes. He disgusted her, but she did not look away. If he were going to try to force himself upon her, she would fight.

But if I fight, they may not give me any more of the Nectar.

She did want more. Already she could feel her head and shoulders beginning to ache.

Acquilano lowered his head, put his nose to her full head of dark hair and breathed in deeply.

She kept her body rigid, eyes glaring straight ahead.

He seemed to come to his senses and stepped back. He removed the collar from around her neck.

"Then get to it. Signor Count is expecting you for dinner in exactly a half hour. When you have bathed and dressed yourself, press this button beside the door. I will come."

He walked around her, pulled open the door then paused.

"Be grateful. Signor Count is a kind man. You will be fed. We have plenty of clean acqua here. And, if you are lucky, Signor Count may even let you live with him, in his quarters."

She felt her stomach turn.

Acquilano continued. "You'll get used to it, and fast. All you little teases do."

The door slammed shut, the lock thundering into place. For a moment she only stood there, eyes wandering back to the revolting dress. Then she undressed before getting under the spigot.

When she had bathed and dressed herself, she walked to the button on the wall. Before she could press it, the door cranked open. Acquilano stood leering, appearing to Sienna much like a hungry weasel.

"Such a little angel! Signor Count was right about you! An angel sent to us from Heaven above."

Her hair was still wet, the tiny cloth on the shelf beside the spigot not being nearly large enough.

Acquilano stepped into the room. In one hand was the collar, in the other the chain. She did not fight him as he put it around her neck.

Down several corridors she was led, all of them with high walls lined with golden beam-torches. Upon these walls, between the bright torches, hung great silken tapestries, all bearing the crest of Noble House Antino.

Finally, they came under a tall archway to a sprawling chamber, the ceiling flung so high that she found it staggering to gaze up at it. The far walls were lined with tall windows, all equipped with heavy grates. In the center of this great chamber stood a massive generator-stove, cranking out heat to warm the room.

The Knight-Scoutsman led her to the other end of the chamber. At a small, round table, sat Count Antino. He wore a flowing robe of ebony silk, as well as an assortment of beast furs. Every finger of his bony hands was clad in boisterous jewelry. Upon his bald head sat a thin crown that appeared to be of some precious metal.

Acquilano guided her to the table and removed the collar. Behind the Count, perfectly rigid, stood a giant of a man, the one the Count had called Del Razzo.

For a moment, Sienna stood before the table, eyes lowered to the heels she now wore. She did not dare try and run, not in such awkward shoes.

The Count raised a massive metal goblet to his lips. This also bore the crest of House Antino. He drank of the wine deeply, all the while staring intently at her.

Finally, he set the goblet back onto the table.

"Sit."

She did so.

"Acquilano, you may go prepare our meal."

The Knight-Scoutsman bowed low. "As you wish, Signor Count." He disappeared down a hallway into shadows.

She felt the Count's ancient eyes upon her, touching her.

He groaned deep in his throat, cleared away phlegm. "You look as I expected you would. Yes, I must have won favor with the gods to be rewarded with such a treat. Acquilano told me you'd be worth every credit."

He took up the bottle from beside the goblet. "Wine?"

"Water. Water, please."

The Count tilted his head back, roared laughter. Phlegm ratted in this throat. "You truly are a peasant, child! I have all the acqua you could drink! Del Razzo!"

The burly Knight-Guardsman turned, took up a metal pitcher and goblet from a nearby shelf. He brought them to Sienna, poured it for her as the Count looked on.

She drank eagerly. It was clear and cool, no grit, no stink.

"Drink all your belly can fit, my little angel. It's quite clean. I have a generator-purifier in my manor. And enough clean acqua to sate the thirst of every peasant and straggler in the Wastes."

She drained the goblet, set it back down. Del Razzo filled it again from the pitcher. Again, she drank.

"Drinking water from a chalice!" The Count grinned wickedly. "Yet somehow your beauty justifies it."

When she had drained the second cupful, she set the goblet

down and trained her gaze on the Count. He appeared to her like a raven; his ebony robe so dark it glinted in the golden light of the beam-torches. Yes, a rook perched there, intently watching its prey.

At last, she spoke. "You have stores of clean water here, and you horde it all for yourself. Every last drop? You could quench the thirst of all the people in the villages, yet you hide it. Their throats dry and crack, and they die of thirst. What greed."

The thought enraged her, but she needed to stay calm. She needed to keep her emotions in check.

"Yes, yes, what greed!" The Count waved both hands over his head. "Greed! Beautiful, glorious greed! Greed is what afforded me my empire, child!" He held his hands forward now so she could see the precious gems that glinted on his many rings.

"It is greed and greed alone that has allowed me to live this long. Allowed me to push out all the other Noble Houses! They bicker and chortle amongst themselves, but they quiver at the very thought of raising sword to House Antino! At the very thought! Greed has allowed me to claw my way to the top, to collect the wealth that is so rightfully mine. But my wealth is not in coin or credit, young one. No, that came with the territory. My true wealth is in a far more precious currency. That currency is you, little angel. The female creature. Young, flesh so tender, face so beautiful it could cause a man's heart to cease mid-beat! Ah, and even more precious yet are you little angels with cunts ripe for bearing children. You have become so rare in these darkened days. So sought after. And that's not just in the Wastes, either, my dear. That's the world over!"

The Count took up his goblet and drank deeply. He had hardly set it back on the table when Del Razzo was pouring more wine from the pitcher.

"Men ... far, far too many men. Men are the reason this world has fallen to such ruin. But we realized. We realized what the most precious commodity truly is. Not gold or silver or the tar that bleeds from the cracked Earth. No, we realized that the most precious commodity was you. Cunt, female, femmy, women!"

Again, he tilted his head back and howled laughter. Sienna was careful to keep her face blank.

"We all want them. More specifically, we all want that little slice of Heaven you hold between those tender thighs. For decades now I've controlled the market. Yes, we may all want you, but only the wealthiest among us can afford you. I see to it that only men of the coin can sire children. They come to me from far and wide, and I make it happen. Why my Knight-Scoutsman must have sired no less than fifty pups in the past year alone! Those balls of his are always so full. When he isn't allowed to drain them, he starts to become unreliable. Ah yes, Acquilano. I know his poison. Del Razzo here, he's another story entirely."

The Count waved his hand at the Knight-Guardsman standing to his rear. "I can't understand it. He has no desire to mate. No desire for the cunt-silk. The only man I've ever known with the power to resist you little teases."

Del Razzo bowed his head low, his voice thunder as he spoke. "I live only to serve, Signor Count. My only pleasure is in the Great and Noble House of Antino. In his Lordship, the Great Don Pietro Antino."

The Count waved his jeweled hand as if to say 'Yes, yes, get it over with.'

"I don't understand it one bit, but I certainly don't question it. The man is the finest guardsman I've ever had in my employ."

At this comment, the giant guardsman's face beamed with admiration. He bowed so low, Sienna thought he might topple over.

The Count took another long drink from his goblet. The vino seemed to be loosening his tongue. "I've been here, upon my throne in this Manor, for many years, child. And my father sat upon that same throne before I did. And his father before him! Many years. There was a time when these esteemed halls bristled with life! I once had a battalion of men in my service, an army! But indeed, the years have been cruel. And the rivoluzionari... Well, I don't believe we'll have to worry much about them anymore, now will we?"

He hacked laughter, displaying his rotten teeth, stained a sickening brown from the wine. She felt her stomach clench, and fought not to show it on her face. She was aware of another feeling now. A burning in her head and arm. She felt very cold and her body ached. She understood this must be her body craving more of the honey-nectar. But she also knew that the anger she felt fierce in her chest was right. It was justified anger. If she got more of the Nectar inside her, that anger would subside. She would feel that warm loveliness wash over her once again, but it would be false. She may even begin to see the raven-count in gentler light.

Just the thought made fire dance in her belly. This man, this villain, was the lowest scum. She knew that, had to remember that. But the call of the Nectar ... Even as she thought these things, sitting at this table, she could feel that desire grow stronger.

The Count's phlegmy voice dragged her from these thoughts. "Yes, we three are the last. Myself, Del Razzo, and the stud Acquilano."

"The children," Sienna spoke now, her voice smooth and fair, the polar opposite of the decrepit Count. "What happened to the children? Did you not raise the boys to be your soldiers?"

To her surprise, the Count dropped his gaze, appearing suddenly withdrawn. Finally, he lifted those watery eyes back to her.

"It is of no consequence. Things happen, child. Things

beyond the control of even a man of power. What matters is that you are here now. And I have chosen you to bear my child."

She felt her stomach drop. Her flesh became clammy. All at once she felt sick; every inch of her body pulsed with cold pain.

"What an honor it is!" he carried on. "To be chosen to be the mother of royalty. I couldn't choose just any little piece to bear my child, you see. In all my life I've never known a female who deserved such an honor. But now I believe I do."

She struggled to speak. "But, how... You're... You're so old."

"A century and three! Yes, child, that's one-hundred-and-three-years young! But even I won't live forever. Not even kings can do that. In all my long years, never have I seen beauty such as yours. My reward for waiting as long as I have. And believe me, my little tease; I may be old, but I am by no means dry."

The Count slammed his bony fist onto the table. "What is taking Acquilano so long with my dinner?" He removed a little black box from around his waist, held there by a cloth strap. Sienna did not know how it was possible, but upon this box came now a picture of the Knight-Scoutsman. He appeared to be standing in a dimly-lit kitchen.

"Acquilano! What the hell is taking you so long? I'll be in my grave before you finish cooking that meal."

Acquilano responded, his voice crackling through the box. "Cry pardon, Signor Count. The oven took longer than usual to warm up tonight, what with cold from the Wastes seeping in. But it shouldn't be long now."

She felt weak, light in the head. She placed her palms on the table to steady herself.

The Nectar. I need the Nectar. That will make me feel better. That will make this all okay. It will make it so I won't care. Who knows? Perhaps I may even smile...

"Signor Count..." She ran her fingers through her still-damp hair. "I'm not very hungry. Not for food, anyway."

"Ah, yes. You have a hunger of a different kind. I can sate that hunger as well; yes, I can. But first, we must eat. Living in a ratty little dual-unit in the Wastes must have deprived you of any kind of a decent meal for far too long."

No. I must stay hungry. A full belly may make me sleepy.

"No, Signor Count, my hunger is different still. My hunger is for you. I want to make love to you. You have been very generous to me. Very kind. I would like to show you my gratitude for Signor Count Antino's generosity and kindness."

The Count stared at her for a long moment, stared through her, it seemed. Those ancient eyes betrayed a terrible intelligence.

He turned to Del Razzo. "Lead us to my chambers. This little piece of flesh has a point. I'm too old to put such things off for even one meal. I will fill her womb with my spunk and then we will see if that fool Acquilano has my meal ready."

Del Razzo was eyeing her now, studying her. "Signor Count, I don't know if..."

"You were never one to know anything, Del Razzo. You're the muscle. Now do as I command!"

The Count stood slowly, both hands flat on the table to steady himself.

"Yes, yes, my little angel. I can still walk. I can still fuck! A century and three and balls still laden with cum." He turned then to his Knight-Guardsman. "Tell Acquilano to feed the gaggle below. And give them all their Nectar, of course. The two of you can eat the dinner he is preparing if he ever finishes. I'm not hungry, anyway. And you know how I get once I've spent my seed."

At this, he threw out his hands, the wide cuffs of his robe fluttering around him like dancing shadows.

"My little angel will sleep with me tonight. And believe me, child, my bed is softer than that cot down below!"

Del Razzo stepped forward, eyes still locked upon Sienna. "Signor Count, perhaps I should pat the female down, just to be safe."

The Count swung his crowned head with frightening speed to face the Knight-Guardsman. "You will not lay a hand on her. If it's a change of heart you've had, then head below and take your pick from the little things down there!"

Del Razzo bowed. "I am only concerned with your safety, Signor Count."

"Right now, my safety depends on continuing my line with this perfect specimen here."

"As you wish, Signor Count." The Knight-Guardsman turned to the table that bore the pitchers upon it. He reached below to bring up a choke-collar attached to a long chain.

"Forget it, Del Razzo. She won't be running off anywhere. What the hell are you so jumpy about anyway? She's just a little female."

At this, the Count turned back to Sienna and revealed his rotten teeth in a wicked grin.

It took every ounce of strength she could call upon, but Sienna managed to smile back at him. She felt frozen as she stood there, head and chest pounding, craving... hungry for more of the sweet Nectar.

The Knight-Guardsman led them out of the great chamber, down a long, wide hall with an arched ceiling high above. From that ceiling hung giant three-pronged beam-torches, all lit with red neon. This hall had no windows, but upon the tall walls were bloated plaques, all displaying proudly the crest of House Antino. At the end, they came to a massive arched door, much like the door to the cell below, only larger. The Count removed a golden chain from around his neck and held it before his ancient face, the gold appearing finely polished, glittering in the neon blood-light. Upon this chain was firmly attached a crest-key, which fitted the lock to this great door.

The Count's robe flowed out far behind as he placed the crest key into the lock. Thunder echoed down the hall. The Knight-Guardsman pushed the door open with both arms.

Inside was a master bedroom, which appeared, to Sienna, regal beyond her wildest dreams. The walls were not steel sheet as in other parts of the complex but appeared to be of smooth amber stone. Velvet tapestries were draped upon those high stone walls, not just of House Antino. The other Noble houses were on display as well: House Esposito, House Medici, House Valerio, and House DiAugustino, among others. The far-flung ceiling was interlaced with what appeared to be actual wood, carved into intricate patterns. The craftsmanship masterful, at least to her eyes. From the center of the ceiling hung a truly magnificent, many-pronged beam-torch. Its light was neither harsh nor neon, but a gentle warm glow that reminded her of the light from the generator-stove back in her padre's dual-unit.

Against the far wall was a kingly bed toward which the Count began, slowly, very slowly. She followed just behind. Crimson silk sheets adorned the bed, as well as enormous pillows of the same shade. Thick wooden beams jutted out from its four corners, supporting a billowy canopy above. Beside the bed stood a dark, stone hearth like a yawning maw. It did not appear to have been used in some time.

The Count arrived at the bed, turned slowly back toward the door.

"Leave us, Del Razzo. I want no disturbances. And I trust you to keep that Acquilano in line."

The Knight-Guardsman bowed low and pulled the heavy door shut. A deep bass vibrated the walls and floor as the lock latched into place.

The Count turned to face her. "Now, my little cock-tease. I

will give you a son. A boy-child to carry on my noble line." He removed the raven's cape and placed it upon a high-backed chair beside the bed. Under it, he wore loose-fitting crimson skivvies that hung off his skeletal frame like scraps of tattered flesh.

Sienna spoke. "Signor Count, before we lie down together, I was hoping I could …" She rubbed her arm in the crook of the elbow where the needle had penetrated.

The Count hacked laughter. "Oh, little angel. Sweet, sweet little angel! Already you crave your fix. My Nectar is quite potent, is it not?" He took the chain from around his neck and made his way inside that gaping hearth beside the bed. He used the same crest-key to unlock a metal door set in the back wall of the hearth.

A secret room. She thought. This must be where he keeps the Nectar.

He brought out a syringe full of the brown liquid and shut the heavy door behind. She heard it lock.

No. I can't.

She took a step back.

It feels too good, too overwhelming. It will make me laugh. It will make me not care.

"Something the matter, little angel? Did you not just say to me that you wanted your fix?"

Careful. Don't show him how you feel.

But the Nectar!

When she spoke, her throat was dry. Her head and chest throbbed wickedly with cold pain. "I think, perhaps, I should wait until after we lie together, Signor Count. It will be better this way. I should have my full wits about me when I… when I take your child."

The Count groaned. "Make up your mind, you little brat!" He set the syringe on the mantle above the hearth. "Now that I think of it, you do have a point. You should be stone-sober for what is coming. Undress."

"Why don't you partake of the Nectar, Signor Count? I'm sure it will make your release positively... heavenly."

His eyes, aged though they were, took on new intensity. "Never. Do you truly believe I could have forged such an empire strung out on that Nectar? I know its dangers. Now undress."

She hesitated. "N-now?"

"No tomorrow, cunt! We're in the chamber of a Count, are we not? Remove that dress. I need to see that body of yours. I need to make sure you've cleaned yourself thoroughly."

She began to undo the buttons down the back of the clownish dress. The Count's cracked lips twisted into a grin. Even without the robe he still looked like a sickly raven, staring down at carrion from its perch.

She slid the dress past her shoulders and let it drop to the floor in one clunky piece. Lifting her feet in the tall heels, she stepped out of it. She was now completely naked before the Count. Her hair was beginning to dry, thick and lush around her fair shoulders.

"Just as I had imagined. The body of Venus herself, forged in the most pristine marble!" He seemed to consider. "Yes, I do like the look of those heels on your dainty feet. You will keep them on."

He pointed then to the bed. "On your back."

She obliged.

Slowly he approached her; a decrepit old raven clawing down from its perch to savor a meal laid before it. Placing his skeletal hands around both ankles, he lifted her legs into the air and leaned in close. His sharp spine poked up like a mountain peak from the back of his skivvies. He put his face in close between her legs.

She closed her eyes and clenched her teeth. She felt the cool air drawing into his nostrils, and heard him breathing it into his phlegmy nose.

"Cunt smells clean. Turnover. On your belly."

She did as she was told and felt his cold fingers spread her cheeks, felt the air on her anus. When she felt his nasty tongue slide into her, her first thought was to cry out. But she did not. She kept her face cold, placid.

Not yet.

Finally, she felt him draw back. When she turned, his skivvy pants were down around his ankles. She caught a glance of his wrinkled penis, already erect, swollen with blood. She looked away.

He was removing his shirt now. In another moment, he tossed it to the floor and stood naked before her. He kept the golden keychain around his neck. He was nothing more than pallid, leathery skin and bones. His skin had a sickening hue to it, the color of raw chicken flesh. He crawled onto the bed, propped himself on his back, head against a giant pillow. His frail body was sprawled across the crimson sheets, his penis poking up from between his legs.

She got to her knees before him, legs and feet resting beneath her.

"I'm old, child. I may not be as versatile in my craft as I once was, but as you'll see, these balls are quite full. Now I'm going to lay here, and you're going to ride me until I release into your womb. Don't you worry, my little angel. If you're as tight as I suspect, it shouldn't take long."

"Of course, my Count."

She reached behind, sliding one foot from its heel.

"Ah, I knew you'd come to see the light. I'm really not as bad of a man as you've likely heard." The Count closed his eyes. "You seem like a smart enough little cunt. I really am sorry about your fratello, but I'm sure you understand. Desperate measures must be taken in these dark days to ensure one's business. A business transaction is really all it was. Nothing personal. You'll begin to understand, in time. I really do care about all my little angels. I keep you all safe. Safe from all that cold waste out there. Safe from all the criminali out there. I'm sure you can imagine what they'd do if they got hold of a piece like you. And any time at all you need a fix of the Nectar, you need simply say so. Any of the other little puttani down below can attest to that."

She hesitated.

Anytime I want.

"You know what I want now, Signor Count?"

His eyes remained closed. He wore a sickening grin upon his cracked lips. "And what would that be, my little cock-tease?"

"Your heart."

Phlegmy laughter rolled from deep in his chest. "Oh, child, sweet child. Never in all my long years have I given my heart to anyone. Least of all a female."

In an instant she was on top of him, the heavy heeled shoe held in one hand. She rested her weight on his belly, keeping sure to avoid his penis.

The Count's eyes popped open, but her free hand was already over his mouth, pressing down hard, making sure no sound could escape. She watched his eyes take on a ferocity, glaring up at her.

She leaned forward her lips so close to his they were nearly touching. "I wasn't asking."

She brought the long heel down onto the base of his sternum and pressed with all her strength. She felt the crunch and heard brittle bone snap. The chicken flesh gave out as the heel sunk in.

The Count struggled, but it was a pathetic struggle. She did not need to use much strength to keep him held down.

She drove the heel further in until it was all the way up to the base. Hot blood poured between them.

"Old fool. I am the captain of the rivoluzionari."

She watched his eyes become wider at the realization. Leaning back, she removed the shoe from his chest and tossed it away. Keeping her hand tightly over his mouth, she dug the fingers of her other hand into a hole the heel had created. As his eyes rolled back in their sockets, she worked her fingers deeper and deeper until her entire fist was in up to the wrist. There she felt around, felt the quickly beating heart, warm, slimy. Wrapping her palm around it, she squeezed. With one brutal yank, she ripped it from his chest. Blood sprayed hot, nearly black across her fair, supple breasts. It spurted up, staining her beautiful face.

She held the heart over the old man, staring down at the gaping hole in his chest. Black blood pooled there as still more flowed out. His eyes had rolled back nearly completely now. He ceased struggling. She removed her hand from over his mouth.

Affording one last glance at the heart, tiny, so dark as to be nearly black, she tossed it across the room. Her own chest rose and fell in quick succession, lungs thirsty for the cool air around her.

She removed the chain from the dead man's neck and studied it for a moment. She pulled off the other heel and flung it across the room. With bare feet, she hopped off the bed and darted silently over to the cold hearth. Placing the crest key into the lock, she felt it turn. The door was a thick metal, incredibly heavy. It took a considerable amount of her strength to pull it open. A white beam-torch burst to life inside the secret room.

Standing before her was a room three times the size of the cell she had been in below. It was stacked nearly to the ceiling with crates. Row upon row, all of them loaded with jugs full of brown liquid.

Nectar.

Beyond these were yet more crates, full of clean syringes waiting to be used.

Her heart leapt at the sight, lips bursting into a smile. At the very front of the room, just to the left of the doorway, stood a crate full of syringes already loaded with nectar. She took one, turned it over in her palms and held it firm as she pushed the door shut.

No. Not yet. The guards.

She walked out of the hearth. The blood was beginning to dry on her skin. She liked the way it felt there. Invigorating.

Never again would she put on that ridiculous dress. She would rather be naked than clothe herself in the robes of the dead raven-Count. So naked was how she remained.

She glanced at the giant door of the master bedroom chamber. There was no way she would be able to open it, not on her own.

Another door. In the floor beside the hearth.

Small, barely large enough for one person to pass through. She almost hadn't noticed it. It bore a lock with the insignia of House Antino. Just as she had suspected, the crest key fit. She turned it, felt the lock click open. It was a heavy door, like the others it was made of thick metal, but she was able to lift it open with both arms.

Below was dark, a narrow steel-mesh staircase leading down.

She had no choice. She didn't know how long it would be before one of the knights came to check on the Count.

Placing the chain around her neck, still holding the syringe in one hand, she descended into the darkness.

Down many steps she went, twisting in a spiral all the way.

It was cold, lit only by dim orange torch-beams on dirty walls. Finally, she found herself in a long, dank hallway, much like the one in which she'd been housed earlier. Down this hall she crept for what seemed like quite some time. Her naked body shivered, and her bare feet scraped on the gravel floor. The hall seemed to go on and on, lined with a row of heavy cell doors on either side.

She heard a voice to her right, faint at first, no more than a whisper.

"Sienna? What are you doing?" There was terrible worry in that voice.

She turned to see the small grate-window of one of the doors.

"Santina? Is that you?"

"Yes, Santina Coltani. I talked to you earlier. I was in the cell next to yours. What are you doing out?"

"He is dead, Santina. The Count is dead. I killed him."

"What?! You did what?!" The voice behind the door raised into a frantic cry: "Why would you do such a thing? Do you have any idea what you've done?"

Then, a thunderous roar from somewhere far above. It bellowed down the high walls and shook the cell doors.

"THAT LITTLE BITCH! I WILL CRUSH HER SKULL WITH MY BARE HANDS! MORTO! MORTO! SIGNOR COUNT ANTINO IS MORTO!" The roar was followed by weeping, a terrible anguished weeping.

"It's Del Razzo!" Santina called from behind the door. "The Knight-Guardsman. You must hide. He'll kill you if he finds you!"

From behind another door on the opposite side of the hall, came the shouts and muffled cries of many people.

"You have to hide!" Santina was pleading. "You can't let him catch you!"

Sienna looked down the hall in both directions. There was nowhere to go, nowhere to hide.

The stairs. Under the stairs.

She darted back the way she had come, chain dangling around her neck, syringe held tightly in hand. She reached the bottom of the tall, twisting staircase just as she heard the stomp of heavy boots come running down from far above. There was just room to squeeze herself in the nook behind the cold metal staircase.

And she waited.

The boot steps came closer, faster. Still she waited, perfectly still, perfectly silent in the shadows beneath the stairs. Her dark eyes focused on the hall where the last step ended.

Finally, the boots were just overhead, frantic. Then the massive knight, Del Razzo, stepped onto the gritty dungeon floor, his back to where she hid. He stared down that long, long hall for a moment, before letting out a roar that echoed down the length of it.

"WHERE ARE YOU, BITCH?! THERE IS NO WAY OUT FROM DOWN HERE!"

She leapt.

Like a cat from the shadows, in perfect silence she leapt. She was on Del Razzo's back, one arm wrapped around his neck, both legs squeezing his torso. Immediately he lifted a massive arm to grab her hair, but he was too slow. She already had the needle sunk deep into his neck, emptying the Nectar into his veins. She felt his arm drop away, felt his body become unsteady. She hooked her nails into the soft flesh under his chin, dug in fiercely. He roared in pain and anger, lifted his arm once more to tug at her hair.

But the Nectar was already taking effect. He was weak. She screamed as she sunk her nails deeper into his flesh and lowered her head, sinking her teeth into where the jaw met the neck. Yanking her head back, she took with it a long strand of flesh. Hot blood spurted out across her face, down her throat. With it came a sound like wet fabric being torn. Still the Knight-Guardsman held firm to her thick hair. She hooked her nails now into this fresh wound, dug her fingers deeper. She felt something hot and pulsing, tubular in shape and hooked her fingers around it. Del Razzo's roars turned to wet gurgles, chunks of blood spitting from his mouth.

She yanked her hand out, bringing with it a long, unraveling rope-like organ. The giant of a man topped over, but Sienna jumped free as he did, landing on her feet. He was seizing, gurgles growing fainter, dying off.

She felt this fresh blood warm on her face and shoulders, felt it running down the gentle ridge between her breasts. She waited, watched until all sound and movement had finally ceased.

Then she heard the voice from a way down the hall.

"What's happening?! Sienna, what's happening?"

She spit blood from her mouth. After catching her breath, she began back toward the voice.

"Sienna, is that you?"

"Del Razzo is dead."

Hesitation from behind the door. "How? How could a girl defeat that man?"

"Easier than I thought."

More hesitation. Finally: "Why would you do this? The Count has been good to us. He kept us fed, gave us plenty of clean aqua. All the Nectar we ever want. And you kill him!"

Sienna took a step closer to the door. "You're a prisoner here. All the girls are prisoners here. They kidnapped us. You call this being good to you? I'll free us. I'll let you and all the other girls out."

"What about the other knight? Acquilano?"

"Don't worry. I can handle him."

For a long moment, there was only silence from behind that thick metal door. When Santina finally spoke again, her voice was withdrawn: "No. I don't want to leave the manor. Where would I go? Where would you go? Back to the Wastes? Your father sold you, remember? He doesn't want you back. This is all we have, Sienna. We have shelter here, stores of food and water. And the Nectar … You've tasted it. Why would anyone want to abandon the Nectar?"

She considered. Santina had a point. Even now her body was pulsing at the thought of all the Nectar just sitting upstairs. She had nothing left out in the Wastes. Massimo was dead, and the rivoluzionari would be scattered by now. She would have to deal with Acquilano, but she was sure she could handle that. She had an entire palace here, all for her taking.

More muffled voices from across the hall. They sounded scared, confused. She looked down at the crest key.

"You know, I believe you may have a point, Santina. Perhaps I won't unlock the doors just yet. How does the Noble House Alligretto sound to you?"

Joe DiCicco deals in horror, thriller, suspense, and other dark (literary) arts. He lives in New York with his dog Peppino.

19

JUNE, 2013

BY TANJA CILIA

Hey, Posse of Sweetie-pies. Wait. Let's try that again. Friends, Romans, Countrymen...ah. Better. Allow me to introduce myself. On second thoughts – I won't. Just call me Woman...on a Mission.

That loud noise you just heard was my acolytes, bolting the doors. You don't know how many of us there are, do you? No, don't get up – you'll be shot between the eyes if you do. We have telescopic laser-sights. Oh! I knew that there would be a couple of you who just wouldn't listen. Ain't that a pity, though. Ten down. Five hundred or so to go.

I bet you remember your Chief – oh, there he is, peeing his pants, no doubt – quoting your hero, Rush Limbaugh III on the news. Pfft! That racist, sexist, misogynist, pervert who, according to his biographer, Zev Chafets, spent the greater part of his life gaining his father's respect and approval.

You made him your god. Thus are the Mighty fallen.

I bet you belly-laughed when on air, he sexually harassed and insulted Sandra Fluke, telling her he wanted to see dirty videos of her, because she was a slut and a prostitute like the rest of the women who use contraceptives, and that her parents ought to be ashamed of her. Oh, all right – so he later issued a fauxpology… but more than 100 advertisers left him, anyway.

This is kinda heady. It's my first time making a public speech like this – and I didn't come here in peace, you know.

Y'all call us Feminazi. I think we ought to do something to merit the title, apart from Rocking the Slut Vote, dontcha think?

Gender parity is not a joke. Your personal dictionaries say we are fanatical, ridiculous, crazy, irrational etc etc etc. You want fanatical, ridiculous, crazy, irrational? I'll give you fanatical, ridiculous, crazy, irrational.

I hear rumbles at the back of the house. My girls are getting antsy it seems, and anyway we really have to git, because we'll need to take long, hot showers when this is over. Because we'll have a Celebration to attend.

I'm sorry-not-sorry to have interrupted your Blue Films Extravaganza in air-conditioned, no-expenses-spared luxury! How fun! How old-fashioned-values! Speaking of old-fashioned…do y'all hear that fine-tuned whirr? It's the chainsaws. This speech will go down in History.

Let the Carnage begin.

Tanja is Maltese, Mediterranean, European.

2 0

APPRECIATING BEAUTY

BY KELLEY FRANK

I'M SITTING IN A TREE, WATCHING XAVIER THROUGH my camcorder. I zoom in as he takes off his shirt. His wife sits on the bed, waiting for him. Their lips are moving – something romantic. He takes a sip of red wine – his throat gleams in the candlelight – then moves toward the bed. I zoom in on him, doing my best to keep her out of the frame as they move together. His wife is always just a collection of parts and pieces in my digital library. He, though, is the star with top billing.

Imagine love or some other emotion where there is barely familiarity. Awkward, right? How can someone love, or for that matter hate, a person she's never met? Now think about how people cried out when Princess Diana was killed, or when Michael Jackson died. There was real mourning there, even though the relationship was based on observation instead of a mutual bond. When we fixate on a person, follow him, obsess over him, this makes people uncomfortable. Movies dramatize this kind of obsession: every so often a movie comes along where a woman is obsessed with a man. Sometimes it's a cute Rom Com, sometimes it's more of a *Fatal Attraction* kind of thing. For the most part our society does not condone obsession. If a man becomes obsessed with a woman, it quickly gets creepy. We women have a bit longer before the object of our desires takes out a restraining order. Society says it's every man's fantasy to have to beat women off with a stick.

Xavier and his wife are really getting into it, and I zoom in on his back as he moves. I have to brace my elbow against the tree trunk to keep the picture steady, but I'm still getting all of it. Next time Xavier comes in to work, I'll think of him like this as he nods to me on the way to his cubicle. I've never shown him the least bit of interest, neither at work nor anywhere else. Coming on too strong is a big mistake. There are social conventions to follow before filming someone as he screws his wife. Most relationships never get that far. It isn't that I want Xavier to screw me like he does her. I'm not really a sexual person, to be honest. But I do have an appreciation for beauty.

Other than my lack of interest in sex and my penchant for beauty, I'm pretty normal. I was an average student in high school, graduated from community college with a decent GPA then got a job as a market analyst, not as spectacular as it sounds. I quit that job and moved South to work for a manufacturing company. I do charity work at the Food Pantry from November until Christmas; it's important to show empathy. In January, people pay me to do their taxes. In the summer, I work as a lifeguard for the local YMCA. I'm pretty normal really. In fact, some people tell me I'm a charitable person, that I have a nice even temper because I never show when I'm angry, and that I'm good with tiny details. It's funny how little effort it takes to be overlooked.

I don't know when it began, but I found myself purposefully cultivating a calm, normal image. I've never gotten a tattoo, not because I dislike them but because it could be used to identify me in a police lineup. I've only been fingerprinted on rare occasions: for my driver's license and of course as a baby. I'm not married; I have a high credit score, and I am always friendly. I bring chocolates for the candy bowl I keep on my desk at work; it endears my coworkers to me and brings me the latest gossip.

Xavier's wife is screaming her head off. It's a great sound, even if she's obviously faking. It'll make things easier.

Is there some enlightenment that comes from killing our own kind for pleasure, insights that those who have not taken the same path cannot imagine? Serial killers are both idolized and feared in our society. There is probably some primal reason for this. Serial killers seem to be most in control of their minds when they are planning their attacks or disposing of bodies. It is a frame of mind that differs from a wartime battlefield or from gang violence. They are lone hunters preying in the shadows. They have self-reliance and strength of character.

Xavier and his wife are finally finished. The candles extinguished and the room dark. I wait a few moments, then the light goes on in the kitchen. Xavier always gets food after sex while his little wife cleans herself up and prepares for sleep. She'll be alone. I pull the revolver from my satchel and move along the branch toward the balcony. I know it is unlocked because I watched them go outside to drink their wine before heading back in for sex. Neither turned the latch. I peer inside. She's got her back to me, checking her phone. I open the door quietly. She's typing. I put the revolver to her back.

I'm wearing gloves. I've already collected Xavier's fingerprints, from his coffee cup at the office using plain scotch-tape and put them on the gun the way a gunman would hold it. I swiped the gun from Xavier's collection days ago. I've been practicing with it in the woods. I won't miss. I squeeze the trigger just as she hits SEND.

She screams and falls forward from the impact. I drop the gun and make for the window. There isn't a moment to waste; I can already hear Xavier racing up the stairs. I head for the woods behind their property. Poor Xavier. How confused he'll be when the police find his fingerprints on his gun.

The best killers hide in plain sight but have enough solitude to make sure their work is well-planned and uninterrupted.

It takes me 10 minutes to reach my car. It's parked off road near a lake. No one is about, not on a weeknight. It won't take me long to get home. I'll clean my clothes, bleaching them to make sure there's no trace of blood spatter.

I drive home, prepared for a vastly more interesting work week.

Kelley M. Frank is a horror artist and author. She also writes film reviews for *Dead, Buried, and Back*.

21

#FF0800

BY GINA RANALLI

YOU THINK YOU KNOW A PERSON, BUT I CAN TELL YOU right now, you never really do. Not until they see their own blood dripping down your chin. That's when you see their real soul. That's when the beast emerges.

Ronnie seemed like a nice enough guy. He played it up, of course. Most of them do. Not all but most. He was in the majority, polite, full of flattery, the whole nine. Wanted to buy me flowers. Jewelry. Fancy clothes. Whatever. To me he was just another john who didn't know what he was getting into.

"You're so beautiful, baby," he said, stretched out naked on the motel room bed, stroking himself, his eyes on my fully clothed body, leering; a stupid smile under his stupid mustache. "Why don't you show me those titties?"

I cocked my head at him, noting that whenever he spoke to me, he never looked into my eyes. Or even at my face. I licked my lips and said, "You want to see my tits, huh? You know that's extra."

"What?" He sounded surprised. "Come on, baby. I'm ready now. Don't play me like that."

I smiled. I couldn't help it. "Hands up, big boy. Over your head."

"Oh, yeah? You're into that kinda shit?"

"You have no idea." I was grinning, but I doubt he noticed. "You're gonna squirt harder than you've ever squirted, Ronnie, my friend."

He laughed. "You're the one gonna squirt, Kelsey; if that's your real name."

It wasn't but I said, "It's what my momma calls me, big guy. Now, come on. Hands up. No skin until I say."

Reluctantly, he obliged. They always do. As long as you have them beating themselves off for long enough, get them close to popping on their own, then they'll beg for you to finish them. They'll do whatever the fuck you tell them to. It's almost too easy.

Once his hands were fastened to the headboard, I did a sexy little dance for him, feeling like an idiot, making a show of bending over and wiggling my ass around. What I was actually doing was snatching his nasty briefs from the floor before whirling around and shoving them hard down his throat when he was in the middle of saying some other stupid shit.

Old Ronnie's eyes went wide then, maybe a tiny flicker of alarm, but he was still hopeful, thinking he'd bagged an extra kinky bitch or some bullshit like that. I suppose, in a way, he wasn't wrong.

"Now the real game begins, Ronnie."

I extinguished his optimism by yanking the pillow out from under his head and putting it over his crotch so I wouldn't have to look at that disgusting purple-red pencil dick anymore.

He squirmed on the bed, grunting protests, but that was fine. It was far from my first rodeo.

"I just want to taste you, big guy," I cooed, leaning over him, assessing his body. Not the best I'd ever had but not the worst either. Not too chubby. Not too slim. Not too hairy, which was always an absolute mood killer for me. Some fuzz around his stomach and on his chest, but luckily most of his hair was on his upper lip and his head.

Finally, he was making eye contact.

"Well, that's an improvement," I said, knowing perfectly well he'd have no fucking clue what I was talking about. "A sign of respect. Do you know what that is, Ronnie? Respect? Have you heard of it before? I bet you have. I bet you respect your daddy. Your buddies. Maybe your boss, if your boss is a dude. He probably is though, right? You don't seem like the kind of guy who'd work willingly for a woman. That stupid mustache says more than you think, and it doesn't say anything good." I looked down at him and shrugged, realizing I was babbling. "Anyway..."

I trailed off and dropped my face to his side, sinking my teeth hard into his love handle, breaking the skin easily and shaking my head back and forth like a wolf with a rabbit. A chunk of him tore free, a nice bite size. His thrashing became almost unmanageable. He did his best to shriek as I spit the hunk of flesh into his face and took the opportunity to shove the underwear deeper down his throat.

The taste of his blood on my lips and tongue was intoxicating, and the sight of the mattress darkening beneath his body gave me a shiver of pleasure. It was a good bite. Deep.

I studied the wound, somewhat disappointed by the color. Candy red. Boring. Common. Unremarkable in every way. Most people don't realize how many different shades that blood comes in. My personal favorites are the darker ones. Reds that are so ruby they're almost black. Sangria. Maroon. Berry, wine, Merlot. All good. All tasty. You'd think the candy would be the sweetest but what are you gonna do?

The cords in Ronnie's neck stood out as he attempted to free himself. He was sweating, his whole body shiny and taut. His pupils dilated, huge, like a cat in the dark.

"You should probably get out of the habit of buying women, Ronnie," I told him. "I mean, it's kinda too late now but maybe this will send a message to other idiots like you. Don't pick women up off the street. At least go through a reputable source, you know what I'm saying?"

I don't think he knew or cared what I was saying at that point, so I stopped bothering to explain and took another bite. This time I went for his cheek, taking care to avoid facial hair. I immediately regretted my decision. He bucked wildly, bashing his forehead into mine. If I hadn't pulled back, he'd have broken my nose. That would have sucked royally.

"Easy there, tiger," I said. "I'm just fascinated by your color." I wasn't, really, but it was something to say. "In case you hadn't guessed by now, I'm not a prostitute. I'm a graphic designer. I see everything in hex codes at this point." I laughed. "That's something they don't tell you in college. How programmed your own mind becomes. But here we are. And your hex, my friend, is FF0800. Very ordinary. But we can't all be special, can we?"

He was going into shock. Fine by me. Tears streamed from his wild eyes as he bucked his hips up, knocking aside the pillow I'd placed over his junk. I noted with some amusement that his arousal had diminished significantly.

"If you think about it though, Ronnie," I continued. "You might be special, after all. These wounds are going to scar badly, and you'll have quite the tale to tell. *If* you survive." I thought about it for a moment, observing the colors of his face. "Huh. Are you having trouble breathing? I guess I might have shoved your underwear a little too far down your throat." I paused before quietly adding, "Oops."

My mother used to joke to everyone that I was her little

shark. I bit all her boyfriends. Every single one. Eventually, she stopped thinking it was funny, but I never let that stop me.

Ronnie's eyes rolled back in his head, showing bloodshot whites. I bit into his jugular, closing my eyes as blood spurted into my face, dousing me in the warmest red. His legs kicked madly as his body spasmed. The headboard banged against the wall, but they were used to that kind of thing in places like this. I had plenty of time.

Slick with FF0800, unhindered but already bored. Anxious to locate the next, hoping against hope for one of those elusive, beautiful shades. They're out there somewhere, trolling down some desolate city street in the dead of a lonely night. All the most gorgeous reds encased in meat and begging to satiate my incessantly thirsty eyes.

Gina Ranalli is the author of nearly twenty novels and novellas in the horror and bizarro fiction genres.

22

THE GENTLE ART OF
NOMINICATION

BY KENZIE JENNINGS

I was at my first client meeting when I decided I'd be working for Loni Wylde for the rest of my career.

Okay, it wasn't really *my* first client meeting. I'd just been pouring coffee for everyone, and I sat in the back afterwards, blending into the wall. I don't think anyone even remembers I was there. Then again, it wasn't like anyone would remember anything except The Incident.

Jason Dowling, a suckwad who'd been with the company for several years, had brought in the glass supplier company reps. They wanted to see how Loni could make their skyscraper window glass "shine" in the age of virtual offices. During the meeting, Jason kept talking *over* Loni, like if he pissed on the client, he was marking his territory. He thought he was being slick, but he knew better than to take over the meeting. It was like he *really* didn't care.

He said, "I figure we could emphasize the *durability*. Like a wrecking ball couldn't even crack it."

Loni asked if that was true, and Jason-the-Dumbass had the audacity to speak for the client. He laughed and said, "Yeah, it can withstand anything. Like, a tornado could tear everything down, but their windows would still be left standing."

I'll hand it to Jason for getting everyone talking. Loni sat quietly, a smile teasing the corners of her lips. Had Jason been more observant, he would've known that smile signaled something awful.

Everyone else must have sensed it, because the room became uncomfortably silent. You know the saying 'like the air had been sucked out of the room?' Whenever Loni got quiet, the oxygen levels would drop.

"Why don't you show us?"

Jason cleared his throat. "What?"

Her smile broadened. "Show us how durable it is, Jason. Try to crash through the window behind me."

Jason looked around at everyone to gauge their reactions. The clients shifted in their chairs, exchanging uneasy glances. Everybody from the office seemed enthralled, like they'd been waiting for something to happen.

"Go on," Loni cooed. "If it's as durable as you say it is, you'll be fine."

One of the reps cut in. "Ms. Wylde, we don't need to have the ad all about the durability. Our glass is tempered so it's just storm proof. We can go with that. There's no need for any of this."

"No, no. He brought it up. If he's that convinced, it shouldn't be a problem." Loni swiveled in Jason's direction. "Show us, Jason."

"Fine, whatever." Jason pushed his chair back from the table and got up.

He approached the window, took a couple of steps back, and hurled himself hard against the pane.

I'll give him credit. He'd been right. The glass didn't crack, but Jason-the-dumbass, who'd obviously cheated his way

THE GENTLE ART OF NOMINICATION | 237

through high school physics, fell right out that 23rd story window along with the windowpane that had completely dislodged from its frame.

We never heard back from that company, but word got around. All The Incident did was enhance Loni's cutthroat reputation. The cleanup had been a nightmare. The impact of Jason's body striking the concrete of the parking lot below was like someone had taken a human-sized balloon filled with blood, bones, and viscera and had just smacked it to the ground.

Vann Thomas' precious Porsche 911 was on the receiving end of Jason's remains. It took Vann several thousands' worth of detailing. There were teeth and bone fragments embedded in his baby's paint job. Vann should've known better than to complain about what had happened. Like I said, word gets around.

AFTER LONI RETURNED from a business trip to Tokyo, she was all about the customs over there. Kind of hard to explain customs from another country when there's no basis of comparison in your own. Japan has some equivalencies, I suppose. Like, there were formal business greetings, but instead of a handshake, you bow. Oh, and the gift giving. The company had presented her with a beautifully wrapped box of chocolates that she kept at her desk and shared only with a select few. Crystal March, another of Loni's junior associates who was into bogus health cures, morbid trivia, and toxic gossip, crowed to us in the break room that it was like biting into chocolate nirvana.

Loni hadn't really changed after her trip. Tokyo had merely *enhanced* some of her personality quirks that had been dormant since The Incident. So, imagine our surprise when we all got the email, insisting we join her after work at a karaoke bar for a little "nomination". None of us had any idea what she was talking about.

This isn't a cosmopolitan town by any stretch of the imagination. There's a decent outdoor mall and a dine-in multiplex. Karaoke bars though aren't our thing. What we have are sports bars that have occasional karaoke nights where a portion of the bar is sectioned off as a stage, and there's always some surly beardo named Phil working the microphones and karaoke player.

We met up with Loni on a Wednesday night at Mad Mike's, the only sports bar near work that had a karaoke night. By the time we arrived, Loni and a couple of her "friends", dudebros-in-suits, were on their second tequila shots.

"Drink, Petra," she purred as she handed me a shot. "In Japan, you'd *have* to keep up with the boss."

It set fire to my throat, painful evidence that Loni had ordered bottom shelf tequila. I knew the game she was playing, and I didn't like it. But I *respected* it.

Everyone had had their drunken turn crooning '80s anthems into the mic. Vann and his friend, Russ Mayhan, ordered another round, asking what Loni preferred because she was all who mattered.

"What's your poison, Loni?" Vann shouted over the din. He turned to Russ and said just loudly enough, "We could order straight up Drano, and she'd love it, man."

"Fabulous idea!" she shouted back. She had on her half-smile when she waved over the bartender and asked if he had any Drano; he stopped what he was doing to bring out some drain cleaner from storage.

Vann's face went grey. "I was just playin', Loni."

"Vann's just being a dick," Russ chimed in. "You know how he gets when he's had a few."

"Yeah, I know how he gets," she said, staring right at me. It felt as if she was daring me to watch and learn.

She then turned around, facing Vann. "Bottoms up, Vann. Show us the steel of your insides."

It sounded like a challenge from a warrior queen to her soldier. And like an obedient soldier, Vann poured himself a shot of drain cleaner. It had to have been industrial strength. The pungent odor alone was enough to eradicate anything the drunks attempted to flush from chunky spew to tampons.

I tried to move away from what was inevitably going to happen, but instead, I turned right into Crystal. I was so close to her I could see all the pores and creases clogged with banana-colored foundation. She grinned, revealing lipstick smudged teeth.

"Listen, I'm not responsible," the bartender said to Loni. He'd recognized a queen when she was out among the commoners, but he wasn't willing to risk his livelihood. "If he goes down, *you're* gonna call the ambulance."

Loni wasn't paying attention. I doubt if she'd heard him at all. She, like everyone else, watched Vann tip back the glass and swallow the liquid like it was a shot of whiskey.

Crystal drunkenly leaned in. Her breath reeked of bar wine and garlic. "You know the ingredients in Drano?" she mumbled in my ear.

Vann plonked the shot glass on the bar top, his face tightly scrunched.

"Lye and bleach," Crystal said. "That's gotta burn."

As soon as Vann started coughing, the bartender poured him a glass of milk while Vann's buddies thumped him on the back, whooping and hollering. Loni pried the glass from Vann's grip and set it down.

"Let it settle first," she said.

Vann nodded, grimacing, still dry coughing. She rubbed his back up and down, murmuring to him. The words were obviously meant for his ears alone, and that made my insides curdle.

He finally had her attention. No greater reward.

And I understood.

After downing a third shot of drain cleaner, Vann had earned a stint in the hospital. Crystal told everyone that his mouth, esophagus and stomach had suffered severe chemical burns. He couldn't speak, which was a blessing for some of us. Vann had enjoyed playing devil's advocate. Vann-speak for finding the argument in everything, especially during staff meetings. So, I liked that he couldn't talk.

What I didn't like was seeing Vann in his new corner office overlooking the city. Granted, the square footage wasn't as large as his previous space, a glorified cubicle, but he had an actual *office* with huge windows and a door with his nameplate on it.

Want to know how Loni recognizes your value? You take a few shots of Drano for her.

Vann didn't go "nominicating" for some time afterwards. Russ kept inviting him, but Vann always had an excuse not to go. He'd write on his portable whiteboard, letting us know he had plans with his girlfriend. An office joke, his girlfriend. No one had ever met her. Crystal said she once saw a magazine ad with the same girl in the framed picture he had on his desk, leading some to believe he'd clipped the picture out of the magazine and photo-shopped it into a picture of him at the beach.

I didn't examine the picture. I just didn't care. Whatever Vann did during his off hours was his choice.

It was always about choice. That's how Loni framed everything.

"We learn more from our choices than we do from lectures and seminars, all that academic nonsense," Loni said to me one evening.

She'd stopped by my desk when I was shutting down for the

night. "This idea that formal schooling is *learning* was thought up by liberal elites who needed to seem relevant in the world, while never contributing anything to the economy."

She pulled up the other chair across from my desk and plopped down with a sigh. I took it as a sign that she wanted me to relax, even while my stomach coiled.

"There's something I've been meaning to ask you," I said, figuring it couldn't hurt to change the subject. "What does 'nominication' mean? I looked it up, and I couldn't—"

"You're not gonna find it in your dictionary app. It's difficult to explain, better to experience. Roughly translated, it's 'nomimasu,' the Japanese word meaning 'to drink' combined with 'communication'. In other words, drinking and socializing."

"Oh, that makes sense."

"Tell me something, Petra, what would *you* choose?"

"What would I choose...what?"

That smile of hers widened. "Everyone who chooses does so on their own. You know...Crystal wasn't in today."

I knew Crystal hadn't been in, and that was fine by me. Whenever she cornered me, I got sucked into her lectures about the health benefits of kale smoothies and sprouted brown rice powder. I didn't want to hear the gory details about what had happened to Vann's insides after he'd swigged that shot. She'd had a crazy gleam in her eyes whenever she talked about that night.

Loni chuckled and said, "She's the worst." Like she'd read my mind. Then she propped her feet up on my desk. "Always going on about the bullshit benefits of hot yoga and reishi mushrooms."

Another reason why I respected Loni, she was observant. Scratch that. She was *supernaturally* observant. The mind-reading thing, she had that down.

"So, I suggested she try the tea I brought the other day. Remember that?"

I vaguely recalled Loni pouring a cup of tea from the Thermos she'd brought in along with her fancy bento box lunch.

"It was just black tea. Plain, old, supermarket brand black tea, but she believed I'd bought it from some Japanese herbalist. She *chose* to trust the authority figure."

And there it was, dangling there in front of me, tempting me to ask. Loni knew I would.

"So why didn't she come in?"

Loni shrugged. "People get sick. They call in. It's what sick leave's for."

"What was in the tea?"

"Honey and lavender. Though the honey was produced by bees that loved my azaleas."

"Will she be all right?"

"Oh, she'll be fine. Some vomiting. Minor heart problems. She had sick leave built up anyway. She would've lost it otherwise."

"Why did you do that?"

Loni gave me the side eye, looking at me like I was a kid who needed to learn. "Remember now, *I* didn't do anything. She chose to drink it, Petra."

"But why did you spike the tea? I mean, wasn't that *your* choice?" I hated myself for asking. It was Loni after all, and I wanted her respect more than anything. However, I didn't understand her motives, and I needed to know. If this was what a successful leader in one of *Forbes'* top 100 was supposed to be like, I had to know.

"What are you implying? That I intentionally set out to hurt my employee?"

"No, I would never—"

"That sort of accusation can easily be taken up with our

attorneys." Loni's tone had grown acidic. "Is that what you want, Petra? I've Frank Haverty's number, and I'm sure he'd be happy to address your issue in the middle of dinner. You know he loves dinner, especially Jackie's Thursday night meatloaf. I'd hate to have that famous meatloaf go cold while he dealt with an internal complaint against an executive."

"Loni, I—"

She laughed, waving at me to stop. The kind of laugh that chilled an employee to the core, a laugh that signaled it wouldn't *really* be all right. "You should see your face. Jesus Christ, Petra, get a sense of humor. It's why no one invites you anywhere."

"I get invited. I was there when Vann drank the—"

"Only because *I* invited you. You see, anytime *I* bring up anything—an idea, a task, an invitation, or whatever—Whenever *I* do it, everyone drops what they're doing to take part. *That's* authority, Petra. I can make people choose without *forcing* them to choose, understand?"

"I think so." I didn't, but I wasn't about to admit it.

"All I have to do is urge them in some direction, and that's it." She slid forward in her chair, put her elbows on the table, and cupped her head in her hands as she stared at me with those unreachable, peculiar eyes. They weren't exactly green or brown. They were muddy pools. Go for a swim in there and you'd never touch the bottom.

"For instance, I could tell you to take out that baby spoon you always bring in your lunch bag. The one you use for your yogurt."

I swear it was instinct that made me unzip my bag and take out the little silver spoon, my very first utensil, the only thing with any sentimental value I owned.

"And I *could* urge you to dig out your left eyeball with it."

"What?"

"Just dig it in deep at the edge of the socket and scoop it right out."

I stared at the little spoon held between my fingers and thumb, like it had answers for me.

Vann did get a nicer office, it whispered.

Loni nodded. "There it is. That *choice*."

I brought the spoon up to my left eye. A wave of heat spread down my spine.

"Go on, Petra. It's just one eye. You don't really need it."

She was right. What would I need it for? After all, balance and periphery were highly overrated.

I slid the edge of the bowl of the spoon underneath my bottom eyelid and then pushed it right in.

NO ONE ASKED WHAT HAPPENED. At work, it was out of respect. The eye-patch gave me some cred.

My family assumed it was an infection, and the doctor had no choice but to get rid of it. It was an adjustment, physically, but my overall *confidence* had never been better.

I owe that to Loni. She just knew.

LONI ISN'T HERE ANYMORE. So much for working for her for the rest of my career. A week before I moved into my new office, the one that used to be hers, the police searched through her desk, her wastebasket, her shelves, and her computer. They couldn't find any clues as to who might have done it.

That's because I kept the note in my purse, the one with Vann's message.

Two words, straight to the point, a message that had brought

Loni running to the parking lot where we were waiting: *Our choice.*

We'd closed her in. Vann held the canister of gasoline. I had the matches.

I remember Crystal whispering, "Do you know how long a body can burn?"

Crystal had been right. It took nearly seven hours.

Afterwards, we went out for a late-night beer. Nominication is essential to office morale after all. I think it's what Loni would've wanted.

Kenzie Jennings is a Florida-based horror author whose boss at her teaching job is actually pretty swell.

ABOUT THE EDITOR

Carmilla Voiez is a proudly bisexual and mildly autistic introvert who finds writing much easier than verbal communication. A life long Goth, living with two kids, two cats and a poet by the sea.

She is passionate about horror, the alt scene, intersectional feminism, art, nature and animals. When not writing, she gets paid to hang out in a stately home and entertain tourists.

Carmilla grew up on a varied diet of horror. Her earliest influences as a teenage reader were Graham Masterton, Brian Lumley and Clive Barker mixed with the romance of Hammer Horror and the visceral violence of the first wave of video nasties. Fascinated by the Goth aesthetic and enchanted by threnodies of eighties Goth and post-punk music she evolved into the creature of darkness we find today.

Her books are both extraordinarily personal and universally challenging. As Jef Withonef of Houston Press once said - "You do not read her books, you survive them."

Prizes - Starblood was nominated for the Commonwealth Book Prize in 2013; Carmilla won the Horror Author of the Year (2013) (Horror Fans Asylum) and FearVenture Author of the Year 2014;

The Starblood Trilogy was voted best horror release of 2014 by The Three Bookateers.

YOU MAY ALSO LIKE

Black Magic Women
TERRIFYING TALES BY SCARY SISTERS

Edited by Sumiko Saulson
Select authors from "100 Black Women in Horror"